The Desires of My Heart

The Desires of My Heart

Marcia Harrison Carpenter

Carpenter's Son Publishing

The Desires of My Heart
©2023 Marcia Carpenter

Published by Carpenter's Son Publishing, Franklin, Tennessee

Edited by Gail Fallon

Cover and Interior Design by Suzanne Lawing

Printed in the United States of America

978-1-954437-90-6

Part 1

Prologue

August 20, 1876

*G*it back! Yer too close!" a man's deep voice commanded from the crowd. Someone else yelled something Addie Kate Flockhart couldn't make out. She glanced back over her shoulder.

She didn't know who hollered at her, but she ran as fast as she could across the grass toward the Centre House's burning great barn. Awakened in the darkness of night by the clanging of the rising bell, seeing a red glow in the night sky, and hearing the frantic shouts of the men, she stared in horror while holding tightly to a water-soaked bedcover, ready to help the Shaker Brethren fight the spreading flames, now roaring.

"This was deliberately set, no doubt," she muttered breathlessly.

She gritted her teeth witnessing the chaos of those dashing about and the hoarse voices shouting to one another as they formed a bucket brigade. The buckets, though filled to their brims at the well, were passed from one Brethren to the next, the water sloshing over the edges so that each was only half filled by the time it reached the fire.

She shivered at the voices barely audible above the horrific clamor of the holocaust.

Footsteps came running up from behind her.

"Stop! Stop!" a man barked.

She did. She stopped so abruptly that the man plowed into her, knocked her to her knees, and caused her to drop the sopping blanket to the ground.

Without saying a word he took hold of her by the wrist and helped her to stand. His touch was commanding, even slightly rough, as he guided her away from the roaring conflagration. He released his grip on her and retraced his steps, snatched up the cover, and raced to the structure, now flaring like an enormous torch with high flying sparks.

The man wasn't a Shaker. She could tell that much by the clothes he wore. He was a person from the world. What was *he* doing here? *One of them* boarding in the Trustee's Building? Or was he the perpetrator of this calamity—returning to the scene of his crime looking like someone trying to help? Though not a big man, he was solidly built with a stocky neck and a prominent nose.

Addie Kate wanted to do something, but she was suddenly helpless. Frozen in dreadful fascination, she watched the frantic scene in the Centre House's yard. Beyond her, flames shot up from inside the farm building, ran along the ridgepole of the barn's roof, and blazed brilliantly against the summer's darkness. The red, blue, and yellow tongues of fire were fierce, leaping over the treetops, embers hurling into the air. She rubbed her eyes with her fingertips hoping to take away the sting of the smoke billowing thick and black. But her efforts failed. Tears formed. Her nostrils stung, and the stifling stench made her cough. Wherever she turned the roaring and crackling sounds of the out-of-control inferno were deafening and the heat so intense it stung and set her face to prickling.

"It's the dark side of the moon. Nights with no moon are as dark as a pocket. No light to expose the culprits who come to steal and destroy. Why do people of the world commit such wicked acts? Why are they so cruel to us? For sure, they've waited until the grain's been harvested and stored. Meanness on their part, for sure. We've endured this kind of persecution time after time."

She spoke the words out loud but mainly to herself.

From the place she stood to watch the actions of many Shaker Brethren, the air grew much too hot to breathe deeply. She gaped at the man from the world as he made his way into the cavernous interior, toward the heart of the blaze. Without warning and to her horror, there was the thunderous crack of a huge beam. A second later it groaned, gave way, and crashed down before him. A shower of glowing coals flashed up in all directions and pieces of debris landed on his forearms, setting fire to his shirt. He slapped at the sleeves— and kept thrashing away at the firestorm.

The bucket brigade couldn't overcome the fast-eating fire, and finally Brother Elijah Turner cupped his hands about his mouth and shouted, "It's too little too late, men. Let it burn."

One by one the men passed the order along. They backed away from the fire, coughed from the dense smoke, and watched helplessly as the massive barn was reduced to piles of charred wood and ashes.

Addie Kate clinched her fists. *Why are the Shakers such easy targets? The work of many for a full year now destroyed in one short night. Why won't the hateful people of the world ever leave us alone?*

She turned to see the man waver on his feet, stagger, and crumple to his knees onto the grass, still holding the blanket, which was now in a state of tatters. For years she'd heard of people from the world, but this was her first time to come close to one.

She knew he would need nursing care and she was the Shaker Sister assigned to the infirmary for the month.

Lord, I ask for strength and courage to help this man.

socket of each sconce that hung on the turned pegs of the pegboard that belted the walls. She struck a friction match—its rasping sound echoing through the quiet sickroom—the light flaring as she touched the flame to one wick after the other. The room brightened.

Doc Spears hovered over the patient. "Would you come here, Sister?"

Addie Kate shimmied into the space beside the doctor. Her back tightened, her hands shook. She was not normally nervous. But then again, she was not in the habit of caring for a non-Shaker, either. He grimaced but kept his eyes closed.

"What about him?" she asked, indicating the stranger.

"The man has some angry red burns. Thank God there's no charred skin, so it's not as bad as it could've been." Doc frowned, shook his head, and made tut-tutting sounds.

She took a peek at the injured man from the corner of her eye. His eyes remained shut. Thank goodness. She wanted to stare at him, but she didn't dare. Doc would notice that, so she considered the man covertly. When she thought he might open his eyes, her focus changed.

He had broad shoulders. His nose was large, his jaw firm, and his eyebrows and lashes, though scorched, were so fair they were scarcely perceptible. His neck was short and thick. His face had the leathery, weather-beaten appearance of one who was frequently outdoors. The skin from his high white forehead down to his chest was tanned to a rich bronze and made quite a contrast to his copious, ash-filled shock of wheat-colored hair that stuck out like bristles of a brush. He didn't come across to her as dangerous, but he was a man from the world.

She made him as comfortable as possible, plumping his pillow, and pulling off his shoes. She knew without a doubt she would do whatever she could to help him because that was the Christian thing to do. She had a strange feeling taking care of a non-Believer, but something about him made her heart swell with compassion for him. Perhaps it was that he fascinated her.

"Any questions on what to do?" Dr. Spears asked as he stepped away.

Addie Kate shook her head and bent over the man. She feared he would look at her.

And he did. Their gazes met for a second.

She looked square into his eyes. They were beautiful—clear and a vivid blue. She quickly turned away, her cheeks growing warm— an unusual experience for her. Never, until now, had any man's eyes interested her. She doused a square of gauze in the water, wrung it out, and with shaking hands, placed it upon his right arm and hand, careful to avoid touching the tender flesh.

The man moaned softly. His nostrils flared. He sucked in air through his clamped teeth and squeezed his eyelids tightly shut.

"Sorry," she whispered.

He barely nodded, furrowed his brows, and kept his eyelids squeezed shut.

"The water's got lavender oil in it. It'll help take the sting out and start the healing."

Why was she telling him that? She had no idea.

She wetted down another square and placed it on the man's left arm and hand. It caused him to stir. Her glance connected with his once again before she dropped her gaze.

He never said a word but bit his lip and grimaced.

Fine with me, she thought. *Shaker women aren't supposed to talk with men anyway—especially men from the world. Only if a third party is around are we even allowed to speak to a Brethren.*

She shook her head and sighed heavily. Those were the rules of Shakerism. She'd lived with them all her life, all twenty-seven years— more than a quarter of a century.

Addie Kate avoided looking at the man's face again, something she found extraordinarily difficult to do. What was the man's name? Was he married? What would it matter if she knew?

Curiosity nagged at her. He was a vagrant, probably—a non-Shaker who she would minister to while he recuperated. She shrugged. Well, he may have a wife and family. Shouldn't they be informed of his injuries? He may have to stay at Pleasant Hill for a while until he healed enough to handle the horses' reins and travel on his way. Why was the man boarding here in the first place? It should have been of no concern to her. The main point now was that the Shakers never turned anyone away who needed help, and obviously this man needed them.

She became completely absorbed in her task and, working methodically, deftly lifted the gauze, rinsed it, and wrung it out—first for his right arm and hand, then for the left. She repeated the process over and over to keep the man's arms and hands moistened with the cool, lavender-infused water.

The night dragged on. The candles dipped and guttered, burning low in the sconces. She lighted fresh ones and set them in the sockets. The air grew sweet with the aroma of melted beeswax and lavender. Finally, the man appeared to have fallen asleep.

Addie Kate peered at Dr. Spears, at the man, then back at the doctor. She stifled a yawn. She was more than tired, but no one would be coming to relieve her. She was the Sister assigned to the infirmary for the month. There was a dull pain between her shoulder blades, and her back felt stiff and sore. She stretched. *Lord, I ask for Your help in dealing with this situation.*

"You must be exhausted, Sister. Better go to bed. I'll stay the rest of the night," Dr. Spears said. "Looks like he's settled down."

She stared at the man a moment in the dim light. He dozed, his breathing long and even. His face calm and peaceful. She stopped, amazed that a tenderness toward him had arisen in her. Caught off guard by the sentiment, she shuddered. No, she could not have sympathy for him because he was not a Believer.

"Guess you're right. Goodnight," she murmured, and went gratefully, so weary she could hardly stand on her feet.

She tiptoed to the door, pushed it open, her head snapping to her left and her right. No one was there. Closing the door quietly behind her, she went out into the shadowy hallway of the Centre House where the stench of the still-smoldering ashes sickened her.

Staggering in the hall, she limped down the stairs to her bedroom and groggily flung herself—fully clothed including her shoes—upon the bed like a sack of flour. She rested her hand on her chest and slept the deep sleep of exhaustion.

The following morning, Addie Kate listened at the door of the sickroom. Holding her breath but hearing nothing, she opened it and stepped over the threshold. She closed the door carefully and moved farther into the sickroom. The room's air smelled strongly of the lavender.

The man stirred in the bed, grunted and groaned, and turned his head away, not giving her so much as a glance.

She held up a basket. "Breakfast," she said in a small voice.

He gave a negligible nod saying nothing. That was all right. She hadn't expected him to speak anyway. She carried the basket to the little table at the bedside, removed the linen towel, and lifted out a plate. She poured steaming and fragrant coffee from a glass jar into his cup, picked up the knife and fork to cut a sausage patty into bite-sized pieces, and salted and peppered the eggs. Holding a forkful of food in front of the man's lips, she began to feed him. After a few bites she held up his cup of coffee for him to take a sip. He did not resist her and peered over its rim as he drank.

Through the entire meal he remained silent, indifferent to her. She kept quiet too. After all, she was not accustomed to any conversation at mealtime since Shakers ate in silence—men on one side of the room and women on the other.

Doc Spears, sitting in a corner of the room, squinted up at them every now and then, but never spoke to them. He was busy with his mortar and pestle crushing herbs to mix with honey, oil, and beeswax for a salve.

The doctor came near as Addie Kate finished feeding the man. "How's our patient's appetite?"

Immediately he turned his attention to the man and said, "We're going to grease and wrap those burns so those blisters don't break open and allow your fingers to grow together because of the raw flesh. I want to make sure no infection sets in. Rascally germs are always running around loose."

She stood to stack the dishes and found the man watching her rather than the doctor. His stare was so intent, a little chill rippled from her heels to the roots of her hair. Her heart turned over. Her hands trembled. No man had ever looked at her like that, and although it frightened her, it also excited her. She gave a quick survey of the room to see if anything else needed to be emptied or carried out.

"Do you have everything you need?" she mumbled at the doctor.

"Yes, thank you, Sister. You may go."

When she reached the doorway, she decided that she was not going to like the man.

"No," she whispered, "I do not like him at all." Then she quietly left the room.

* * *

Ella Beth came unhurriedly into the kitchen of the Centre House. "I haven't seen you all morning. Where have you been?"

Addie Kate, her hands in soapy dishwater, scrutinized her older sibling. "What are you doing here, and why are you looking at me like that?"

"You're not having to nurse that man from the world, are you?"

Addie Kate looked at her sibling soberly and dried her hands on her apron. "Yes, I have to. The infirmary is my assignment this month."

"You shouldn't have to be the one who tends to the likes of *him*, though."

"I wish it wasn't me, too. I don't like it any more than you would."

"Why didn't the Elders have one of the Brethren do it?"

She shrugged. "No idea. The poor man's been burned . . . in the process of helping *us*. Even his eyebrows and hair have been burned. He must be tended to. And we better give him the best attention we can."

"Don't you go and pity the man. Don't let yourself get to liking him."

"Oh, I won't. Don't you be a fussy old hen, Ella Beth. Just listen to yourself. I never said I was. I *meant* I *have* to *give* good care to him." Addie Kate put a hand on her sister's arm. "Why are you getting all worked up? He's not a Shaker, but he is a human being."

Ella Beth snorted. "I'm not making a fuss. He could be an awful man. You better be careful what you're doing, Addie Kate. How long will he be confined here?"

She shrugged. "I'm not the doctor. Maybe a couple weeks."

"That long?"

"It's not really. I'm sure the man's harmless enough."

"Just refuse to do it. He's a man from the outside world and you're not, and them two never go together. You'd best be remembering that." She slapped the back of one hand into the palm of the other as she said, "Stay away from him. Have one of the Brethren nurse him."

Addie Kate rolled her eyes. "I can't believe this. I don't see how he can be so bad, just because he's from the world."

"Believe me, he is."

"Ella Beth, I think you're worrying unnecessarily. I'm to do as I'm assigned. Doc Spears will be right there with me all the time I'm with the man. For goodness' sake, he's helpless! He can't as yet hold an eating utensil." She made a face. "Sounds to me like you've already made up your mind to dislike him. Don't be so mean."

"*Mean?* You don't know anything about him. And you better make sure you never do! Think of the Shaker's tenets. They're what they are because they're safe."

Addie Kate glowered at her. "I am aware of the rules, Ella Beth. Stop it! I've only been with the man for a few hours. Doc Spears was present, too. So there. Don't get all tensed up about it."

"I don't want you to like him—"

"For you, it's because he's not a Shaker, isn't it? He's someone who needs our help, though," Addie Kate shot back. She shook her head. "Now hush. Don't be such a worrier. Couldn't we—"

At that moment, Sister Jerusha Lingenfelter strutted purposefully into the room and crossed straight over to the sisters, huffing her way. She was a formidable woman, good-sized, middle-aged, with small, closely-set eyes and a big mouth with prominent rabbit-like teeth— her lips covering them only with effort. She was the Eldress in charge and reigned supreme over the Sisters living in the Centre House who went about in fear and trembling of her. Order and strict discipline were the greatest forces in her life. Eldress Jerusha was spoken of in hushed whispers and referred to many times simply as *Her* or *She*.

Addie Kate glanced up from washing dishes and met Jerusha's stare without faltering. The Eldress then glared back and forth between Addie Kate and Ella Beth, her eyes flashing.

"Is something wrong, Sister?" Addie Kate managed a smile through gritted teeth. Her face glistened with sweat, beads trickling down from her right temple to her chin. She rubbed a cloth over a sizable copper kettle.

"That is a question you should ask yourself." Jerusha spoke in a harsh voice.

The Eldress's tone nettled Addie Kate. "I'm not sure I understand what you're getting at."

"I think you know well enough." The Eldress twisted her mouth in an ugly way.

"I'm sorry. No. No, I don't." Addie Kate wiped her brow with her apron and turned back to her dishwashing.

"Sister, people do not turn away from me while I'm still speaking to them!" she snapped. "It shows great disrespect. How dare you!"

Addie Kate froze, her skin prickling. She met Jerusha's gaze, held her breath, and waited for the Eldress's tirade.

With a sniff and a lift of her nose, Jerusha spun around to face Ella Beth. "Sister, pray tell what are *you* doing in here? Your duties do not include the kitchen."

She said it loud enough so all the other Sisters could hear. They went rigid, for when Sister Jerusha "prayed," it meant she was really annoyed.

"I wanted to check on Addie Kate. I had no opportunity to see her this morning and thought I'd take some liberty to talk with her. The kitchen is not her assignment, either."

A puffing sound emerged from Jerusha's lips and, in a flash, she thrust her liver-spotted hand in the air and jabbed her claw-like thin, veined finger at Ella Beth's chest.

"That will be enough! I don't like your back talk. Addie Kate knows where she is to be. She sees to her duties. You're not to take liberties, and I'll do the checking on your sister. You go on, now, with your assigned work or you'll face humiliation. Do you hear what I say? Do I make myself clear?"

Ella Beth kept her eyes downcast and nodded.

"Answer me!" Jerusha barked. "Step over here and put your head up to see my face."

"Yes, ma'am," Ella Beth said in a tiny voice. She stood submissively before the Eldress.

Jerusha's lips formed a pout and she glowered at the two sisters. She made the familiar choking sound in her throat which always sounded more like a grunt, turned abruptly, and as suddenly as she had swooped in, she swooped out with her nose in the air.

When Jerusha was gone, Addie Kate looked at Ella Beth and said, "You didn't deserve that kind of treatment."

The older sister nodded in agreement. "Why does that woman hate me so much?"

"I wouldn't take it personally. Eldress Jerusha is . . . uh . . . a little difficult sometimes."

"A little *sometimes*?" Ella Beth said, befuddled. "She's difficult and domineering *all the time*. I imagine she's always been a terror."

"That's true because bitterness eats at her soul. She can become angry over the least little thing . . . about almost anything," Addie Kate said in an exasperated whisper. She hung up the dish towel and came toward her sister. "It's not hard to tell when Jerusha is displeased. Her mouth gets tight."

Ella Beth held out both her hands, palms up, in a gesture of helplessness. "The problem is, though, we have to figure out what she's displeased about."

"I know. We spend much of our time trying to avoid her wrath."

"I see her as abrasive and tiresome," Ella Beth offered. "She always seems to be very pleased with herself. Why does she act so?"

"That's her way. She uses fear to get what she wants. I feel sorry for her because she's a wicked old woman," Addie Kate said. "Don't you think so, too? Look at her eyes. They're just like a pig's. She even grunts like one."

A stunned silence hung over the Sisters in the kitchen who had just stood there and listened to Jerusha's upbraiding of the two. But the siblings exchanged silent messages with their eyebrows and snickered.

Chapter 2

*T*he sun had not yet dropped over the horizon. In the west the clear eggshell-blue sky held deep rose streaks edged with orange and gold. "Truly," Addie Kate said aloud, "the heavens declare the glories of God." She climbed the stairs to the second floor, stood in the threshold of the infirmary before entering the room, and studied the non-Shaker.

He rested in a chair with his eyes closed: legs stretched out before him, head tipped back against the wall, and arms propped up on feather pillows. Was he meditating or praying or sleeping?

She shut the door firmly behind her, expecting him to glance up, but he did not stir. Hadn't the doctor come yet? He'd promised to always be present in the room. Those were the rules, and he was aware of the dinner time. She'd wait a few moments for him. During her whole life Addie Kate had never spent five minutes with a man—even a Brethren. But here sat a man from the outside world and she was alone with him. Horrors! She busied herself unfurling the towel that covered the food, then spread it as a tablecloth, and smoothed it out. Trembling within, she avoided peeking at the man while she emptied

21

the basket and fussed over arranging and rearranging plates, bowls, and cups. Finished, she cleared her throat.

The man stirred but said nothing. He acknowledged her with a short nod.

She swallowed hard. "I . . . d-dinner," she stammered, and pointed.

"Cain't yuh look at me? Why yuh keep a tryin' tuh avoid facin' me. Yer about as friendly as a porkypine."

Addie Kate raised her head, her eyebrows twisted, but she never responded.

"Don't yuh talk? I'm tryin' tuh make some conversation here. Wantin' tuh be polite, yuh know?"

She chose not to speak directly to him nor even pay any attention to him for fear there might be someone hiding nearby, spying on her. She looked around and, not seeing anyone, she said, "Yes, I can talk, but not to you."

"How come?"

"You're from the sinful outside world."

"*What?* What are yuh talkin' about?" he asked, wobbling his head.

She ignored him and occupied herself with cutting up the beef and boiled potatoes.

"Yuh seem likeable enough. Yuh kin feed me, but yuh cain't talk tuh me?"

She bobbed her head. "Not supposed to."

"Who says?"

She breathed a little fast—a moment of panic sweeping through her. "Shaker tenets, and I must follow the dictates."

He stared at her. "Yuh got *laws* as tuh who yuh kin talk tuh?"

She quirked her mouth and nodded.

"Why're yuh botherin' tuh be muh nurse then? Ain't I a bother tuh yuh?"

What would happen if the doctor came and heard her talking with the man? She might face humiliation. Just thinking about what the

Elders and Eldresses might do made her stomach ache. She decided to take her chances, however. The man deserved a response.

"This is my assignment," she said.

She scrutinized him. In the almost dark room, his face appeared to be softer and kinder, but, oh my goodness, here she sat, conversing with a non-Shaker. Would she die from disobeying the directives? Her heart beat loudly enough she thought surely he could hear it. She took a deep breath and said, "You are needing to be tended to for your burned hands and arms."

Why was she blabbering so much? Nervousness? Probably. She seldom spoke to any of the Brethren whom she was familiar with— and this man was a total stranger.

He squinted. "Yuh ain't very big tuh take care of me, but suppose yuh's healthy and fit." He grinned at her.

"I am. I may be small, but I'm strong," Addie Kate told him. His smirk was friendly enough, which did nothing to lessen her feelings of guilt at paying attention to this man.

"Yuh have a beautiful smile."

"It's lopsided," she said softly.

"Still is splendid. Yuh got a name?"

She nodded. He didn't need to know it, and then she shrugged, not being sure what to make of him. Certainly, he was a curiosity.

"Cain't yuh at least tell me what it is?"

She frowned. "Why should I?"

"Would be a cordial thin' tuh do."

She rolled her eyes and sighed. He was persistent. Hopefully by the end of August, he would be recovered enough to leave and resume his journey to his destination, and if he weren't able, another Sister would be assigned to replace her.

She didn't want to be headed for damnation if she continued chatting with the man. Though he was more amiable than Addie Kate had anticipated, she feared being condemned if the Elders learned she fraternized with someone from the world.

"Yer a goodhearted woman, but yuh shore ain't too sociable."

She clicked her tongue, and after taking a breath, said, "Adelaide Kathleen."

"Adelaide Kathleen," he repeated.

"Addie Kate," she corrected.

"Oh, a bobtailed name."

"What do people call you?"

It didn't in the least make any difference for her to know his name. He was someone she would tend to while he recuperated.

He inhaled and puffed out a snicker. "Wouldn't be at all fittin' tuh tell yuh how a few people address me, but I was christened Beckett Hollin'sworth Claycomb. No one ever calls me that, though. Too high and mighty. When they feel favorable toward me, most of 'em call me Jib—because of the shape and size of muh nose. See?" He turned his head sideways to show his profile.

It was, indeed, shaped like the jib of a sailboat and of quite considerable proportion. He smiled at her, but she turned her head, looking for the doctor, fearful she would get caught breaking the mandates.

"I take after muh pappy on the Claycomb side," he went on. "I'm the only one in the family what resembles him, exceptin' muh pa. Anyhow, if I call yuh Addie Kate, I don't think yuh ought tuh call me anythin' but Jib."

Absorbed in cutting up the mutton on his plate, she never answered.

"Ain't yuh gonna say muh name?"

She shook her head. "Eat!" she ordered.

His gaze rested steadily on Addie Kate. "This community's got some puzzlin' rules if yuh cain't even talk tuh people like me."

"Yes. Here." She held the chunk of meat close to his lips, poked it in his mouth, and watched the muscles in his jaws work as he chewed and swallowed it.

She glanced at him. "Anyone left behind . . . who we need to send word to about your misfortune here? To . . . let them be aware of . . . what's happened to you?"

He shook his head. "No, it ain't necessary."

"No family? No wife?"

"No. Ain't married. Never been and don't recollect wantin' tuh be, neither."

"Don't you like women? You afraid of them?"

"I ain't. Do I act like I'm scared of yuh?"

"Perhaps your affections are engaged then."

"No. Why're yuh askin' me these questions? Yuh got a husband? Ain't he bothered a bit with yuh havin' tuh come here and feed me every meal? I mean, since yuh ain't supposed tuh talk with me."

Addie Kate bristled. "There is no husband."

"No? I'll be. How come? Figgered all women concocted some kinda idea in the back of their minds about havin' a family."

"What makes you think you're knowledgeable about women?"

"Whoa! Don't yuh wanna make the circle of life complete? Ain't yuh desirous of the joys of marriage?"

Her cheeks grew warm. "You have no right to ask that . . . it's of no consequence to you. Just so you know, we don't marry."

Living here had been her only experience with family. Though she had, in past years, allowed herself to wonder what her life might have been like if she had escaped from the village at age twenty-one as her brothers had done, she remained at Pleasant Hill. Deep down, though, she wanted to live where she would be free to wed. By staying, she would never get married, because she was a Shaker, and they vowed to celibacy. What could a woman do if her desire was to marry and her religion said no? She would need to leave, but how could she without help?

"Beg yer pardon. Yuh'll hafta forgive me for askin'."

This man from the world irritated her. She turned her face away from him.

"I'm sorry."

"I just don't want to talk about it!"

"Cain't swallow the fact yuh all don't marry." His eyes widened. Then he burst out laughing—a long, loud laugh, his blue eyes crinkling. "Ain't yuh joshin' me?"

Was he making fun of her? She pinched her bottom lip between her forefinger and thumb. "No. Don't deride us."

"Come on, Addie Kate. Yuh don't really hold tuh that nonsense, do yuh?"

"Yes, we do."

"Why? It ain't a natural thin'."

"It is to us. We practice purity through celibacy. We believe the celibate life places one's self in a position of complete surrender to God's will. The scriptures tell us that no one can serve two masters. The flesh lusts against the Spirit, and the Spirit against the flesh. For us, wedlock has no place in Christ's Kingdom."

"Interestin'. What else goes along with what yuh believe?"

"What are you implying?"

"Nothin'. I jist wanna listen tuh what rules of faith yuh all follow."

Addie Kate let out an indignant snort. "Our religious persuasion maintains that Jesus represented the male principle and Mother Ann manifested the female to worship. Christ is the spiritual Son of God and Mother Ann is the spiritual daughter. Our 'rules' as you call them include the open confession of sin, separation from the world, celibacy, and common ownership of property."

"Yer people here hast tuh be the most fascinatin' who ever lived."

"I don't appreciate sarcasm. You don't really think that."

"I tell yuh, I do. Meanin' yer thinkin's weird. It ain't what the Bible says we're supposed tuh do. We're not tuh withdraw from the world, and people is tuh have children."

"How is it you are familiar with what the Bible says?"

"I read the words muhself. I always been a believer in the Almighty and the power of prayer."

She scowled at him. "I read the Holy Book, too."

"Dutiful chapter, no doubt? Is yuh aware that Christ Himself is the bridegroom? Yer beliefs hardly match up with what God says."

"I'm not arguing the issue."

"I ain't quarrelin'. Where do all the younguns I see around here come from, then?"

Addie Kate blinked. Annoyed, she said carefully, "They're orphans. Or they're children from broken homes. Some come from families who can't afford to keep them. Doc Spears makes several trips a year gathering those who want to come. It's our charitable work. They are given meals, clothes, and shelter. They receive an adequate education, and they develop skills and learn trades."

"Let me git this straight. The Shakers are too pure tuh marry and beget offsprin', but they ain't too pious tuh accept younguns provided by the ole sinful world? More I find out, the crazier it sounds."

"We do not condemn marriage among the peoples of the world. But with Believers, it can never be considered."

"Yuh all agree tuh live like this?"

Addie Kate sat quietly and clenched her fists tightly in her lap, out of sight.

"Tell me the number what's comin' here and stayin' and bein' converted tuh this way of livin'? Cain't be very many?"

The two glared at each other for a long moment.

She wanted to defend the Shakers, but the fact was that very few converts were coming in. They used to, anyway, she amended in her head. Desertions were increasing, though—women being the biggest renegades. Over the years, ever since she had been brought to Pleasant Hill, the membership had been dwindling. It was no longer in its prime.

She turned away, too angry to face him. Though he was speaking the truth, she did not want to give him the satisfaction of agreeing with him. How dare him talk this way about these hardworking people. Try as she might, Addie Kate could not overcome the prickle of hostility his comments provoked in her. She reminded herself there were only a few more days to be with him. He was healing well and the beginning of September would bring a different caregiver, if need be. Perhaps she would find an easement from the commotion going on inside her.

"Folks here is peculiar. Two front doors, one fer men and the other fer women. Two stairways, too. Cain't believe yuh think men and women ain't tuh get together in matrimony and bear little uns."

"What's more important for us is to live a holy life as a celibate than it is to propagate. We're molding ourselves for Heaven."

"Fiddle-faddle. Sounds ridiculous tuh me. Men and women is made tuh be together, two by two. If they are normal, they couldn't hold tuh no celibacy."

Addie Kate made a snorting noise. "Sure they can. A person can do whatever he came to think was right."

Jib cocked his head. "Yuh reject what the Good Book says, that it ain't a satisfactory thin' for the man tuh be by himself. Didn't God make a helper suitable for the man? Ain't he commanded tuh be united tuh his wife, and the two'd become one? Tuh be fruitful and have children? Yet this is a whole society of men and women believin' what one earth woman says and not what the heavenly Father says. Seems cultish-like tuh me. Appears yuh live in a unreal world where the real thin's never said or done or even thought. Cain't believe you choose tuh do that."

Addie Kate said nothing to Jib's tirade. She gathered the dishes and rammed them into the basket, her chin trembling.

He held out both wrapped hands in a gesture of regret. "Sorry for upsettin' yuh."

"Well you should be." This man was outrageous.

Before she left his bedside, she said, "You don't understand our ways. Don't judge us, Mr. Claycomb. We live comfortably here. There's no pretense of extravagance . . . only simplicity and order . . . and security. I happen to like those qualities in my world and find comfort in the predictability and sameness of the assignments. The mundaneness is a sort of meditation. Nobody objects, and if they don't like it, they can leave."

"*Security?* Is that what yuh said? This place has jist had a plumb powerful fire."

"True. I think the enemy sees us as easy targets. I wish the hateful people of the world would let us be."

"Yuh called 'em the enemy because they dishearten yuh. Still, yer tellin' me everyone's satisfied with livin' here?"

"No, I'm not saying that. I'm simply hoping to give back what I can to the work of this village in a positive way. I intend to be an agreeable Sister—never having to decide what to do for myself, always knowing what is expected of me, and doing things in the manner they want. They expect nothing less than perfection."

"Don't yuh mind? What about wantin' somethin' jist for yerself."

"At one time I wanted a husband and a family, but those desires are not the Shaker way. My life here is all right the way it is."

"Yuh happy?"

"I don't think about happiness the way most people do. I'm not chasing or seeking it, if that is what you mean."

"Fiddle-faddle, woman! Sounds tuh me like yuh ain't swung over tuh this way of life. If what I'm sayin' is true, I'd say yuh ain't bein' honest with yerself. Appears tuh me like yer tryin' tuh be what yuh want tuh be and, at the same time, tryin' tuh be what they want yuh tuh be. Sooner or later, yuh'll hafta decide."

She glared at him. "I don't lie, Mr. Claycomb!"

"Oh? Yuh enjoy workin' from sunup tuh sundown? What do yuh git in return? Yuh cain't work all the time. Yuh gotta have some rest time, too."

"Hard work is a spiritual and virtuous thing and beneficial to a person. We have what we call release days, but, for the most part, we believe leisure leads to evil deeds. We seek to be actively doing something worthwhile every waking minute. We're hand-minded, you might say, not head-minded. Our motto is 'hearts to God, hands to work.'"

"Cain't yuh sit and let life settle in around yuh or take time tuh think about thin's?"

She furrowed her brows and shook her head in short jerky movements. "No. Not without feeling guilty about it. Our doctrine doubts the advantage of too much mental activity."

"That's the craziest thin' I ever heard."

Addie Kate huffed, jumped to her feet, faced him, and put up a hand, motioning him to be silent. "Mr. Claycomb, we ought not say any more."

"Hows come?"

"You don't understand the first thing about us. You've just made assumptions."

Why was she bickering with this man? It was absolute folly to do so. "I shouldn't have told you all that earlier."

"I'm glad yuh did."

Just then there was a stir at the door and the creaking of the floorboard sounded in the doorway. Someone was coming in.

"Doc's here," Jib announced.

Addie Kate followed his gaze to where the doctor stood, looking at them. She waved in his direction, as though seeing an old friend.

He held a basin of water. "Hello," he said. "How fortunate for me you're still here, Sister."

Her jaw dropped. How long he had been standing there Addie Kate did not know. Her mouth closed for her to swallow, her heart storming within her chest.

Doc Spears came forward. "I've got fresh lavender water and strips of muslin to bind up his wounds."

He went to work. Addie Kate edged her way along the bed and stood beside him as he cut off and pulled away the old, stained bandages from Jib's draining burns.

The patient let out a yelp as his raw skin became exposed. He held his hands out for examination and cringed when his palms came in contact with the water.

"Still painful, huh?" the doctor asked. He gingerly washed and generously salved first one hand and then the other and wrapped gauze around Jib's hands, his wrists, and up his forearms to his elbows, slowly and methodically. When he fastened the last bandage, he said, "Thank you for staying and helping me, Sister."

He gave Addie Kate a curt nod of dismissal.

She grabbed the dish hamper and started toward the door. When she got to the threshold, she stopped for a moment and peeked over her shoulder. She found Jib looking at her. She bit the side of her mouth and shuddered inwardly. Then she wheeled and walked out, closing the door behind her.

* * *

Beckett Hollingsworth Claycomb focused on Addie Kate's back as she left the room and pondered the youthful-looking woman. He reckoned her honey-colored hair, all but concealed by her head covering, and her creamy white-and-unflawed skin contributed to that impression.

Her eyebrows were so light they were scarcely visible. Her wide-set, large eyes, enhanced with long, thick black lashes—curled up at the ends—made him look twice at her. It was her eyes he remembered best. He thought they were her treasure, the most magnificent green he had ever seen—the color of jade. She was a soft-voiced, extremely well-spoken petite woman, slender and graceful. He was reminded of a china doll he had seen displayed in a store window while at St. Louis.

He could not put Addie Kate's image out of his mind. Why couldn't he? It was odd because women had not interested him to that extent before. A smart man would put all notions of her aside and keep his distance from her. She was a Shaker, and they never married—unless, of course, they left the community. There was nothing carnal about his thoughts. So what was it then? Her spunk? She had plenty of that. Her sense of propriety? She was faithful to restraint. Her loyalty to the Shaker sect? He wasn't sure what to make of the little woman. But there was something about her haunting him, that made her fate sound sad to him—a life of menial labor. How could he help her? What could he do about the situation? Could he find her a mate, for starters? Someone who would take her away from here? It would be a difficult task. What kind of man should he look for? Come to think of it, what about himself? It's conceivable he should be the one who took Addie Kate as his wife. He thought she was pleasant enough, and he'd be nice to her, but he wasn't in love with her. Maybe he never would be. He would be willing to marry her though—for expediency rather than for love.

He remembered wives who followed their husbands in the war and became widows along the way. They simply married another soldier—maybe not even knowing the man before taking his name as hers, and he personally knew mail-order brides brought to Virginia.

Yes, he would marry Addie Kate because, somehow, he knew that *without* her, his life would not be the same. On the other hand, his life would not be the same *with* her either.

Chapter 3

*J*ib, whistling softly between his teeth, his legs stretched out in front of him, his heels crossed, looked up as Addie Kate sauntered into his sickroom with the noon meal. He paused and said, "I been waitin' fer yuh. Muh dinner bell's aringin'."

She ignored him. Not seeing the doctor, and, for propriety's sake, she walked around Jib, giving herself a wide berth, honoring the Shaker's prescribed distance between men and women. It was awkward. Where was the doc?

She set the basket on the little table, stretching to do so, and at once realized to her chagrin that she had misjudged the distance. Reaching too far she wavered, flailed her arms to clutch something, anything, to keep from falling. In making an attempt to stand upright, she grabbed hold, of all things, Jib's shoulder.

"Whoa!" he said.

Once she had gained her footing, she relaxed her grip and gasped at his closeness. She turned away, her hand jerking instinctively to her throat. Breathless, she whispered, "I'm sorry." She stood quietly, shaking. A strange tingling sensation ran through her whole body.

Jib nodded. "That's all right. Did yuh hurt yerself?" He kept his gaze on Addie Kate and she focused on him.

She struggled to gain her composure and worked to keep her face calm, but for her hands, it was a lost cause, and her legs were as unsteady as her hands. How on earth would she be able to feed the man now? Her face grew warm, mortified at the idea. She drew her hand close to her side so as not to let him see it tremble. "Dinner," she managed to say, her voice fairly steady, but she wouldn't look at him as she lifted everything out of the basket and set it on the table.

"I'm hungry as a bear. What do I git tuh eat?" He sniffed the air. "Smells delicious."

She smiled faintly, and took a quick peek at him. "Fried chicken and cream gravy, hot biscuits, baked beans, mashed potatoes, and apple pie."

He returned her smile and she hurriedly glanced away. He hunched forward on the chair. "Addie Kate, everybody's got a life story. Shore like tuh hear how yuh ended up here."

She clenched her fists, moved her tongue over her lips, and kept silent. Over the last few days, she had been talking with this non-Shaker, and, in doing so, she risked the probability of suffering humiliation. Nevertheless, she discovered more about Jib than she ever knew about any of the Brethren—or Sisters for that matter. Would it really make any difference if she told him? Probably not, she decided.

Addie Kate cut the meat off the bone as she spoke. "My parents died in the cholera epidemic of forty-nine. For years no one told me a thing about them . . . and our past. Guess they figured it was better I didn't know. 'Gone away,' the Shakers put it. I was five years old before I understood what that meant."

"Sad tuh lose a loved one, ain't it?"

She quirked her mouth. "It's odd, but I have absolutely no memory of them."

"Yuh're too young tuh remember about yer ma and pa."

She nodded. "Neighbors carried me and my siblings here. Shakers've been kind to us. They provided everything we've needed."

"Family still here?"

"The Shakers are my family," she said.

"That ain't what I mean. Yuh know that."

"My older sister is Estella Elizabeth. We call her Ella Beth. She's still here. Our three brothers didn't like the way of life here, so they all left when each turned twenty-one years. Got itchy in their feet, they said. Wanted to spread out."

"What happened tuh 'em?"

"Don't know. Guess they went west. Haven't had any contact with any of them since. They might be somewhere out in the mountains or on the plains. None has ever returned. Seems like they've been guzzled up by the world, simply disappearing out of our lives."

What made her talk so much? She shook her head, turned away, and said, "Forgive me for rattling on." Was he that interested in what she said? She took a long breath through her nose, held it, and let it out through her teeth, puffing out her cheeks.

"How yuh managin'?"

"Mr. Claycomb, life is an adventure wherever it is—even in the mundane."

"That so? I'm gettin' the impression yuh see yer life here as not too interestin'. What yuh goin' tuh do about it?"

"Nothing I can do."

"Shore there is. Always a way tuh do somethin'. Ever think of escapin'?"

The question panicked her. Escape? She held her breath, covered her mouth with her hand, and raised an eyebrow as though the thought had never occurred to her. But the truth was that, over the years, her thoughts from time to time had turned to that very idea. She released her breath gradually and closed her eyes, opened her mouth, but could not speak. Besides, there was danger in answering. Her fear was that she might be betrayed. After all, there were eyes everywhere watching—and of course, ears always listening. Had a word been dropped to the Elders and Eldresses?

His quiet voice went on. "I figger since yuhs no longer a child, yer old enough tuh leave. How old are yuh, anyway?" he asked.

She clumsily smeared gravy over the mashed potatoes and frowned at Jib, annoyed at the implication she was no longer a young woman. She snorted as she forked a bite of beans into his mouth. "I'm twenty-seven."

"My, my. Practically senile. Poor old lady. Middle-aged and never been kissed. How come yuh've never left?"

"Ella Beth didn't want to. She's accepted the tenets of the Shakers. Besides, I'm all she has now."

"But sounds tuh me like yuh hain't took tuh the rules here," he said, matter-of-factly. "Is yuh a goin' tuh live here with the Shakers— disheartened the rest of yer life?"

She flattened her lips. She had never met anyone who, in the space of a few days, charmed her to the point she talked about herself—especially her deep-down self. If the Eldresses found out she spoke so honestly to this non-Shaker, without a doubt she would face some kind of punishment. Still she chose to take her chances. Somehow, at the moment, it seemed all right for her to share the truth with him.

Addie Kate nodded. "I realize what Ella Beth wants, but that's not quite what I want. Um . . . never have felt like I belong here. Don't quite fit in. Odd, huh? Life is a puzzle, isn't it? I've been at Pleasant Hill ever since I can remember anything at all. Don't know why I'm still here. Would have left years ago, but I never figured out where to go . . . and besides, I have no money." She made a helpless gesture. "I don't know anyone who isn't a Shaker. The village is the only place I've ever been. Resigned myself to staying and signed the covenant because Ella Beth did. Thought I didn't have any choice about it."

Addie Kate immediately regretted using the word "resigned." Ashamed, she just revealed something she vowed she would never tell. For years, she had faced frustration because of the stifling rules—

and feared the mandatory shame for dishonorable talk. Her strategy for survival was to hide her angst from those about her.

She got silent because betraying any loyalty to the Shakers didn't seem fair to them. True, she had wanted much more for herself than what they offered. Once in a while, when meditating as she lay in bed at night, she did her best to picture another way of life in her mind, but she could not call upon any images about what it might be like. As a Believer, she would have zero influence on anything or anyone. If she stayed at Pleasant Hill, there'd be no evidence of her ever having existed on this earth. No possessions, husband, babies suckling her breasts, nor little ones seeking comfort in her arms, not even a name on a marked gravesite. There would be nothing to indicate she had ever lived. It saddened her that because she was a member of the United Society of Believers in Christ's Second Appearing, she took the vow of celibacy and chose to live communally for the sake of the Society—always at the expense of her own individuality. Sadness pricked her because a deep painful hunger she had was to be a wife and mother. She wanted a child who would be connected to her for the rest of her life and, therefore, be her legacy—*something* of herself remaining behind when she left this old orb—to show that her life did have some significance.

"How're yuh able tuh stand it? Don't yuh feel frustrated? Why do yuh think yuh need yer sister's approval? The faster yuh stop hopin' fer that, the better off yuh'll be."

She and Jib stared at each other for several seconds—not speaking. Then she turned her attention to the food on the plate, swishing a piece of meat in the cream gravy. "Enough talking. You better finish this afore it gets cold." She shoved the forkful into his mouth.

Jib munched away, swallowed, and said, "I git the idea that yer the sorta person what'd be happy with a man and little ones runnin' around."

"You aren't that familiar with me to say something like that."

"I see kindness and gentleness . . . and somethin' naturally motherly in yuh," he said. His expression made her shudder.

"How do you mean 'natural?'"

He shrugged. "Some people pretend about life. I suspect yer pretendin' nicely."

"What are you talking about?"

"I'mma thinkin' yer actin' like yuh don't like me, and yuh hafta like me."

"Why do you say that?"

Jib pursed his lips. "Because I ain't a bad person, and I believe yuh kin see that. What I'mma wonderin' is if yuh have stopped tuh consider who God Almighty made yuh tuh be? Jist maybe He made yuh tuh be a wife and a mother. I kin tell from listenin' with muh heart and not jist muh ears that this ain't the kind of life yuh wanna live. Addie Kate, the Lord don't want us tuh live in frustration and fear. Everyone deserves a chance for happiness. Do yuh even know what'd make yuh happy? Shorely yuh got one thin' yuh want more'n anythin'."

She recoiled and turned her head away. Had this man truly understood what she was feeling and empathized with her?

"I expect yer a might wary of me and afraid yuh betrayed too much. Don't worry about what yuh told me."

Why had she babbled on so much? Why couldn't she keep her mouth shut? Someone should have stuck a gag in her mouth. For a fact she found him easy to talk to, and she had begun looking forward to her visits with him, but she'd failed to follow the warning about not revealing too much about herself. Holding her head high and her body rigid, she stood and said, "We ought not to say any more."

The conversation ended. "I better go," she said, at once needing to be away from Jib. "I must tend to my other chores. I can't be here."

She tumbled everything together into the basket and made a beeline for the door where she spotted Doc Spears leaning his shoulder against the doorjamb. How long had he been there? How much had he heard?

She froze like a statue for a moment, her heart pumping so force-fully it was hard to breathe.

The doctor had been within mere feet of them while she and Jib talked. He'd listened to everything they said. Would he report her to the Eldresses? She shuddered at the thought.

The doctor moved and let her pass by him. She went out without looking at either of them.

* * *

Wednesday morning, Addie Kate arrived with Jib's breakfast. She placed the filled plate of scrambled eggs, ham, fried potatoes, kidney beans, wheat bread, and apple pie before him and poured a tall glass of half milk and half thick cream. She peered at the man sitting in his chair as he sat back and watched her, smiling broadly at her. The way he grinned at her made her heart leap.

She seated herself on the stool opposite Jib. "Hungry?" she asked, regarding him.

He nodded. "Reckon I'm pretty shaggy since I ain't been cleaned up yet." He rubbed a wrapped hand against his chin stubbled with whiskers.

She glanced toward the door, hoping to find the doctor standing there. He's supposed to be with her when she's with this patient. Didn't he care about the rules, or was he lazy about doing his job? Shame on him for shirking this duty. Was it that he was sympathetic to her, or did he trust her to keep proper behavior? She feared he would sneak in and eavesdrop on their conversation again.

Addie Kate faked a cough. "I realize it's not any of my business, but I'm curious, Mr. Claycomb. What are your plans when you leave us?"

It wasn't any of her business, and she didn't really take an interest in knowing his plans. However, she had built up plenty of curiosity concerning him, and she had come to enjoy his company more and more. She decided to treat him with friendliness, nothing more than companionship. "We've talked all this time about me. What of you?"

"What yuh wanna know?"

"Whatever you want to share. Why not start with your family?"

"Hail from Virginia. Goin' tuh Nebraska Territory." He jerked his head to indicate the west.

"Brothers? Sisters?" She cut up the ham, speared it with the fork, and held it to his lips.

Jib leaned back in his chair, cocked an eye on her, took his time chewing, and swallowed before he said, "Feared it ain't a happy one what's happened tuh muh family."

"Do you hate to talk of it?"

He nodded.

"I'm sorry. I don't mean to pry."

He bent forward. "Sisters're married. Maw's a widow. Pa was a hard worker. He and muh oldest brother . . ." He took a deep breath and shuddered, staring off into space. "A evenin', years ago when it was threshin' time . . . I was, as best tuh recollect, eleven years . . . him and muh brother drove our loaded wagon ontuh a ferry. The post what held the float broke—wagon tipped straight down intuh the water where it turned over. The horses, still harnessed, fell backwards smack on top of 'em. No one could help and they both drownded." He shook his head.

Addie Kate shut her eyes, sucked in a breath, and put a hand on her chest. "How awful! What a tragic story."

Jib nodded. "Ma's never got over it. Ain't certain that any of us has. Got another brother who dint come home from the War Between the States. Warned yuh it was rather gruesome." He glanced her way.

She changed her position on her chair. "What a sorrowful past."

He bobbed his head. "I went off tuh war a week after muh seventeenth birthday—May of sixty-three. Wasn't like the rest of muh family, not exactly a traitor tuh the South—but I jined up with the Army of the Potomac—the Union. Dint believe in the South's cause.

Found muhself in the second battle of Fredericksburg and right away got introduced tuh the horrors of war. North won that one." He sat silent for a while. "Two months passed and I landed at Gettysburg, Pennsylvany—absolute terrible." He caught his breath on a shudder.

Addie Kate shivered and waited for him to speak. But he said no more. He looked vacantly out into space.

She said, "It must be difficult to talk about what happened. What do you aim to do now . . . in going to Nebraska?" she hesitantly asked.

Jib sat up straighter. "I'mma itinerant photographer. Wanna take pictures. Lots of 'em."

"Of what . . . or whom?"

"Anythin', anyone. Everythin'. Everyone. Wanna take pictures of the West recordin' what I see. Indians. Mountains. Streams. Cowboys. Buffalo. Wanna preserve true history while it's a bein' made. Pictures'll be memorials tuh the past. Like monuments tuh how people lived."

"It is fortunate you get to decide what you want to do. Some of us are not able to pick and choose the way we'd like our lives to go. Most of us have to take what life deals us."

Hearing a floorboard creak, she turned her head toward the door. She gasped as a shudder went through her. In the threshold stood the doctor with his hands behind his back, watching them. Her face became warm while she hastily gathered up the dishes, her pulse throbbing. Wary of the doctor who remained where he was, her glance shifted from him to Jib, and she whispered, "Oh, my goodness." Addie Kate caught her lower lip between her teeth and pressed tightly. Would Doc Spears ever stop eavesdropping on their conversations?

Jib turned in that direction. "Mornin', Doc."

Before she walked out of the room into the hallway, Addie Kate peeked over her shoulder at them.

That night, Addie Kate lingered at the window of her bedroom. She smelled the acrid odor of the barn's still-smoldering remains and took note of the rhythmic breathing and soft snoring of the Sisters' sleeping. She pondered Jib's story as she climbed into bed and squeezed her eyes shut. The man had experienced misery and heartache. Why should his past bother *her*? Why should she concern *herself* about him? What was he to *her*? Though she had been told time and again to be suspicious of anyone from the world, she couldn't help pitying the man.

She gulped a deep breath, turned on her side, and fluffed her pillow to summon sleep. But when she closed her eyes, the image of Jib sat right behind her eyelids. What was going on?

Trying to convince herself to never like him, Addie Kate confessed only to herself that he had started to grow on her. The two characteristics she had grown to appreciate about the man were his honesty and common sense. She was shaken by the realization that she and Jib were slowly becoming friends. For a while, she sorted her muddled thoughts and then fell asleep.

The next morning, Addie Kate caught the sound of muffled voices coming from the sickroom. She tapped on the door before entering into the room. Doc Spears stood at Jib's bedside, finishing with the bandaging by laying aside his scissors. "Give me another minute or so, Sister Addie Kate. Sorry to slow down Jib's breakfast."

She crossed the room. "Morning, Mr. Claycomb," she said in a sing-song inflection.

Jib raised his head. "Mighty chirk, ain't yuh?"

She gave a slight shrug. "Morning's the best part of any day."

She smiled at him and he smiled back. After that, neither said anything to the other. Quiet prevailed, and the doctor left as soon as Jib finished eating.

Addie Kate dillydallied in stacking the containers and putting them into the basket.

"Doc says I'm a healin' up real good." He lifted his hands. "See? Bandages gettin' thinner. Won't need tuh be a stayin' here too many more days."

She flinched. Was he serious? Would he be leaving for Nebraska so soon? What had happened to her animosity toward him? Since she learned about his past, her negative feelings toward him seemed to have vanished. She admitted to herself that he had a certain magnetism and was the most interesting person she had ever met. And she admitted that every time she was with him she saw a new facet of his personality, and what she saw she liked, more and more. But she said, "Good news, isn't it?"

He nodded. "Doc's as pleased as a coon in a corn patch."

She quickly looked about the room. "Anything I can do for you before I leave?"

He shook his head.

"Fine, then, I'll come at noon."

She started off in the direction of the door.

"Wait! Come back, Addie Kate," he called. "I wanna talk tuh yuh."

"I don't want to talk to you," she said coldly and remained where she was.

"Come on. I'm beginnin' tuh think yuh don't like me," he said. "Makin' me take offense. Yuh could fall in love with me if yuh'd let yerself. I ain't a heathern. Some people like me a lot."

Addie Kate licked her lips. "Is that right?"

"Shore is. I ain't sure I'll ever have a better chance tuh say muh piece. Sit down, won't yuh?" He waved her over and indicated the chair.

She stood still hesitating with a moment's caution. It would be inappropriate for her to stay, she recognized that, but she did as he ordered, ignoring the likelihood of humiliation. She put the tote on the little table, stopped a short distance away from him, and spread her upturned palms in a gesture of surrender. She then sat stiffly on the very edge of the chair beside his bed and waited for whatever was coming next. What if someone found her in this room alone with this non-Shaker? Oh, *shameful!*

He leaned back, took in a deep breath, ran his tongue under his lower lip, and blew out a stream of air. "Addie Kate, this here is what I gotta say. Yuh don't belong with the Shakers."

"So you say. Being a Shaker means—belonging. And just where do you think I belong?"

"With me. I think yer sweet, Addie Kate, and I wanna take yuh away from here. I wanna give yuh the opportunity tuh have a life of yer own. I like yuh. Yer gonna hafta choose between me and Ella Beth. Yuh like me, too, don't yuh?" He met her gaze with a penetrating stare.

She inhaled deeply and gawked at him. "No!" she barked. A shiver ran up her back.

"I don't believe yuh."

"I don't care whether you do."

"Look, I'mma tellin' yuh tuh marry me. I'm a hopin' yuh'll say yuh will."

Chapter 4

Addie Kate met Jib's gaze while he sat quietly, but neither of them said a word for a long stretch, her mouth opening and closing like a dying fish.

"Yuh don't hafta say nothin' now," he said.

She couldn't have spoken even if she tried. His words shocked the breath out of her. His proposal came so unexpectedly that she could not think about it clearly. Bringing to mind a picture of escaping from Pleasant Hill and starting a new life with him terrified her as much as it thrilled her. She went to the opened window and looked through, staring off. The air smelled of ripening tomatoes and green beans hanging in clusters from the vines.

At last she swung around to face him and said pettishly, "You got some nerve. You either lack common sense or are insane . . . or stubborn."

"I'm a votin' for stubborn, if I git a vote." Jib bent his head back and laughed.

"You don't need to marry me," she said.

"I wouldn't mind marryin' yuh."

"I thought you didn't want to get married."

"Ain't come across a woman I wanted tuh git hitched tuh. Yuh changed muh thinkin'. Yer different from any woman I know. I'm sorry yuh don't like me much, but I like yuh . . . a awful lot and I wouldn't mind makin' yuh muh wife." He smiled at her.

"Well, your idea is completely foolish. I don't even know you very well," she argued. "You're presuming too much."

"No, I ain't," he snapped. "Yuh jist might like me if yuh'd let yerself go. I ain't too hard tuh look at, do yuh think?"

"I haven't thought about it. At the very least, your proposal doesn't make sense."

"People hardly ever do what makes sense. I'm a hearin' with muh heart that yuh want more outta life than what yuh're gittin' here."

"Whatever gave you that—" She came back to the chair and plopped down.

"Listen. Tell me this. Yuh satisfied with yer life now?"

"I never said I'm unhappy." The words came out more snappishly than she intended.

"Ain't none of muh business, but I'mma thinkin' yuh need a bigger vision, Addie Kate. Don't yuh wanna know the awesome thin's yer heavenly Father has planned tuh give yuh?"

"I'm doing well enough. Now, tell me . . . what difference does it make to you?"

"I care. Yuh got a whole life ahead of yuh. Don't rule out God's intervenin'. Don't accept thin's far less than what He's got in store fer yuh. Yuh wantin' a sign? Jist maybe I'm it. I'm a thinkin' our Lord has brought me here tuh be the answer tuh yer problem."

The room grew silent, and not knowing what else to do, she sat. *Had Jib been summoned here for her?* she wondered. *The Almighty does work in mysterious ways.* She grimaced. What was she thinking? She shot Jib an annoyed glance. "And . . . what is my problem?"

"Leavin' this place. Sounds like yuh ain't never been yer own person . . . nothin' but chattel tuh 'em. Holy Book says there's a time for everythin'. I'm a thinkin' the time has come tuh leave. Yuh gotta take charge of yer own destiny. Don't be a doubter, woman. Yuh may not figger out how life's gonna pan out, but God has done already got the solution. Yuh gotta keep believin' that. Remember, He wouldn't have give yuh the dream unless He had a way of bringin' it tuh fruition. I been prayin' fer yuh."

"You pray? . . . For me?"

"Why yuh surprised? Didja figger me a pagan?"

She quirked her mouth and shook her head. "Oh, no. I didn't mean that. But you're talking about matrimony and leaving, and I don't waste time imagining impossible things."

Untrue. The ideas of wedlock had lurked in the back of her mind for years. Most of the time she would not take them out and inspect them, but they were there, all right.

"Marriage is a sacred commitment," she said. "You're speaking about a convenient arrangement. That is not a reason for a couple to wed. So don't talk to me about it."

"How come? I hear sadness loud and plain. This ain't the kind of life yer a wantin'. Yuh been dreamin' of somethin' better than this. Why won't yuh let me help?"

"I don't see how you can."

"That's ridiculous. Yer considerin' nobody but yerself."

"I don't think so. Your habits and beliefs are too different from mine. How can there be happiness in that kind of relationship?"

"Bein' happy is a matter of the mind. I'm certain many a woman is a dutiful wife tuh a man she ain't in love with. I have a special feelin' toward yuh, Addie Kate. Don't yuh think a union kin succeed well enough on companionship, respect and . . . likin'? I'd be faithful tuh yuh. And I believe yuh'd be content—jist gimme the opportunity tuh prove muhself. Cain't yuh trust me, even a little?"

"A little wouldn't do."

What had happened to her animosity toward the man? At this point, she confessed only to herself that she enjoyed being with Jib. She believed her feelings were not strong enough to call it being *in love* with him, but, at the same time, he intrigued her. "If you were to be my husband, my hope is that you would want me as your wife more than anything else in the world."

For a minute they sat looking at each other. Jib ran his tongue under his lower lip. "Reckon plenty of married men play that game."

"The question is, how can an escape from here be accomplished? I've never yet figured out how it could come to pass."

"Easy enough."

"Nothing ever is."

"Can be. Jist come with me. Climb intuh muh wagon and we ride off. What do yuh say?" It took some time for his grin to form while all his attention was fixed on her.

She said nothing, inhaled deeply, got to her feet, and exhaled loudly. "You can't help me! Nobody can! Being a Shaker is my lot in life."

"That's jist it, Addie Kate. Yuh ain't a Shaker in yer heart. Are yuh sayin' yer givin' up on freedom?"

"No, I'll never do that."

"Then come with me." Jib pursed his lips. "I ain't a enemy, Addie Kate. I'm hopin' yuh'll accept me as a friend."

"I can't."

"Why not?"

"Have you considered that I may not want you for a friend?" A bold-faced lie. As she had become acquainted with him during his time of recuperation, she found him to be an interesting man. The Brethren, cut from the same pattern, talked and dressed alike, and their manners, with only some slight variations, were identical. Jib stood out. He had seen the world and experienced freedom.

He arched his brow. "People's mysteriously drawn tuh each other—or they ain't." He smiled then, and she caught her breath. "I cain't force yuh tuh like me, Addie Kate. But listen here, I'm aimin' tuh be yer husband. 'Tis the right thin' tuh do. So there."

She squirmed. "I can't. I'll wed someday, all right." She glared at him, never blinking, and tried to imagine what it would be like to have a husband.

"Who yuh goin' tuh marry?"

"Someone. Some man. Some day. I'm not giving up, I'll have you know." She stood and folded her arms across her chest. "I'm not reaching for the stars either. I just know it won't be you."

"And how many men have appeared tuh help yuh achieve that end? None—only me! Are yuh too scared tuh live yer own life? Addie Kate, here's a warnin', I do whatever I say I'm gonna do."

"I'm not wanting to argue about this."

"We ain't arguin'. We're merely discussin'."

"Then no more discussion."

"Think about it and we'll talk again."

"We've said enough. You know I can't go with you. It's impossible."

"No, 'tis possible."

"It would be absolutely wrong for me."

"Why?"

"Well, because."

"Because ain't no reason. Don't yuh want yer life tuh change?"

"Yes, if possible." She stepped backward, intending to leave the room, having no further reason to linger.

When she got as far as the door, he called out. "Wait! Yuh hafta come back!"

She stopped short and flapped her arms at her sides. "You've tried that trick before. Now what? I've dillydallied long enough."

It was getting late, and she surmised the Sisters would be furious with her if they were aware of where she was and what she was talking about with this man from the world.

"Yuh left the basket. See?" He pointed.

"Oh!"

She stomped his way, making sure of space between them. She furrowed her brows and squinted her eyes.

"We git along, don't we? Yuh wouldn't've give me such tender nursin' attention if yuh thought *nothin'* of me. I'm fond of yuh, Addie Kate. But I ain't in love with yuh."

She was not *in love* with him, either. No, she simply liked him. For the first time, she cared for a man—one who pictured a different future for her, improving her lot in life.

"Yuh'll make a desirable wife. I see a kind and sweet and patient woman. 'Tis sad yuh have allowed Ella Beth's choice decide *yer* destiny. Ignore what she's a wantin' fer yuh. Yuh're a whole other woman than her with a life and dreams different." Jib then issued a challenge: "Be true tuh yerself, woman. One day yuh'll wake up and regret passin' up this opportunity tuh live a life yuh desire."

Addie Kate gasped. She could never remember a time when she didn't want a husband, home, and children, but because she frequently prickled with resentment at his words, she would not wholly welcome them now. She shrugged and released her breath so sharply that it blew her bangs upward.

He continued, "This ain't truly livin', yuh know, but existin'—merely a markin' time."

True. One day, though, contentment would come to her. She saw herself waiting for it. She said, "Marking time . . . to what?"

"Yer dyin'."

Her cheeks burned. She gave him a piercing glare. He was right. He had shown her there was more to life than being comfortable day after day in a dull and predictable manner, similar to waiting for death. But how *dare* he say that!

"I better go," she said without conviction and without attempting to move. Why was she dawdling?

Jib closed the space between them. "Don't go . . . not jist yet, anyways. Promise me yuh'll at least think about what I been sayin'. I'll be clearin' outta here in a few more days. Hopin' yuh come along with me."

She stared at him, scrutinizing his face, her heart beating fast and hard. She wanted to fling herself against him and hide her head in his shoulder, but the wanting of this filled her with shame. She said, "For your information, Mr. Claycomb, we don't appreciate people from the outside world coming in here and meddling in our lives trying to convince us to go flesh. If I left here, I'd be ashamed of breaking my vow and frightened to death for how I will be punished."

"With all respect, yuh won't stand in judgment by breakin' that frivolous promise, so yuh don't hafta remain loyal tuh it when yuh've gained more wisdom. God's a lovin' and forgivin' heavenly Father. Don't give up on what yer wantin' in life."

She did not respond, merely squeezed her eyes shut and, for a second, let herself speculate whimsically on living beyond the confines of the village. Did she possess the courage to leave and live without the stifling rules, to do exactly what she wanted with her life?

Jib put his arm around her and pulled her close. She felt the roughness of his shirt against her cheek, felt his breath on her hair, and heard him whisper her name. She stiffened. What was he doing? Almost faint with shock, she pushed away from his arms and walked a few staggering steps with one hand over her heart. Breathing fiercely as she swayed, she put out a hand to steady herself. He caught her and drew her to him again and then took his time in pressing his lips upon her own.

Hesitant at first, she yielded to his embrace. Her pulse fluttered and her mouth softened. With a tingling beginning at the base of her spine and creeping up her neck, she looked up at him, trying to make sense of what was happening. *This is the last thing I need*, she thought.

"Mr. Claycomb, how could you behave in this way?!" she said in a frightened tone. "Why do this to me?"

She brushed the back of her hand across her jaw. Would he have the audacity to repeat the offense? He lowered his head and did just that with so much feeling, the fine hairs on her body tickled. She had not expected such a soft, warm, and gentle kiss. This put her in undiscovered territory. She knew she was playing with fire.

"No!" she jerked herself free and moved away from him, her mind a jumble of thoughts, her fingertips touching her cheek. "You kissed me!" she cried.

He grinned and stroked the underside of his chin with a wrapped hand. "Forgive me," he said repentantly. "Shows I like yuh . . . but . . . yuh kissed me back. Perhaps yuh do like me and yuh ain't accepted that fact yet."

She raised her index finger in warning and shook her head. "What we did was sinful. My fear is that someone saw us." She retreated from him. "I must go."

"Are yuh runnin' away?"

"No, I'm not. I need to get to the kitchen now. In all likelihood, they're wondering where I am and will come looking for me."

She hooked the basket over her arm and stomped out of the room giving him a view of nothing but her back. Addie Kate suspected there was a good chance her world would never make sense again.

"Remember this, Addie Kate," he called after her. "I'm aimin' tuh marry yuh. Mark the words. We'll be happy forever after and have a fine life with the two of us workin' together."

* * *

After climbing into bed, and long past midnight, Addie Kate, still awake, stretched out on her back to her full length, her hands locked under her head. She listened to the Sisters as they slept—inhaling, exhaling—almost in unison. She had not wanted to think of Jib—but there she was—and considering matrimony. That would mean she'd have to be with him day *and* night.

She shook her head at the ridiculousness of it all. What was wrong with her? *Everything!* The memory of his mouth on hers came to the forefront in her mind, clear and vivid. Guilt washed over her because she had no will to drive the recollection away. Had she committed a wicked thing that would bring punishment to her? She worried about the indiscretion with Jib earlier that day and confessed to crossing the line into forbidden country—a move that could have severe consequences in her life if anyone knew.

"He wouldn't have been able to do it if I hadn't let him, and I did. It was reckless of me. I wish nothing'd happened," she mumbled. Part of her anguish was that she had discovered delight only to be left now with an overwhelming sense of regret. That was the only time it was to happen, but she hoped the ability to remember his kisses would stay with her forever. He admitted he wasn't in love with her. She pondered possible scenarios until she felt heartsick with the hopelessness of ever experiencing marriage.

"I suppose Jib'll eventually meet someone," she told herself. "He'll probably be very happy, too."

She groaned in disgust at the idea of him living happily ever after with another woman. It should be of no importance to her, yet that possibility sent a shudder down her backbone and made her stomach ache.

"Shame on me for acting like a jealous woman of the world."

She rolled to her side in order to rest more comfortably, pummeled her pillow, and tried to empty her mind of Jib, but his image remained there. The day had been unsettling. Jib was right. She was trapped here. She would be better off leaving with him.

* * *

Jib lay in bed. He thought about the little Shakeress named Addie Kate Flockhart. He let out a huge sigh. Of course he cared *about* her, but *for* her? Would he admit he was captivated by her? He faced the startling realization that he desired to marry her and father children with her. The hitch, though, was that he feared he was pressuring her too much to leave the only home she had ever known. Would she agree to go with him?

"Lord, I'm askin' that Yuh'll bring us together some day," he prayed. "It's gotta be Yer way and timin' tuh be right."

Chapter 5

Saturday evening, Addie Kate sought privacy with her thoughts. She fretted over Jib and lacked a calm spirit because of it. She wished she could confide in her sister, but knowing Ella Beth would be mortified if she knew, Addie Kate dared not divulge anything to anyone. The only thing to do was to keep quiet.

She wandered leisurely toward the Meeting House, entered the building's cool recesses, and found the stillness profound. Addie Kate paced about, and, appreciating being alone, she sat on a long oak bench and leaned forward, covering her face with her hands, and spoke aloud in the silence. "If I could be still for a moment, I might pray, for I do not know what to do."

"About what?" a male voice said.

At the unexpected sound, Addie Kate's heart leapt into her throat and caused her to spring to her feet. She spun around, looked across the room's expanse, and froze.

"Oh! You can't be here!" she cried out.

"Too bad. I already am," Jib Claycomb said.

She had not heard him enter the building, but there he was standing no more than several feet away.

"You need to go!" She pointed toward the door. "You must leave!"

He remained where he was, ignoring her authoritative order, sweeping his hat from his head, holding it at his waist, and turning it in his hands.

"I ain't goin' until I've said muh piece. I don't wanna say goodbye tuh yuh."

He never waited for a response and ambled toward her, his footfalls echoing across the bare wood floor.

She put her hand to her chest, not entirely pleased at his company. "We've got to be cautious, Jib. It isn't proper for us to be seen together. Eyes are everywhere."

"Jib? What d'yuh know? That's the first time yuh've called me that."

He put up a hand and rubbed the underside of his nose with the back of a knuckle. "Look around. Ain't nobody else here. No Elders or Eldresses. Jist yuh and me," he said as he swept his arm in a gesture, panning the room.

She released the breath she held and moved farther away from him.

"You must leave," she said in a firm voice. He came close to her and put his hands on her shoulders. "Slow down, woman. No one's here but us. Relax."

Her thumping heart quieted a little. "How soon are you going away?"

"Tomorrow."

"I'm not going with you."

"It's a pity, too. Addie Kate, yuh's the one who wanted tuh leave somethin' of yerself behind on this earth. Yuh won't be able tuh do that by stayin' here. Yuh think it over. If yuh wanna change yer mind, don't hesitate. Come with me."

She glared at him. "We've settled that issue."

"No, we hain't. Yuh keep pushin' me away. Listen. This is a perfect opportunity for gittin' outta here."

He smiled at her as he took hold of her hands and lifted them to his lips.

She gently drew them away and stepped back from him. "Please, not now."

He studied her. "I know yuh ain't been convinced tuh go along with their way of thinkin', so yuh oughta consider breakin' yer vows."

"You may be right, but that decision is not yours to make for me."

"Don't believe yuh've worked it out that way. Appears tuh be Ella Beth's choice." He swiped his forehead with the back of his hand.

She shook her head. "My sister is looking out for me. What're you after?"

He raised an eyebrow and quirked his mouth. "I'm givin' yuh a chance tuh make a new beginnin'. Fact is, I don't like seein' a splendid racehorse hitched tuh a plow. Tryin' tuh git yuh tuh see the possibility for escapin' this place. Cain't yuh understand that?"

She considered him several seconds. "Stop it," she snapped.

He pressed the air with both palms. "Jist sayin'. Mayn't ever come back this way. Life takes mighty strange twists and turns. Yuh gotta realize the people here has got it all wrong."

"You might be right, but I love these industrious, cheerful, peaceful people."

His gaze fixed on her. "This way of livin' is not goin' tuh last. Utopia's don't exist. No one kin make Heaven on earth . . . leastwise in this lifetime. The members here is growin' older and they're not gittin' enough young converts tuh keep the community goin'."

"Come here," he demanded, extending his hand. She grasped it, and he pulled her to him, wrapping his arms tightly about her, holding her to his chest.

She bent her head back and gave him her attention, her heart slamming inside her. This was sinful. What if someone walked in on them? Yet she wanted to relax and let him kiss her and hold her close.

He leaned forward and put his lips on hers. When he let her loose, they stood facing each other. "Will yuh think of me, Addie Kate?"

"My life will never be the same without you. Everything's different. I thank God every day you came. I wish you only the best," she said, managing a feeble smile. "Be safe," she added, her voice catching on the words.

He stroked her jaw with the back of his hand. "I aim tuh be." His lips barely brushed hers. "Goodbye."

They both stood together without speaking, neither of them ready to part. Then he wheeled on his heel leaving her and walked across the room.

She looked after him for a moment, then hissed, "No! Not that door! It's the women's entrance."

He switched his direction, abruptly stopped, and retraced his steps. "One last thin', Addie Kate. Why are yuh givin' up so easily on yer lifelong dream?"

He again headed to the door, turned and looked at her as though he intended to say something else, but suddenly left the Meeting House without saying another word.

Addie Kate dashed to a front window, slumped against its frame, and observed him settle the floppy Stetson on his head, nonchalantly pulling it down on his brow. "Turn around, Jib. Look back for me."

He hunched his shoulders in a shrug and clumped down the stairs without so much as a backward glance, shoved his hands in his pockets, and made his way to the Trustees' Building.

Addie Kate shivered and took a few deep breaths, making her chest heave. She reached up to touch her lips, smiled, and held locked hands to her heart. "Thank You, Lord, for my friend. I ask that You will bless him in his travels and bring him back to me someday."

When Jib was no longer in her line of sight, she opened the door and sat on the top stone step. She propped her elbows on her knees, her fists supporting her chin, and stared into space.

"I'll live out the rest of my life at Pleasant Hill with all their stifling laws. Father in Heaven, haven't I prayed for years that someone would rescue me? Was my rescuer Jib?"

With sadness in her heart and a stabbing pain in her stomach, she trembled and rested her head in her hands.

The amethyst light of the twilight dwindled to darker shades of gray as the singing of the night insects increased in intensity. Neither brought solace to her. For the umpteenth time in her life, she daydreamed of a husband.

"Wait, Jib," she said, under her breath. "I'm almost persuaded." Would the moment she could actually leave ever come again?

After a long silence, Addie Kate stirred. "Well, that's that. I wanted to go with you, Jib, but the Shakers' way always wins."

Husband. Children. They weren't going to happen to her. She hoisted herself up and reached for the railing to steady her. Then she trudged across the turnpike and walked purposely toward the Centre House, glancing around to see if Jerusha or another Sister had been spying. She saw no one and slowed down to breathe easier.

That night, after climbing into bed, Addie Kate could not find peace. She meant to stop thinking of her encounter with Jib earlier in the evening, but instead she lay wakeful and sick at heart. The hours went by as the day's events moved like a kaleidoscope through her mind. She tossed and turned, sighed, buried her face in her pillow, tossed and turned again, and finally boosted herself to a sitting position. She swung her legs over the side of the bed, dropped her feet to the floor, and slipped out of her bed to crouch beside Ella Beth's slumbering form. Grasping her sister's hand, Addie Kate whispered, "Wake up."

"You all right?" Ella Beth mumbled.

Addie Kate shook her head.

"What's wrong?"

"Jib's leaving." She caught her lower lip between her teeth.

"The man from the world? About time *that man* left us," she said.

"*That man,* as you call him, has a name. Beckett Hollingsworth Claycomb. He's the pleasantest person . . . *really* he is. He's not just some other man from the world."

"I don't want to hear anything about how he is." Ella Beth said the words in a snarky tone. "We're in dangerous territory discussing him. If we're overheard talking about a man, we'll face disgrace. Remember the rules?"

"They don't matter."

"Yes, they do. What is going on with you? What are you even thinking?"

"Ella Beth, the less you are familiar with my thoughts, the better."

"You care for him, don't you?" She sounded accusatory.

"I didn't, at first."

"What about now?" Ella Beth persisted.

"I'm afraid of the way I feel about him . . . it isn't in the same way as I do the Brethren." She stopped. It startled her to put words to that fact. "Jib is very affable to be with. He's congenial and . . . a charming man. Now that I have become acquainted with him, I do like him. He's a good man. Before you say anything, nothing's going on between us."

"Are you sure? Sounds to me as though you've fallen for him in the world's way. I'm not surprised this happened."

"How do you know anything about the world's way?" Addie Kate furrowed her brows. She liked Jib—more than she should for the short time they had spent together and more than was wise.

"Just do."

"I'll admit there's a fondness for him, but it doesn't mean something is 'going on.'"

"I warned you. Why didn't you listen to me?"

"I'm sorry," Addie Kate said. "I didn't want it to happen, but there you are. I hadn't paid enough attention to what was going on. If I had seen it coming, I would have stopped it."

"How?" Ella Beth asked.

"I don't know. Perhaps nothing. The truth is . . . he . . . he's . . . kissed me."

"Little sister, no-o-o! Don't show lack of sense!"

"I'm not."

"You're doomed."

"No, I'm not."

"We don't permit such . . . disgusting liberties. What'd he go and do that for?"

Addie Kate shrugged. "Guess he wanted to. He told me we'd get married, and, before I realized what was happening, he put his arms around me and kissed me."

"Where'd he kiss you?"

"On my mouth, silly."

"Pay more attention to what you are doing. Be more careful. You'll suffer humiliation if the Eldresses find out."

"They won't unless you tell."

"You must get over your attraction to him."

"Easy to say now. I'm overcome with shame."

It was another black lie she told. May God forgive her. "Honestly, Ella Beth, Jib's got a big heart. He's an honorable, worthy man."

"Forget him. Plain and simple. Leave him alone."

"I can't," Addie Kate said sharply.

"He's going back to his world, and you're committed to the Shaker way."

Ella Beth surveyed her younger sister in the moonlit room.

"Nothing can come of your foolishness. Why didn't you heed my warning?"

Addie Kate blew out a puff of breath.

"He's been very gracious to me. I can tell this is the news you want, though, isn't it? That he's left."

She went back to her bed and crawled into it, chastising herself for sharing the information with her sister.

Jib had proposed a marriage of convenience. Love was good, but it was not terribly vital, not in a world where security was so seriously important. But what if he *did* fall in love with her?

Addie Kate reminded herself that at least he'd honored her enough to want her as his lawfully wedded wife. Now what had he told her to remember? That if she stayed at the village, she would leave absolutely nothing behind as a lasting legacy. He didn't need to remind her. She was well aware of that and moaned. *God knows who I am and that's all that matters.* Or was it? Not to her, anyway. She squirmed, tormented by the heartache of being invisible to posterity. Jib was right. She didn't belong here. She wasn't a true Believer in her heart. Signing the covenant made her a hypocrite. She should have accepted his offer to leave. "I'm a foolish woman," she muttered.

Addie Kate jerked the pillow under her head and thumped it, crooked her arm against it, and stretched her legs trying not to think of her future days. The quicker she got used to the idea of a shattered dream, the better. As she drifted off to sleep, she vowed that for the rest of her life the memories of his kisses had to be snuffed out.

On second thought, she stuffed them away.

Chapter 6

$\mathscr{S}$ixteen days after the devastating fire at Pleasant Hill, Beckett Hollingsworth Claycomb, now sufficiently healed from his burns, carried his belongings from the room in the Trustees' Building to the roadway where he parked his hack.

The shiny black wagon served not only as his conveyance but also as his photography studio. Black oiled canvas curtains stretched across both sides and the back, with each section able to roll up when he pulled a rope. It had been a two-seater at one time, but he had removed the second seat to give more room for his safari's worth of bulky camera equipment and all the necessary chemicals for developing the photographs.

His span of mules, Hezekiah and Keziah, shifted their weight in their harnesses, shook their heads, and swished their tails. He talked to them, his voice low and soothing, and gave each of them a pat between their ears—his customary greeting—and "Hez" rewarded him with a playful nudge. "Kez" started with a whinny and ended with a hee-haw. Jib laughed. The animals were gentle, intelligent, and dependable. The Shakers had taken good care of them during his convalescence.

All morning he thought of Addie Kate and hoped she might change her mind and go with him. He hefted a trunk effortlessly into the confines of the hack, his arms taking on definition as he moved and twisted, and clambered in to place it. Jumping down and standing at the back, he brushed his palms together, pulled a handkerchief from his back pocket and mopped his forehead, taking off his hat to do so, and looked up as Addie Kate came strolling toward him. A broad smile swept his expression.

He called to her. "Yuh comin' tuh tell me yuh're goin' with me?"

* * *

Addie Kate knew it would be a mistake for her to stop by the Trustees' Office and watch Jib pack up. What purpose would it serve? But the thought of him leaving and her seeing him for perhaps the last time caused an actual ache in her breast. She had to talk with him once more before he left.

She came closer to him, glancing around to see if any Shakers might be watching. "Hello," she said.

"Hello," he answered and stroked his jaw with his knuckles. "Yuh need tuh leave Pleasant Hill."

They stared at each other until she barely nodded. "I must say you are persistent."

"Maybe I wanna be. If yer stayin', yuh'll live a life between a rock and a hard place . . . and fight the dragon."

She flinched. "The dragon?"

"Ain't her name Jerusha? Addie Kate, I want the best fer yuh. If yuh'd leave this place, yuh'd be livin' yer own life, and believe me, there's no feelin' in the world like that."

"I suppose so."

"What about yer dream?"

She shrugged. "Waste of time."

"Don't think so. But, I ain't gonna git intuh it with yuh tuhday."

"I don't want a rehash, either."

"Figgered we ought not quibble on the day I'm a leavin." Jib spoke without glancing at her. He bent over and tossed to his right a spindly fallen twig. He peeked her way and dusted his hands against his trousers.

They both spoke at once.

"Addie Kate—"

"Jib—"

Then she was in his arms, and he hugged her. They stood together for another minute just holding each other.

"I think yuh've guessed, hain't yuh?"

She pushed away enough to see his face. "What?"

"I'm gonna miss yuh somethin' terrible," he said. "Never considered marriage till I met yuh."

She breathed fast and shook her head as she squirmed out of his arms. "No rehashing, remember?" She returned his gaze without blinking.

"If yuh could marry, yuh'd choose me, wouldn't yuh?"

She never responded. What would he have done if she actually uttered the "yes" word instead of merely thinking it?

He took in and held a huge breath, then emptied his lungs in a long slow stream. "The trouble with you people here," he said abruptly, "is that you hold to a weird idea that to be a Shaker is to be a little better than other people."

If only she could answer, but she could not say a word and did not. She covered her face with her hands, nodding. She lowered her arms, but never moved away and neither did he. "Will I ever see you again?"

He rested a finger beneath her chin, lifted it, tilting her head. "Does it matter?"

She looked into his eyes and said, "Of course."

"Difficult tuh say. I'm aimin' for Indian Territory. Don't know what'll happen."

They stood close together in broad daylight, not concealed in any way.

"I hope everything goes all right for you," she said. "I'll be praying that God will protect you wherever you go."

He rubbed a knuckle over his lips. "If I come back again, it'll be tuh carry yuh off. So be ready. Don't want yuh backin' out another time on me. Afraid, though, that you'll forget me and that I was ever here."

"I'm sure I'll think of you from time to time."

He tipped back his head and laughed.

Addie Kate grasped his arm and let her hand slide down until their fingertips touched. "May things go well with you."

"Yer leavin' me with disappointment and heartache," he said. "Commitment tuh this way of livin' is foolishness."

"To me, it's called loyalty."

"Tuh what? Tuh rules made up by a woman from the world? Open yer eyes, Addie Kate!"

She flinched and backed off. "I've changed over the time you've been here. I have come to realize I have some say in what happens to me. But . . . I can't leave."

He embraced her. "Time tuh say goodbye."

"Yes," she whispered, with her breath and lips close to his ear. "Good luck to you."

That was all she could manage. Fearing her strength would not hold up and send her into his arms to sob, she turned, took a step back, and raised an arm in a gesture of farewell. Only once did she glance over her shoulder as she walked out of his life, back to her own. He had remained standing in the same spot, watching her.

* * *

The hack was nearly full, but not so much it wouldn't take what remained scattered on the ground: A camp stove, tent, rolled-up bedding, and an Indian rubber sheet which would be placed on the ground before rolling out the blankets. A coffee pot, an iron spider, and a bake oven were already stowed away as well as a candle lantern placed under the front seat. What should he load next?

Jib surveyed the pile of paraphernalia gathered about. His frying pan, dishes, and water pail were waiting to be stored inside. He went to and fro, manhandling everything up into the conveyance, stacking and roping it as securely as he could so that nothing would fall out.

Brother Hans Borg ambled over. "Taking your leave, eh?"

"Yep. All healed up. Good as new, thanks tuh Doc Spears and Sister Addie Kate." Though the scars of pink and red splashed across his hands and arms were an ugly, horrible reminder, he flexed his fingers in demonstration of their suppleness.

"Don't see many drays like this in these parts," Hans commented.

"Reckon not. Perfect fer muh purposes, though. Serves as the darkroom—tuh develop muh pictures," Jib said.

"Ah, ja sure, you betcha." Hans nodded. "Be pleased to help you load up," he said. "What d'you want?"

"Much obliged. Keeps me from havin' tuh git up an' down. That tripod'll do." He pointed.

"Going home?" Hans asked, hoisting the piece of equipment up to Jib, who laid it on the floor of the wagon against one side. He needed to leave a walkway down the middle.

"Travelin' tuh the 'Big Country.'"

"West? Wide open out there. Where's abouts?"

"Nebraska."

"Heard tell it's wild out there. Could be a dangerous trip."

"Only the Lord knows what's ahead. Wanna git tuh St. Louis so's I kin board a stern-wheeler tuh head up the Missouri River tuh Omaha."

"Nebraska, eh? Isn't that where General George Custer and his troops got massacred this past June? Read all about it in the newspaper. Ja, called the Battle of the Little Bighorn. And you want to go out there?"

"Shore do."

"Why?"

"Jist tuh git where I ain't now. Itchy feet, I reckon."

"How long will it take you?"

"Right smart while. Takin' muh time and gitten some pictures of the prairie and frontier life . . . Indians . . . buffalo hunters."

"Not any cowboys, eh?"

"Cowboys? Hope so."

Hans surveyed the boxes remaining on the ground. "What d'ya want next?"

Jib indicated. "That black thing."

"Looks like a death shroud."

"Camera cover. Called a focusin' cloth." Jib shook out the dense material, then smoothed and folded it before he placed it on the floor of the wagon. He rejoined Hans.

"What's so interesting about the open spaces to risk your own safety and comfort?"

"Jist wanna git some pictures of life out there. Hopefully capture the history what's bein' made. I'll take that haversack now." He gestured. "Careful. They's glass plates for the camera."

He piled the awkward bundles of equipment where they would have some cushioning from the jouncing of the wagon. The boxes of chemicals came next with the camera last.

"There. That's everythin', ain't it?" He turned, brushing his palms together. "Thank yuh, Brother Hans. Yuh the one in charge o' the broom factory?"

The man nodded. "Ja, sure."

"Tell yuh what." Jib jumped down out of the back opening. "I'll buy six if yuh got 'em tuh spare. Figger if I need a little pocket money on muh travels, can sell one er two."

Hans bobbed his head. "You betcha. Pull on over. I'll get you fixed up." He sauntered on toward the shop.

Jib ambled around to the front of the wagon, paused and gave Kez a pat on her flanks, and made his way up to the seat. He ran his hand across his cheeks and felt the two-day growth of whisker stubble on his face.

"Feelin' rather woolly tuhday. Ain't shaved in a while. Probably look like a vagrant."

He released the brake, clucked to his team, and flapped the reins. The mules heaved and the hack lurched forward. Jib stopped in front of the broom factory and jumped down.

Hans came out carrying six flat woven brooms with natural hardwood handles. After receiving payment for them, he went back to the shop.

Jib pulled on gloves, yanked his Stetson well down over his forehead, and climbed into the driver's seat. He clenched his hands tightly on the reins he held and drove away—from Pleasant Hill and out of Addie Kate's life. It wasn't what he wanted. But his mother had always said, "When yuh cain't do what yuh want tuh do, do somethin' else, and do it hard." He would have plenty of pictures to take along the journey. He knew that much. He would keep busy. He had to.

Was Addie Kate watching from some window?

* * *

Addie Kate walked away from Jib and crossed the wagon road. Trembling, she entered the Centre Family House.

"I'll live through this because I won't die from it," she said to the air.

She climbed the stairs to the upper level and knelt at a window overlooking the turnpike. With an elbow resting on the sill, she leaned her forehead against the glass pane and stared out the window at him. What was the point of wondering if she would ever see him again?

But didn't he say he might come back? It was awful watching Jib climb into his hack, seeing him disappear, taking her dream with him.

"If only the circumstances had been different," she said with a lump in her throat, an emptiness in her heart, and a longing to go with him.

Slowly tears blinded her and spilled over. As she made no effort to wipe them away, they rolled down her cheeks while great shuddering breaths came faster. She dropped her head upon her arms and wept for him—and for herself. A sob choked her, and she caught herself, straightened, and stood still, shutting her eyes. When she opened them, he was gone—out of her sight. Just like that. She better get hold of herself or she would definitely suffer punishment for acting in a worldly manner. "God, I ask for Your help."

"They need me here," she'd said. "No," he'd said, "they need your hands and your back." He was right, of course.

"Lord, I cannot go on without Jib. You gave me a chance to leave, and I didn't take it. I ask that You forgive me . . . now give me the strength I need to stay."

Addie Kate, engrossed in her own troubled thoughts, did not hear the door open and close. She did not know what made her turn around, but she sensed she was not alone—that someone stood near to her. She wheeled about to face, of all people, Jerusha—mere inches away. In her immediate panic, Addie Kate screamed and brought her fingers to her mouth.

"I . . . I didn't know you came in. How long have you been there?"

"Should that make any difference?" The Eldress's voice had the menace of a knife. She folded her arms across her chest, pursed her lips, and narrowed her eyes to slits. "Pray tell, what are you doing up here, Sister?"

Addie Kate's face grew warm. She clenched her teeth, swallowed hard, and turned away, not replying.

"Answer me!" Jerusha shrilled—and continued, "You seem to have the habit of ignoring me while I'm still speaking to you. You know the rules, yet you keep disregarding them. Your willful and headstrong behavior is improper conduct. You have behaved disgracefully too many times and there is no possible excuse. I cannot tolerate or permit these qualities."

It was not hard for Addie Kate to hear the venom in Jerusha's accusations, and she longed to make the hot retort which rose to her lips, but she suppressed it and prayed silently, *Lord, help me get away from this overpowering woman. Is she simply biding her time, waiting for the opportunity to catch me in some folly? I suspect that is so. Then she would be able to raise heaven and earth to have me face humiliation.*

Addie Kate stepped to the side, but Jerusha blocked her path, and for a moment they stood staring at each other, neither giving way. Addie Kate said, "I'm beginning to think it is impossible to please you."

Jerusha, wheezing for air, made a faint choking sound and hesitated for a beat. "How dare you speak to me that way," she snarled. She opened the door, scuttled out without a backward glance, and marched off, much to Addie Kate's relief.

Noticing the slight tremor of the Eldress's mouth and jowl, Addie Kate immediately pitied the older woman but became gripped by a sudden chill that left her weak and trembling.

Chapter 7

"*T*hank goodness you're here." Ella Beth raised up from her bed when her younger sister entered the bedroom. "Where have you been?"

"Around . . . somewhere." Addie Kate lit a taper and put it in the sconce.

"What were you doing?" The older sibling sat on the side of her bed, her legs dangling.

"Nothing in particular." Addie Kate yanked off her muslin head covering, laid it aside, and touched her hair, cropped short—the Shaker requirement. *What would she look like with longer hair?* she had wondered at times.

Ella Beth snorted indignantly. "You're being awfully secretive. Have you done something against the rules?"

Addie Kate swallowed wrong and choked and could not respond. "No!" she finally said, irritated. She undressed quickly by removing the bib, the shirt, and full skirt—the traditional garb. Her abrupt movements sent air currents that caused the candle's pointed flame to dip and tilt. She hung each item of clothing in its place on the wall pegs.

"Something happened. You owe me a simple explanation."

Standing in her shift at the oak washstand, Addie Kate poured tepid water from the heavy stoneware pitcher into the basin, the splashing water making a cool sound. She wiped her face, neck, and armpits.

"Nothing's wrong. Why would you think so?" She wriggled her nightdress over her head.

"For the fact that you are coming to bed later than usual says there is *something*. Tell me everything."

"Nothing to tell." She could talk more freely with Ella Beth than with other Sisters, but she did so guardedly. "I simply wanted a little private time to think." Pictures of Jib flashed through her mind as she blew out the light and flung herself across her bed. "To be honest, you wouldn't be interested."

"Try me. It's not a question of interest, but of concern."

"Shut your eyes," Addie Kate ordered and lay back, closing her own eyes, staying still until she heard her sister's rhythmic breathing indicating slumber. Then she cried into her pillow until she fell asleep.

Awakening with a start during the night, she tried to find a comfortable position but, in the end slipped off the bed. She stood over her sister who was sleeping soundly. "Ella Beth, wake up," she whispered, touching her sister's hand.

The woman opened her eyes and rolled out of bed to crouch beside Addie Kate, their heads together, their voices no more than whispers. "What's the matter with you?"

"Shh! What do you mean?" Addie Kate asked, bewildered.

"*That man*. Is he gone? Or is he still here?"

Addie Kate shook her head, putting a finger to her lips. "Shh. No. He left today."

"Thank Heaven. You think too much about him."

"Why do you keep calling him 'that man' the way you do? He has a name."

"I don't care what it is. I'm glad he's gone. Now you'll be able to get back to your old self. Everyone sees how different you are since you have been with him."

"I'm not any different."

"Yes, you are. I've made excuses for you, but you don't make it easy for me. You're on dangerous ground, little sister. I realize it, and so do others."

Addie Kate bit her lip. "I wish I hadn't told you about him," she muttered.

"You didn't need to. I could see with my own eyes how you are conducting yourself shamelessly. I was about ready to give you a necessary talking to."

"What am I doing so improperly?" she demanded.

"You like him . . . don't you?"

"I didn't at first."

"Does that mean you do now?"

"He's a fine man."

"You love him, don't you? You may not even know it, but you're in love with him. It sticks out all over you. Think, Addie Kate . . . there isn't any happiness in this for you. What will your feelings for him bring you?"

"Shh!" she said. "The truth is, I want to leave Pleasant Hill and he's my way out."

Ella Beth's eyes grew wide and she placed a splayed hand over her breast. "Be sensible. Don't say that." She made a little tut-tutting noise between her tongue and teeth. "You've become a stranger to me. My own little sister. How could you forsake us? You told me you two were just friends. What happened? You need to forget about him, that's what you need to do."

"I can't. Our friendship developed into something more, and I'm not saying I'm in love with him. So don't get all-overish about it."

"He's a stranger—whom you mustn't trust at all."

"Shh! Shame on you. Jib's a nice man."

"He's taking advantage of you, Addie Kate. You surely can see that."

"I enjoy being with him. You apparently never loved a man."

Ella Beth flinched. "Not true, I love all our Brethren."

"They're not who I mean."

"I don't know any other men. So there."

"Too bad for you. Jib is a decent person. He's a man of faith who is reliable and trustworthy—so unsophisticated yet wise and experienced."

"He's made quite an impression on you."

"He's an impressive person."

"I can't believe you would be so blind. You better hope you're as discerning about him as you think you are."

"He's become a friend."

Ella Beth shook her head. "He's not a Shaker—enough of a reason to stay away from him."

"He's opened my eyes about a lot of things," Addie Kate said wistfully. "Now I'm not sure what I am going to do without him."

"Maybe you built up something which wasn't there. So be quiet, little sister. Stop the sinfulness. Consider the impact on the village if you renounced your vows to Mother Ann."

"It doesn't matter a mound of beans to me what they'd think."

"Now you shush. Yes, it does. Are you saying you want to hurt them?"

Addie Kate paused, groping for the right words. She glanced away, then back at her sister. "You're . . . content living here . . . aren't you?"

Ella Beth caught Addie Kate's hands.

"Of course. This is the kind of life I want. This way is the best one for you, too. You won't be—"

"Happy? No, you want me to be satisfied to the same degree as you are."

"Listen, Jib's life is out there." The older sibling made a sweep with her arm.

Addie Kate nodded.

"Yes, but for many years something has been missing from my life. All I have ever wanted are a husband and children, and I don't want to argue with you about it, either. I didn't like Jib at first, but as I paid more attention to him, what he said sounded reasonable to me. I see his point of view about our doctrine."

"Hogwash!"

"Shh! I'm telling you he's a most companionable man. I'm very fond of him."

"He saw that you are a soft touch. He's turned you against us."

Addie Kate shrugged and wagged her head. "Not true. These desires have been in my heart for a mighty long time."

"How irresponsible and shameful of you."

"I don't believe so. What if . . . the very thing I want for myself is also what God wants for me? He works in mysterious ways, you know, and is mindful of my fears in reneging on my covenant and leaving Pleasant Hill on my own. It is entirely possible that God brought Jib to me . . . to give me the courage I needed to leave this place. It might be that He is saying, 'Decide what you want in life.' Anyway, I can't think of anyone or anything else. Jib's the best friend I ever had." She patted Ella Beth's arm. "Except for you, of course."

"You poor girl. You shouldn't have disclosed so much to him."

Addie Kate nodded and looked off into space. "He's different."

"Of course he is. The nonsense with you and *him* must end. Ignore him."

"Impossible."

"You knew him only a few weeks."

"I know, but I felt safe around him."

"Be still. Sakes alive, little sister. He would take you out into the cold and heartless humanity."

Addie Kate folded her hands in her lap. "He wanted to marry me, but I had vowed I wouldn't live after the flesh. Have you ever wondered what it'd be like to be with a man and birth a baby? Well, I have." She furrowed her brow, looking at her sister. "It's not absurd to think about things like that either." She may be a Shaker, but she was a woman, too.

"Shh." Ella Beth pressed her fingertips to her lips. "No, never, and you better not either henceforth. It isn't going to happen to you. So move on. If you keep talking about that, Sister Jerusha will find out, and I don't want to suffer punishment because of you."

Addie Kate waved a hand at her. "Don't be ridiculous. She's out of earshot."

"How do you know?"

"I just do. The woman makes me go gooseflesh. I can tell when she's around because my skin gets all creepy crawly. She's always spying."

"It does seem she's right there when we least expect her. Sure is spooky. As far as I'm concerned she's never been one who's dipped her toes in the milk of human kindness."

"Ha," Addie Kate added, "I want to sulfur-smoke my clothes after being with her to prevent catching any wickedness."

They both stifled a chuckle.

Abruptly, the door flew open. Sister Jerusha burst in from the hall and swept haughtily into the room. The light she held high cast shadows that swayed across the room and made her long white nightdress appear as a ghostly illusion. The Eldress stepped closer and leered down at them crouched on the floor together, her gaze darting from one to the other. "What's going on here?"

Terror shot through Addie Kate like a knife to the stomach. Did Jerusha sense the two women had been talking about her, and though they had spoken in hushed tones, had she listened in on their conversation about Jib?

Bile now burned at the back of Addie Kate's throat, and she dug her fingernails into her palms. "What do you want, Sister?"

The Eldress took a deep breath and, with a harsh chicken-squawk sounding voice, said, "Sisters Addie Kate and Ella Beth, pray tell what are you two doing . . . huddled together down there?"

Neither woman made a sound as they exchanged glances. Both stood. Addie Kate's heart beat rapidly and a shiver ran down her back.

"Answer me," the Eldress growled. Her eyes blazed. The veins on her neck stood out. "And don't lie to me."

"Your accusation is false. I have always been truthful with you," Ella Beth said.

"Is that right? Somehow I do not believe you. You have always been difficult to deal with."

Ella Beth opened her mouth, but Jerusha silenced her with a wave of her hand. Addie Kate interceded, "I'm sorry if we were praying too loudly."

"Enough!" Jerusha barked. "Now get back to your own beds, and don't let me catch you two disobeying the rules again."

"Yes, ma'am," they said, almost in unison. Each climbed into her own bed and waited for Jerusha to say something else.

But the Eldress lowered her candle, glowered at the two, drew a wheezy breath, and went into a coughing fit. Without looking at them, she spun around on her heel and tottered out of the room into the darkness and out of sight.

Addie Kate turned on her side to face her sister, leaned on one elbow, and propped her head with one fist. "That was most unfortunate . . . her finding us together. But she can't prove we weren't praying. She doesn't like to be wrong, and she's suspicious of us. Of me, at least . . . that's pretty obvious. She doesn't like me, and she knows I am aware of that fact."

"Addie Kate, you were so convincing I must say I think you should be on the stage."

"Didn't you think she looked quite smug?" Addie Kate asked.

"I think she resembled warmed-over death," Ella Beth offered. "Choking and gasping for air after that rant. The woman is hopeless. She has the need to pick on others for some reason."

"She's very likely hiding her own weaknesses."

"Actually, I think she would find fault with the angel Gabriel himself."

"She's infuriating, for sure, if you ask me. Do you suppose we'll be like her in twenty year's time?"

"Heaven forbid." The two peeked at each other and chuckled.

"I can't imagine her as ever being young. I think she's always been an old grouch."

Addie Kate stretched out on her bed. "She's an unhappy woman. Otherwise, she wouldn't be so critical."

Were the other Sisters in the room awake now, she wondered, *and did they hear Jerusha's whole tirade?* If so, none of them said one word.

Though Addie Kate was tired and her head ached, she reflected on the events of the day. It was pointless to wonder if Jib would ever come back, and she, with more than a tiny piece of her heart, desperately hoped that he would. What if he *did*? She asked herself that over and over. If it ever happened, he would probably come back married with a passel of kids. She frowned. For some reason the notion of him married distressed her and she had no wish to dwell on the reason for it.

Chapter 8

*T*he October sky was blue and clear. A beautiful autumn day with the leaves in blazing colors of reds, oranges, yellows, and browns parachuting down; the geese honking in their formations flying south; katydids rasping; corn stalks rattling when the wind gusted; and the fallen apples rolling on the ground, releasing a cidery smell. Addie Kate dawdled making her way to the Sisters' Shop—her new assignment—and hoped to silence the tumult in her heart.

Moving off the path, she hid behind a monstrous pine tree and gave in to the need to let her tears come—not a moderate flow, but a flood—sobbing uncontrollably.

"What's this? Who's there?" a voice called. "Do you need help?"

Addie Kate stopped short, swallowed a sob, and struggled to breathe calmly. "I'm all right."

The voice objected, "No. Something's wrong."

"Leave me be," Addie Kate said sharply.

"I won't."

Addie Kate choked, brought her fingers to her mouth, and peered through her blurred vision to see Sister Esther Breckinridge staring at her. She smiled in a watery fashion at her.

"Gracious, Sister, you are pale as can be." Esther clutched the Sister's arm and asked, "Are you ill?"

"You can let me go," she said, shaking herself free. "I'm simply having a weepy day."

Esther shook her head. "There's more going on than that. Tell me."

Addie Kate stared at Esther a long moment in which she fought hard to control her emotions. "I'm afraid to. You'll find it sinful."

"Try me."

"I don't take any interest in doing anything. I just drift through each day." She wiped her face dry with her palms, drawing in several breaths as deeply as she could manage. She respected the middle-aged woman with dark brown eyes, a broad sweet smile, and who was genuinely tenderhearted.

"Then you are sick," Esther said. "You appear the picture of despair." She drew the younger woman toward her. "I can see you're in a bad way. It doesn't do to bottle things up. I always think it helps people to talk. Confession is good for the soul."

"My life has become so confusing, Sister. I don't understand how to deal with what's wrong. I feel lost and bewildered and . . . old."

"What is your age, Addie Kate?"

"Twenty-seven."

"That is not old, I can assure you, and none of us knows where our paths in life are leading, but we can trust the Lord to guide us no matter what our age is."

"Yes, but I suspect that what'll be waiting for me in the years to come is what is happening to me now. Our life here is so predictable. One day is like another—all work and weariness, restless sleep at night, and then it all repeats. The clock is ticking, and, in a short time, I'll turn around and be forty and then fifty, and I'll just be doing more of the same old stuff and find there is nothing to show for my life."

"I hear you," Esther said softly, and squeezed Addie Kate's hand. "You can honor God in whatever you do, can't you? Now, please tell me what the *real* problem is. Don't worry about telling me. I'm as safe as a locked box."

"I couldn't help doing what I did and am absolutely miserable and so ashamed of myself. Even the rules didn't save me. Sister Esther, I'm like the apostle Paul when he said the things he shouldn't do are the ones he does, and the things he should do are the ones he doesn't. I am a wretched person."

Esther shook her head and furrowed her brow. "You poor thing."

"Most of the time, I'm coping with my thoughts." Addie Kate said nothing more for a time as they walked along scrunching the dried leaves under their feet. "There are times my heart is so troubled, but I'm determined not to show my misery in front of the Eldresses."

"A wise thing. What is the cause of your sadness?"

Addie Kate glanced sheepishly at her companion and said, "A man. One who isn't a Believer. I miss him terribly . . . and . . . I may never see him again . . . and must get used to living without him . . . but I'm finding it's unbearable. There is an ache in my heart every time I think of him. I don't sleep well. My appetite is gone. I'm not even interested in remaining a Shaker."

She and Esther exchanged glances. "Whatever do you think of me?"

"Right off, I'm sorry the man is not with you, but I'm also saddened that you think our mandates here are such a burden."

"Do you understand, then, why this is hard for me to talk about it? What is wrong with me? I do wake up happy when I dream about him." Her cheeks became wet. "You see why I find it difficult to go on. My anguish seems beyond endurance." Addie Kate stopped talking and snuffled. A brief silence ensued.

"In my mind, I'm putting myself in your place," Esther said. "It is hard to carry on with what we must at times. Sister, I do understand what you are experiencing."

"How can you?" Addie Kate splayed her hand against her heart. "I shouldn't trouble you with this."

"Don't think that. The Bible tells us to help bear one another's burdens, and in this way, we will fulfill the law of Christ. Addie Kate, I too, had heartbreak. Years ago, I dreamed of love and marriage. I suspect most women do."

"You cared for a man, too?"

A little snort fizzed up from Esther. "Uh-huh. Sound far-fetched to you?"

"No, I didn't mean it like that. I just never suspected you had ever suffered unrequited love."

"I assure you it's the worst feeling ever."

"How were you . . . uh, able . . . to go on?" Addie Kate pressed her friend to know.

"Life is extraordinary. I live one day at a time. Which is exactly what you must do."

"You don't care for him anymore?"

"That's not what I said. I have merely accepted reality and gotten on with my life. I'm assuming he has, too."

"What happened?" Addie Kate asked, walking along beside Esther.

The older Sister raised her eyebrows. "We grew up together. I thought he was an honorable person, a hard worker and trustworthy. I adored him. Then came the War Between the States. I wished to marry right away . . . he wouldn't. He feared the possibility of leaving me a widow, so we agreed to an engagement. The thought of him returning home sustained me through the years. If he had been killed, I would have mourned forever. Well, he came back in the month of April. We planned to be married in June. My father died from typhoid fever shortly before our wedding, and that was when my family was horrified at what we learned about our economic status. We thought we were financially sound, but the balance we had was infinitely less than what we needed. Everything we possessed went to creditors."

Esther paused. "My thought was to postpone everything until we could straighten the situation out. I discovered, though, my beau felt deprived of a comfortable income. Turned out, he had counted on my inheritance to support us. I released him at once from our betrothal. I can't tell you how devastated I was. It was at that point I joined the Shakers. I had nothing. They required me to have nothing. Worked out fine." She plastered a smile on her face and glanced at Addie Kate.

"I'm sorry. I had no idea."

"No reason for you to be aware. We don't share our life stories with one another. And we definitely don't ask questions of each other, but every one of us possesses secrets."

"No good comes from snooping into the past of others here, does it?"

Esther nodded. "I consider myself fortunate that I came. I'm content with the way life is lived here." She took hold of Addie Kate's hand. "I hate to see you hurting, though. You love him, don't you?" She released her hold on the younger Sister's hand.

Caught off guard by the question, Addie Kate prepared to deny her feelings. Instead, she shrugged and turned her palms up. "Perhaps. I'm not sure. I do appreciate his kindness. He's among the kindest people I've ever met." She lowered her head and stopped walking.

"Here's the thing," Esther said. "Love is something one finds when least expecting it. I'm going to give you some advice, though you never asked for any. If I had it to do over, I wouldn't have given up so easily on my hopes of a home and children. I squelched what I dreamed of and I'll regret that for the rest of my life. I can't tell you what to do. It's your life . . . and . . . your decision to make. What the Believers think shouldn't make any difference to you. They are not your judge. I'm only saying what I think. I can say there is such contentment when being able to live in the custom you fancy. There is nothing disgraceful about wanting a husband and family, Sister."

Addie Kate studied Esther's face. "Thank you for sharing your story with me. It has been comforting to listen to you. I don't dare mention this to anyone else."

"What about Ella Beth?"

Wagging her head, Addie Kate said, "She doesn't understand. She is very happy here and thinks I should be, too." She hesitated.

"I can't do a thing about it now, anyway. He's left. He offered matrimony as a way to take me away from here. I'm afraid I've made a pretty general failure of my own happiness. I told him I couldn't go with him because I had already finalized my vows to Mother Ann."

"For Heaven's sake, Sister, your first duty is to God, not Mother Ann. You weren't true to our heavenly Father, your man, or yourself, were you?"

Addie Kate shook her head. "No, guess not, and I have no idea where he is or how he is, so I cannot contact him. I must put him out of my mind, but I'm simply not ready to do that yet."

"You don't need to erase your memories of him."

"I'll muddle through life somehow," Addie Kate said, expelling a deep breath.

"What you can do," Esther looked around furtively, "is to leave this place when the opportunity comes . . . and go live the life you want."

Addie Kate gasped. "I can't believe you'd tell me to forsake my vows."

"I thought you wanted your man to come back for you."

"Oh I do . . . but . . . I don't, either. I'm confused about it and downright scared."

"I wasn't brave enough to fight for what I dreamed of. Perhaps you are more courageous than I was. I strongly suggest praying about him . . . and the matter."

"Will the Lord listen to me even though I have broken a vow of purity made before Him?"

Esther chuckled. "Of course. He is merciful and forgives us when we ask Him to as long as we are sincere. Life gets easier to figure things out as the days go by—especially when you can stay busy. Keep on as you are doing. How advantageous the harvest season is here. Time, one way or another, is a great mediator. Things do work themselves out. If he's intended for you, he'll be back."

They reached the Sisters' Shop. Addie Kate took hold of the door latch, swung around, and looked Esther in the eyes. "Please don't tell anyone what we've talked about. I don't want Sister Jerusha to get wind of it or she'll have a conniption fit. Promise me you will never say anything?" she pleaded.

Esther nodded. "I would never betray you. Cross my heart."

She leaned forward and patted Addie Kate's arm reassuringly. "Now, you must never give up on what you want. Keep petitioning God until you get some kind of answer. Perseverance is the key to answered prayer."

The women entered the room. The Sisters, chattering away when Addie Kate and Esther walked in, stopped their lively buzz of conversation if at a signal and smiled politely at the two. The room became uncomfortably silent.

Addie Kate strode across the floor, hoisted a ladder-back chair from the wall peg, and pulled it to the window to gain as much light as she could. She seated herself and focused her attention on a Brethren's sock that needed to be mended. After fitting the darning egg into the stocking's heel, she threaded a needle, and while making the necessary tiny stitches, images of Jib skittered through her imagination. She kept turning over in her mind what he'd said.

Suppose she were to go on this way. That was a problem. She was in trouble and it was because she was thinking of him too much. "I must stop behaving this way," she said, but only to herself.

"They're rigid," she heard him say. "They form an opinion on everyone by their own narrow standards. In their spiritual pride, they live separate from the world, but then they depend on it for economic maintenance. They eat and work and sleep and rise up to do the same things again. Always, there are the scrutinizing eyes of the Elders and Eldresses watching over everyone waiting to catch any instance of impropriety." Addie Kate had not been able to dismiss her talk with Esther either. In the midst of her musings the truth hit her, and she dropped the stocking to her lap. Jib and Esther *were* right. She *could* leave the village. Mother Ann was a mere mortal just like herself. The Almighty *would* forgive her.

She lifted her head. The weight that had been sitting on her spirit for weeks now left her in a rush of clarity. Beckett Hollingsworth Claycomb was important to her—for her future. She needed him and pledged to ask in her prayers every day for Jib's return to her, trusting in the goodness and faithfulness of the Lord. What if Jib forgot about her, though, or chose not to come back? What would she do then?

Part 2

Chapter 9

*J*ib let the mules amble at a leisurely pace on the road—which wasn't much more than wagon tracks that had beaten down the tall grass—along the Platte River, a slow and shallow and spread-out body of water with cottonwood trees growing on its islands. As he drove farther west, he listened to the sounds of the plain—the wind rustling the grass, the clomping of the mules' hooves, and the scrunching of the hack's wheels on the crisp, bluish-green buffalo grass. He shaded his eyes as he stared off to where the sun was three-quarters down from overhead. Every way he turned, the prairie spread endless under the vast sky. He scanned the wide reaches of it. He did not see any houses or people, only rippling grass.

"A man is only a speck in the midst of this expanse of green that seems to go on forever," he said out loud to Hezekiah and Keziah. They pricked their ears forward and swished their tails.

He scuffed his jaw with his knuckles. "This here land'll be settled up someday. Has tuh, bein's it's already a state. There'll be towns all along here, and the railroad'll come and people will come with it."

Jib was in Nebraska now. He came via a sternwheeler on the Ohio River to Cairo, Illinois, and from there to St. Louis on the Mississippi, then on to Omaha on the Missouri River. His mules shipped as freight and fared well on the journey.

The sternwheeler had landed at Omaha the day before yesterday. Jib decided to stay in town the first night he was there in order to have plenty of time for stockpiling the necessary supplies needed for his journey. Today, the weather was cool with the feel of fall.

"Whoa!" he ordered, and the animals stopped. He fumbled in a shirt pocket and yanked out a folded piece of paper. Shoving his hat back with his index finger, he unfolded and checked a map by following with his finger along the course of the Platte river. He heaved a sigh, jammed the map into place, and, looking up, spotted two does grazing. They lifted their heads, looked his way, but stayed where they were.

Grabbing his rifle from under the front seat of the hack, Jib clambered down and picketed Hez and Kez, allowing them to graze. He made his way unhurriedly toward the deer, the grass rasping against his boots. He was close enough to take a shot when an eight-point buck, which apparently had been lying down, raised up near where he had spotted the two female whitetails.

Jib squatted on his haunches to hide as it started for him. Hoping to get a well-timed shot, he waited until the buck was within a hundred and fifty yards of him. Then he stood, pressed his cheek against the gunstock, and sighted down the barrel. The animal kept coming on a run, and when it was within range, Jib fired.

The animal never slowed and Jib jumped out of the way.

"Musta missed," he mumbled and shook his head.

It stopped abruptly, turned back toward Jib, came at him again at full speed, then suddenly crumpled to the ground.

"Jumpin' Jehoshaphat! Got 'im after all!"

The animal thrashed convulsively, kicking, snorting, and flailing its legs in the high grass before becoming still.

Jib cautiously approached the animal, poked it with the muzzle of his rifle, and saw that the bullet had gone right between the eyes.

Withdrawing his hunting knife from its sheath, he bled and gutted the stag, then carefully ripped the skin off the carcass.

After he finished the butchering, he cleared a circle from the ground of anything that might burn. "Cain't take no chances for settin' the surroundin's on fire."

That done, he busied himself gathering wood along the riverbank, then laid and lighted a small cookfire. Within the hour he had a choice cut of venison on a wooden spit, sputtering and hissing as the fat dropped upon the flames. The tantalizing savory smell proved almost too much. Jib was hungry. He knelt to poke the coals and added more wood. He sliced off a sliver from the hunk only to discover it was tough and dry like an old leather boot. Its aroma had been far better than its taste. While working the meat in his mouth, he began the action of sharpening his fixed-blade knife by pushing it on the edge of a whetstone, spitting on it now and then to create a slurry liquid.

While pressing the ball of his thumb gingerly to the cutting edge, testing for sharpness, he caught the rumble of galloping horses' hooves and watched as a ragged line of Indians splashed across the Platte. Their scalp locks held eagle feathers that fluttered and spun in the wind.

When Jib saw the ten of them riding toward him, he slid the knife back into its sheath and put it on the front seat of his hack. He wiped his mouth with the back of his hand and, paying no attention to the Omahas, checked on his team as they chomped away. He had seen signs of the Natives' presence and even passed small bands of them camped amid the bluffs. They had been friendly and peaceable enough.

The band galloped up out of the water and rushed toward him, whooping, yelling, and shouting. They were warriors with their faces painted in streaks of yellow, red, and white. A few had guns, but most of them had bows and arrows, and one had a long lance. Jib's heart beat fast.

They gave a war whoop and, brandishing their weapons, charged at him. He stood with his hat off, the breeze ruffling his hair, and scanned them as they swarmed about him. He thought they were bluffing and trying to scare him, that when they got close, they would call out and ask for something to eat.

Instead, they swung in a circle around him, shouting and pointing and waving their bows. One raised his spear. A shiver ran through Jib. Trapped with no means of saving himself, he swallowed hard, his Adam's apple bobbing,

A young warrior halted his horse right in front of Jib, raised his bow, and taking the arrow that he held in his teeth, notched it to the bowstring. He drew it back to tautness, pointed straight at Jib's chest, but never released it.

Jib trembled. He had no way out of the fix he was in.

"Help me, Lord," he prayed and waited for a what-to-do while his mind worked. He remembered from the map there was a trading post about a quarter of a mile away, but there was no way he could outrun these renegades. His throat tightened and his breathing sounded almost as noisy as the rustling grassy landscape.

An older Indian with a pockmarked face galloped up yelling and waving his arms wildly. He made a guttural sound and struck the readied shaft aside, making it drop. He shouted and signaled for the others to pull back, causing quite a commotion among them. At last, after some argument and waggling of weapons in the air, one by one the whole party turned and rode off in the direction of the river as noisily as they had come, their howls and whoops and the hoofbeats fading as they went.

Jib spraddled his feet to steady himself, wiped a sleeve across his forehead, stuffed his hands in his pockets, and kept his gaze on the rebels until the last one was out of sight. Releasing his breath, he went limp and sank to the ground. He lost no time extinguishing and smothering the embers, getting back on the trail, and riding off through the tall prairie grass into the sunset.

* * *

Purple shadows lengthened over the land, and evening arrived. A wolf howled somewhere, or it might have been an Indian. Jib realized they imitated wolves' howls sometimes. As he rode along the rim of the river bluffs, he glimpsed a tiny flickering light far across the waves of green grass. It was visible from far away and up a slight rise of hill. He snapped the reins on the mules' flanks and, with a lurch, the hack picked up speed, pushing toward the beacon.

Getting closer, he recognized the peaked white tents of an Army encampment, and hearing the faint sound of voices, he felt relief as he came upon a detachment of cavalry along the Platte. He pulled his mules into the light of the bonfire before he drew rein. Several of the enlisted men sat around the cook's fire eating their supper.

"Howdy," Jib called, pulling to a halt.

An imposing man glanced up from his plate and called, "Looking for somebody, stranger?"

Jib turned on the wagon seat. "The officer in charge here."

"I'm the one you want to see, then. What can I do for you?"

"Jist passin' through these parts and seen yer fire. Thought I'd check out what it was about."

"Where you headed?"

"Fort Kearney." He pushed his hat back with his thumb.

"You aiming to muster in?"

"Lookin' tuh be a photographer somewhere. Thinkin' that might be a place to start."

"Prospects won't be too bright, I can tell you. Dark time for the military, you know."

"Name's Beckett Claycomb."

"Homer Smith. Captain Homer Smith." The man rose, looming big with coal-black hair, bushy eyebrows, and a neatly trimmed mustache. "You're welcome to join us."

"Much obliged."

A private came and took hold of the bridle. Jib scrambled down from the seat and clasped hands with the captain in a handshake.

Several of the enlisted men glanced over at Jib as they pulled out boxes and pitched the tents. Another private, who introduced himself as James Rooney, came to help with the mules. He unhitched and unharnessed them and put them in with the horses. Hez and Kez lay down first thing and rolled over back and forth.

"Want some grub? Go ask for something."

"I could do with a cup of coffee. Shore smells right pleasin'. Reckon it'd hit the spot. Got a haunch of venison I'm willin' tuh contribute tuh the soldiers mess if yuh'd like." Jib rubbed his left eyebrow with the tip of a forefinger.

"How old is it?" the cook asked.

"Only a few hours. Killed it a little after the noon. Done got it dry-salted."

"Sure enough? Yes, sir, we'll be right glad to take it."

Jib tugged a heavy canvas bundle out of the hack, plopped it on the ground, and unrolled it.

The men stopped what they were doing and came close. A couple of them took a quick look at each other with broad grins.

Jib accepted the steaming coffee, blew over the rim, and took a tiny sip. "Yuh say there's no openin' for a paid photographer at Fort Kearney?"

"That's right. No call for anyone in that position at this time. Now I'm pretty sure there's some little space that's not been appropriated for something else if you don't mind setting up shop in a log shack. Doubt they'd charge you for it. Your income'll be your profits. Might think of looking in Columbus, though. Fair-sized town . . . has better opportunities. Maybe could throw in for a spell with a photographer already established in the business, or leastwise, he could help you find a suitable building to house your own studio."

"Somethin' tuh consider. Thought yuh oughtta know some Indians ran at me over yonder."

"Do tell?"

Jib nodded. "Be obliged if I could pitch muh tent here with yer company fer the night."

"Sure thing."

"Soon's I finish this cup, I'll fetch muh sleepin' gear."

He loudly swallowed the last of the coffee, and, with the back of his hand, he smeared the wetness from the corners of his mouth.

Early the next morning before the camp was astir, Jib awoke. He lay still for a while, done in from yesterday. Then he threw his blanket off and sat up, dug the sand of sleep out of his eyes, and finger-combed his hair. It was dark inside the tent, but he stood. Shivering a little, he dressed and went out into the dawn's dimness. He gathered his camera equipment from the hack and positioned the tripod hoping to take pictures of the sunrise, the troops responding to reveille, and the presentation of colors. However, the day arrived with fog, and it wasn't until midmorning that the haze lifted like a curtain and the sun broke through and shone clear.

Jib remained with the detachment two days and three nights. On the third day, now early in November, as soon as breakfast was over, he left the military camp and started for the town of Columbus. The morning proved cloudy and damp and became cloudier with the wind switching from the northwest. By noon, it began to rain. Toward midafternoon, the winds picked up, the temperature plummeted, and the rain turned to snow. He shook against the chill.

He never expected the weather conditions to get so bad, but it seemed that in the plains, weather was always a surprise.

"I'm a thinkin' it would be best tuh be lookin' for a shelterin' place," Jib said to his team. He no sooner said the words than he came upon a Conestoga going in the opposite direction. A tired-looking man with a stubbly face held the bridle and led his horses as they trudged their way through the powdery white softness.

"Goin' far?" Jib hollered to the man.

"Illinois. Me an' mine is turnin' back. Life's too hard in the West," the man yelled.

They saluted, the creaking wagons slowly rolled by each other, and Jib continued on his way. He had not gone too much farther when a full-fledged whiteout developed with the flakes flying in such a fury they stung his face. Blinded by the whipping and whirling chaos, he could not see where he was going, fumbled around, finally gave up, and trusted the mules' judgment about picking their way. Late afternoon came, and still they plodded on until they halted in front of a mound.

Shivering, Jib scrambled down from his seat, stepping into an ankle-deep drift, causing him to suck in his breath. Hugging his coat firmly against his chest, he floundered through the snow to what he supposed was a sod house.

As he approached the shelter, the door flung open and a bearded man, holding up a lighted lantern, appeared.

"You lost? Better stay the night! Put your mules away in that stable over yonder. We'll give you some hot food and coffee," he called over the wailing howl of the storm and directed his attention to a lumpy form in a little rise of the land. "When you're ready, grab hold of the long rope fastened at the shed's door. The other end is fastened to the corner of the house. It'll guide you here, and just come on in."

Jib flicked the rumps of Hez and Kez, who inched forward into a dark room. He pulled a tin lantern from the floor of his wagon and lit the candle wedged in it. Lifting high the light, he surveyed the low structure built at the side of the soddy and banked around with prairie hay to provide protection from the cold. Grateful to be out of the sharp wind, he spent the better part of two hours rubbing the mules dry and left them with two horses and a milk cow.

Finding and grabbing hold of the rope, Jib made his way to the house, lifted the latchstring, and flung the door open on a gust of wind. He entered, permitting the cold to swirl in with him, and hastily closed the door. The aroma of mouthwatering food welcomed him.

He crossed the threshold in silence and rubbed his hands together as he scanned the interior.

It was a one room soddy, cheerful and warm, in stark contrast to the dark and cold of the outdoors. The home was sparsely furnished with a cast-iron cookstove, stools and chairs, and a table with a glowing coal oil lamp placed in its center. At the far end of the space, a colorful, intricately pieced quilt hung as a partition to shut off the bed against the wall by itself. Several braided rag rugs lay scattered on the floor's narrow-wood planks. Canvas tacked up tightly against the ceiling gave the room a cozy and pleasant look.

"Come on in. You can hang your headgear and coat on that peg by the door," the homeowner said. "Name's Rufus. Rufus Barnard Haines."

Jib reached up and snatched off his misshapen Stetson with one hand and shook Rufus's outstretched hand with the other.

"Beckett Claycomb. Jist call me Jib, though." He shrugged out of his bulky garment and hung it up.

"Well, Jib, I can't deny you shelter in weather like this. And I allow you're more than a might peckish after fighting with the elements and caring for your animals."

"Truly appreciate yer hospitality, Rufus. Shore feels good tuh be snug indoors. Never aimed tuh trouble no one."

"Isn't none. This here's my woman." He pointed. "Her name is Zara Melvina."

She was a short, dainty woman with her hair coiled about her head in sizable, bulging braids. She stood at the cookstove, stirred something that bubbled and smelled mouthwatering in a big black kettle, and peeked at Jib, but she never smiled or spoke.

"Pluck a chair and have a seat. Would you like some coffee?" Rufus asked.

Jib nodded. "Yes, thank yuh." He settled himself and studied Zara as she snatched a cup from an open shelf and poured the steaming drink from a blue-enameled coffeepot. She brought it to Jib, turned away, and went back to the range where she dipped up a plateful of thick stew, hot and fragrant, with plenty of potatoes, turnips, carrots, and rabbit meat. Jib's hands rested beside the plate while he thanked God for His providential care in providing this warm and welcoming home.

"Go ahead and dig in," Rufus said. He motioned to Zara who brought out a pan from the oven and then placed a bowl of butter and a small crock of honey in front of Jib.

"Found a tree full of bees down by the creek. My woman's got a light hand with biscuits, makes the best bread you'll ever eat. They're puffed up and soft and flaky."

Jib ate heartily, then laid down his fork. Picking up his coffee cup, he held it in both hands. "Don' know when I've enjoyed a meal more, ma'am," he said. "For shore 'tis the best I've eaten in a powerful long time. I greatly appreciate yer hospitality. For a fact, yer a fine cook." He bobbed his head.

She busied herself straightening things, came to the table to clean up after Jib finished, and washed the dishes in a pot of water heating on a front burner. Completing her housekeeping duties, she sat beside Rufus and across from Jib at the table.

Their two boys sat on stools across the room, saying nothing.

"These here're my sons." He motioned them forward and each stood on either side of their father.

"Taller one is Raymond Clarence. He's being six years old. Younger one is Wilmer Clifford. He's being four. They're kind of shy. Fine boys, though. Hard workers for their ages."

Jib nodded to acknowledge them. "Howdy." He noted the way Rufus gave each a pat on the shoulder. "I kin tell yer right smart proud of 'em. They must be excellent help fer yuh."

"Yes, sir, they are. I'm very pleased with them."

The blizzard howled and shrieked into the night. Rufus said, "Bedtime for you two young uns. Go help your ma." After directing them, he turned to Jib, adding, "Hope you don't mind bunking with the boys in front of the stove."

The boys obeyed and helped their mother drag the mattress, now stored on their parent's bed, to the floor in front of the stove.

Zara spread a sheet on top of it, plumped three goose-feathered pillows, and added a feather tick to draw up over them.

"Come on now, you young rabbits, and hop into your holes before the wily fox catches you," she teased, kissing her sons as they lay down.

Rufus and Zara pulled the curtain for their privacy. Jib removed his outer clothing, folded each item, and shivering in his under flannels, sank into the well-padded straw tick, exhausted.

Stuffed with dry prairie hay, it held a sweet smell and rustled and crackled under his weight. He pulled the feather tick over his shoulders and marveled at how snug and comfortable he was. Jib straightened out his body and, without hesitation, fell asleep to the moaning and whistling of the winds outside and the whisper of snow against the window glass.

Late the next day the sky cleared, but Jib stayed a second night with the family. The following morning, after breakfast, with the wind still and the sun shining brightly, Jib wound a woolen scarf about his head and ears and neck.

"I'm a hankerin' tuh git tuh Columbus before it gits too far intuh the year," he said as he buttoned himself into his overcoat. "Got slowed down in late summer because of a fire. Kinda behind the time of year tuh be goin' anywhere."

"What's waiting at Columbus for you?"

"Hopin' tuh open muh own photography studio," Jib said with a sort of shrug. "Had a notion tuh git hooked up with the military at Fort Kearney but learned that likely won't happen. I jist wanna record history in pictures as it's bein' made. Settlin' the West, buffalo hunts, Indians, cattle drives. Thin's like that. Folks long time from now needs tuh understand what we're talkin' about. I aim tuh show 'em . . . in pictures."

"Forty-five or fifty miles yet to Columbus," Rufus said. "Country's rugged. Looks level, but it isn't. And with about a foot to eighteen inches of snow, you'll be slowed down, for sure. If I was you, I'd follow the Elkhorn River. Got a little settlement on Union Creek where you might need to stop over. Folks'll take care of you. Columbus'd be about thirty-five miles on with a road you could probably see to follow."

Jib shook hands with Rufus.

"Thank yuh for all yuh've done tuh help me. I'll never forget yer kindness. God bless yuh all."

He shook hands with Zara and said, "Goodbye, ma'am. Thank yuh for yer delicious cookin'." Then he turned to Raymond Clarence and Wilmer Clifford and shook their hands.

"Goodbye. Yuh both are fine young men." he said.

Jib pulled open the door, flinched at the blast of bitter air which smote him full in the face, and headed to the stable to hitch Hez and Kez to the hack. He climbed to the seat, clucked to them, and the wagon rolled forward. He waved to the Haines family, now standing in the threshold, and drove away, breaking a trail through the snow.

He got to Columbus four days later.

* * *

A week went by, then two weeks. No letter came to Addie Kate from Jib. Her life resumed its normalcy outwardly. She was everywhere she was supposed to be and she did everything she was supposed to do, settling down to the old humdrum routine. She arose each morning knowing exactly what the day would bring and moved mechanically through the hours performing her duties. However, she had few words and fewer smiles for the Sisters when they spoke to her, and she became increasingly pale and thin. Jib occupied her thoughts, no matter what tasks occupied her hands. Madness seemed very near at times when the idea of his presence was so strong she turned her head and imagined seeing or hearing him. How could she bear the days or weeks or possibly months ahead of her without him? For the most part, Addie Kate did not deceive herself. Her friendship with Jib was over, gone out of her life as suddenly as it had come. She must forget about him and work from dawn to dark for the sake of the village.

Night after night, she sighed when she climbed into bed and lay there, exhausted. With sleep would come the dreams of him. They were always the same. He would come to her, whisper her name, take her in his arms, and put his mouth on hers.

"There is no one in the world for me but you," she would say.

One time, Addie Kate awoke but struggled to open her eyes. There, to her amazement, stood Jib. She reached for him.

"Hurry and git yerself ready," he whispered. "I'm takin' yuh away from here."

She breathed deeply and closed her eyes, opened them again, and focused. He was gone. Jib was not there. All was quiet and still. Addie Kate stiffened, then sat up in bed, gasping for air. She was helpless here. Would he ever come for her in reality?

Chapter 10

*T*inkle. The little bell above the door jingled.

Jib looked up from across the room. A tall, curly-headed, black-haired man stood on the door's threshold. He was standing in the shadow, so Jib, unable to see the visitor's face very well, scooted his stool away from the work counter.

"Hello," he said, speaking as he moved to greet the visitor.

"Mr. Claycomb!"

"That's me. How kin I help yuh?"

The man came into the room. "Remember me? Name's James Rooney. You rode into our bivouac out on the prairie a while back. Brought a dressed-out buck. Took pictures of our company's encampment."

"I do recall." Jib stuck out his hand. "Pleasure tuh meet yuh again." They shook hands.

"I've mustered out of the military now," James said. "Thought you were headed to Fort Kearney. Looked around, but I couldn't find you. Wondered what happened. Didn't know you were here until I spotted your sign."

"Abandoned the idea of bein' a post photographer when told it was a dark time for the military. Found this place for rent and the former proprietor sellin' everythin' in it. Guess he caught the gold fever and couldn't wait tuh reach the mines. Had a fair price on the equipment and I jist couldn't pass up a good bargain."

"Things going all right for you?"

Jib raked his hand through his hair and puffed out his cheeks.

"Cain't say as much. Business is more'n a might scanty. I'm livin' a hardscrabble way of life. Workin' here and there with muh team. Doin' some carpenter work. Ain't got a steady source of income. Thinkin' tuh hang up muh fiddle and go back East. Folks been affected by the grasshopper swarms the last several years. Ain't had any produce tuh sell tuh give 'em enough cash fer exposures of families and farms. Cain't git muh photography business goin'. Hopin' it'd pick up, but it hain't. Git a day's work here and there with odd jobs whenever and wherever I kin. Gotta make a livin' somehow. Had tuh hire out as a day laborer. Puttin' up hay, diggin' wells, plantin' or harvestin', whitewashin' buildin's, fixin' whatever needs repairin', freightin'. Done cut back on everythin' possible. Thought I was gittin' a deal rentin' this place, but guessin' I got the little end of the horn. Makin' a poor fist."

"Sorry to hear that, but glad you're getting other work to sustain you."

"What yuh lookin' fer from me tuhday?"

"Me and another fella who got discharged the same time as me are wanting to make our way to the Black Hills. Don't know if you would be interested in mining, but sure could take a lot of still proofs on that adventure."

"Seemin' like people have gone crazy about goin' there, don't it?"

James nodded. "We're just asking you to consider joining our party. You could take some shots of whatever you come across. No doubt we'll see some buffalo hunters, some Indian camps. Who knows what?"

Jib rubbed the side of his cheek with his fingers. "Soundin' like it might could be quite the exploit. When did the government open up the Hills for legal settlement?"

"Since February of seventy-seven."

"Is an important time in our history, and I do wanna preserve what I kin through plates. Ain't doin' much jist sittin' here."

"'Think about the possibilities for your images in future years."

"When yuh plannin' on headin' out?"

"If things go well, two weeks ought to give enough time for getting the outfit together. Why don't you think about it?" James glanced around the room. "Nice place you got. Right off the main street. Handy, huh? Sorry things haven't gone well for you. Must not have worked out for the previous owner either. May be the right time to go on to other things."

"Somethin' tuh think about, anyways. Let me show yuh around. This here's not only muh studio but muh home as well."

The space was roomy with a large window facing the street and two doors in the back wall. One door opened into a small dark room with a table and corner shelves. Stored there were a tripod and glass plates. The other door led into his bachelor living quarters.

"A bit tight, ain't it? But for now, suits me jist fine. Got some canvases here rolled up and attached tuh the ceilin'. Use a pulley tuh change tuh different backgrounds for the takin' of portraits." He demonstrated how the pullies operated.

"I'm impressed with what you've got. Not many men batching would keep a place as tidy as you have. Too bad business has been so poor." James Rooney made his way to the front door and turned back to Jib. "Town's all decked out for the party tomorrow. Looking very patriotic. You fixing to participate in any of the activities? Or just taking pictures?"

"Both. Aim tuh toss horseshoes as well as take pictures, too."

James nodded. "Dinner on the ground?"

Jib bobbed his head.

The next morning, he got out of bed and went to inspect the day. Barefooted and holding a cup at chest height, he stepped out the front door, his hair still flattened from sleep, his cheeks and chin fuzzy with wiry whiskers, and stood on the board sidewalk, sipped his coffee, and appreciated the promise of a fine summer day. "Thank Yuh, God Almighty," he prayed, "for such a glorious day. It's gonna be a fine Independence celebration as patriotism is put on display. One of the biggest days of the year filled with a lot of whoop-de-do and doin's honorin' the foundin' of this here nation."

He squinted as the sun edged up above the roofs of the buildings lining the dusty thoroughfare. He took a long pull from the cup and studied the awakening town. Red, white, and blue bunting hung from the fronts of the stores and draped the balcony of the two-story hotel.

At that time of day, the street was quiet with only one horse tethered to the long hitching rail in front of the General Store. Soon, though, the crowd would grow from a continuous stream of buggies, buckboards, and horseback riders. The air would crackle with excitement as the town's people engaged in the fun activities planned for them: a parade firstly; races—foot, wheelbarrow, and sack; a tug-o'-war; a horseshoe pitching contest; speeches; music—group performances, solos, and audience sing-alongs; a square dance before darkness; and lastly, fireworks. *A good day for observin' our country's freedom,* he thought.

He flung the dregs of his coffee onto the ground. *Best git some clothes on.* He grinned, wheeled around, and went to get dressed.

For the next several hours, Jib pitched horseshoes. It was deep into the afternoon when the winner of the event was finally determined.

Drums, horns, and bells provided much noise. Farmers, wives, hired hands, merchants, bankers, and everyone in and around the community joined in the festivities.

People moved about everywhere. Jib bumped into many he recognized and kept pausing to swap a few words with each as he maneuvered his way through the commotion to a makeshift platform.

A man clapped his hands as he stood in the center. "Ladies and gentlemen, may I have your attention?" The master of ceremonies, waving his arms, his voice booming above the racket, waited for the clatter to tone down. "I am pleased to announce the winner of the horseshoe pitching contest is Beckett Claycomb." People applauded. "Jib, come on up here and be recognized."

Jib proceeded to the stage, smiled broadly in triumph, and clasped his hands over his head in the gesture of a champion. Whoops and cheers rose from the crowd. He bowed gallantly and stepped down, his back slapped and his hand pumped by a throng of well-wishers.

A big, muscular, tanned-face fellow approached him. "Congratulations! Fine game. Name's Curtis Knowles." He extended his hand forward to shake Jib's. "Looking for men who'd consider joining with me in going to the Dakota Territory—to dig for gold. James Rooney told me you might be interested. Was he right?"

"Well, sir, muh mind kinda makes itself up if I give it enough rope."

"Better push it along, then, as I'm planning to head out soon."

"Might go with yuh if I could drive muh own hack and mules."

"You sure they can hold up to the journey? Leaving from Sidney. Seems to be one of the starting points for the Hills. Easier course. We can get all the supplies we need there."

"How many're signed up already?"

The man scuffed his chin with his knuckles. "Two plus me."

"How long's the gittin' gonna take tuh git there?"

"Depends. We're at the mercy of the weather and if there're any problems with renegade Indians or road agents. Guess the average jaunt would take a little over a month."

Jib yanked off his Stetson and ran his hand through his thatch of hair. "Sounds mighty temptin'."

"Do some serious thinking about it." Curtis Knowles jerked a nod and touched his hat as he walked off.

Just beyond the town, on a wide meadow, a pit was dug and a pig roasted, with its tantalizing aroma now wafting throughout the area.

The women spread sheets out on a half dozen hay wagons—each over-loaded with many kinds of covered dishes. Rough tables and benches, set up for the people, provided a place to sit and eat the bounty. Men, women, and children milled about waiting for the dinner bell to ring.

Following the meal, the spectators grew livelier, and the revel-ing continued toward the early evening. When the scraping sound of a fiddle could be heard, and the band—seated on the raised plat-form and consisting of three fiddlers and a trumpet player—struck a stirring chord, it was time for the dancing to begin. Canvas had been pegged down to the ground for a dance floor. Jib expected the musicians to play lively tunes, but he wouldn't stick around long to find out. No, he drifted away from the celebration because of all the things he needed to take care of since he'd made up his mind to join with Curtis Knowles's group. However, he wouldn't miss the fireworks display.

By the time he gathered his camera paraphernalia and carted it home, shadows crawled across the land. He could relinquish the gal-lery with no problem. After all, it was a rented piece of property.

Suddenly a tremendous boom, a sound like a thunderclap, stopped the dancing. The sky crackled and lit up with sprays of red and white and blue. People stood still, put their hands over their hearts, and sang "The Star-Spangled Banner" as the band played. The fireworks then began in earnest. There were collective oohs and aahs and some clapping as the display proceeded.

Friday dawned very warm, typical of July in Nebraska. Jib chewed on a toothpick. He had just eaten a substantial breakfast. It was the kind of day a man would want to have to tackle the chores he needed to get done if he were going to rendezvous in a matter of days with Mr. Knowles and his party.

Jib entered the small barn at the back of his place and greeted Hez and Kez. "Glory be, muh two faithful four-legged friends. We're gittin' ready tuh head outta here. We'll start out tomorrow mornin'. Sound interestin' tuh yuh? First, need tuh inspect yer shoes. Don't want neither of yuh tuh git lame on our expedition. Then, need tuh check the wheels on the ole black buggy and git it cleaned out. Wanna make shore it'll make it."

On Saturday, the hack stood parked close to the back door and Jib started loading it early. He kept at it all day, taking his time, and though it was nearly full, he found enough room for the remainder of things in the studio. He boxed his pots and pans and loaded them. He rolled up his bedding and placed it next to the folded tent. Packed last was the precious photography apparatus. Tomorrow, by midmorning, he would shut the door to this establishment and ride away, leaving the building to somebody else who might have better luck with a business.

Jib swept the empty rooms, tidying up. As he worked the broom, the image of Addie Kate flashed through his mind. He scratched his head and winced. What was it that kept putting *her* back in his mind? Was it because he was using a Shaker broom? Or was it because he was leaving a place again? He pushed the dirt out the door and the thought of her to the back of his mind.

Everything was in the hack—all that he owned. He would sleep on the bunk without any mattress tonight. Tomorrow he would get up, take a last look around to be sure he had forgotten nothing, walk out into the sunlight, and start for Sidney.

* * *

The morning light grew along the eastern sky, first faint and pink, then gave way to full sunshine. Addie Kate awakened, still done in from yesterday's work. Harvest season was always tiring.

When the rising bell clanged, she sat up in bed, weariness still in her, her muscles stiff from the previous day, and dressed quickly. She began the duties of the day—airing the beds in the Brethren's rooms and getting to breakfast on time.

Thank goodness she kept busy with what she was doing because Jib kept popping into her thoughts. Why was she wasting time thinking about him? Suppose she were to go on this way? "I am going to stop this thinking about him," she said to herself. "I am going to stop."

But there he was, spinning in her mind like a little wheel. Where was he, anyway? Had he really gone out West? Did he ever think of her? Would he ever come back, or would he be lost to her forever? Her mind went round and round, believing in him one moment, imagining that he'd had second thoughts the next. The worst thing was not knowing, but, then again, she still had hopes of his return.

The passing days grew into weeks. The weeks turned into months. Still she had no peace. She hated the life she was living, but she couldn't help it. As she thought of the years ahead, she envisioned no end to her longing for Jib. Though her assignments steadied her, she was always aware of Jerusha's spying eyes.

Chapter 11

Around midnight the night before he left Columbus, Nebraska, Jib awoke to the flicker of lightning and a rumble of thunder, sounding far away. He rolled over in bed and went back to sleep only to be awakened again by a wrathful storm, with fierce flashes of lightning, booming and clashing of thunder, the splashing of rain on the roof, and the blowing of high winds through the town. In the morning, there was a constant drizzle as he met up with James Rooney, with wetness dripping from everything.

Another man, named Frank Collins, joined the group. He was older than Jib with a touch of gray in his well-barbered dark hair. He was a big-framed man with brown eyes and a grizzled, walrus mustache, neatly trimmed. When he laughed, it was readily apparent that he was missing his two top front teeth.

A young man hung around the three.

"What's your name?" Frank asked.

"Um . . . Elvin Jackson," he said, rubbing the underside of his nose with a knuckle. "But yuh kin call me Elf."

"Very fittin' name," Jib said, "yuh cain't be more than a boy. Take yer hat off so's we kin see what yuh look like."

The young man reached up slowly and removed his misshapen Stetson. He was thin and gangly, with a baby face, a ruddy complexion, large blue eyes, and shoulder-length unkempt sandy-colored hair. He seemed agreeable and pleasant enough.

The group now numbered four: James, Frank, Elf, and Jib. The men wore long oilskin coats as they headed to Kearney where they would board a train, go on to Sidney, and rendezvous with Curtis Knowles. The five would comprise the company.

Jib drove his hack with the mules, the others rode their horses. The men traveled along the Union Pacific railroad tracks for some time even as the locomotives rushed by, steaming and clanging.

Late afternoon, the rain stopped. They came to the Loup River and found it running full, gorged from the heavy rains the previous night. The water was muddy and the current was plunging noisily down a widened course to the Platte.

"I've been looking for a good place to cross and was hoping we could tackle it here," James said. "But the bank drops off pretty steep, and the water's running awful swift. Pert sure we can make it, though. What do you all think? . . . Tell you what, we can rest the animals while I check this out. I'd sure like to be on the other side before dark. Watch how I get along."

Jib nodded and added, "Yuh might wanna leave yer gun in the wagon."

James shrugged, rubbed his jaw while he considered his course of action, and shifted in his saddle toward Jib. "I'll be all right," he said, guiding his horse into the water.

The men stayed on a grassy place and watched James's horse balk. The animal would slide down the slope, would go in so far and then whirl and climb back out, up the ridge. After a couple times of coaxing the animal, it went to swimming depth and almost made it across. But within twenty-five feet from the ragged opposite edge, the gelding lost his footing. He stumbled and somersaulted into the water making a great splash, throwing James clear of the saddle, and came up pawing his front feet into the air, only to go down again.

James had tossed his rifle toward the embankment, but it fell short by a few feet. He pushed himself away as far as he could from the floundering horse and started to swim for the shore. A cottonwood tree, washed out by the roots, had fallen at the water's edge. He caught hold of a branch and dragged himself along the trunk where he got both arms over it, leaned into it, and spat out a mouthful of river water.

Frank and Elf found a suitable place to cross farther upstream. Jib followed. When they got to where James was, they clambered to rescue him. Frank waded in until he was knee deep, then thrust forward the handle of a Shaker broom. "Grab hold! I'll fish you out," he called. He grasped the broom's straw end as he hauled the soaked man up the incline. By that time, the horse had gained his footing and rose out of the water, swishing his tail.

The three men stood around James as he bent over with his hands on his knees and gasped for breath, his shoulders heaving.

While they were waiting for the man to recover, six Indians came from behind and moved in close. When the men wheeled and faced them with pistols drawn, the braves stopped, their faces surprised, and swung their ponies around to gallop off the other way.

James struggled to straighten and breathe normally. Once sufficiently recovered, he removed his footwear and waded barefoot back into the river.

"What do yuh think yer doin'?" Jib protested.

"Trying to find my rifle. Should be around here somewhere." He felt through the shallows for a time, glanced up at the men watching him from the embankment, and grumbled. "Reckon it's gone . . . carried away. Current's too fast."

James scrambled up the incline where he retrieved his boots and socks. He accepted the men's help in boosting him onto his horse and clung to the saddle as the party moved out.

The braves trailed them for a while, never coming near. At twilight, they trotted off toward the south and that was the last the men saw of them.

"Quiet now," Jib said, after he exhaled a pent-up breath. "Lookin' like it's safe. Think they're around here somewhere?"

"Don't trust them," James argued. "Doubt we'll be able to sleep much tonight. We'll post a guard when we make camp. They're probably after our horses."

However, they had a peaceful night, as there was no further trouble with the Indians. When daylight came, the outfit set out for Kearney.

They made fifteen miles that day, stopping from time to time for the animals to rest and cool off. Jib hoped he might be able to take some pictures along the way, but he never mentioned it to the others.

The foursome reached their destination a week later.

Chapter 12

*T*hree men rode at a slow trot down the wide main street of Kearny, Nebraska, the horses kicking up little puffs of dust. Jib followed the trio to the almost-deserted train depot. The clock on the outside of the building read ten thirty in the morning. They arrived early, with seventy minutes to spare. Plenty of time to purchase their tickets, for Jib to pay for shipping his mules and the hack, and for the others to sell their horses to the owner of the livery stable.

That done, they waited on the empty wooden platform for the train to pull into the station. At long last, they saw the billowing plume of black smoke from the pufferbelly's smokestack before they glimpsed the green-and-black steam locomotive. It whistled long and loud, then slowed in its approach. Creeping along, the wheels screeched and hissed as it stopped with a final groan and the doors swung open.

Strangers stepped down from several cars, hauling their baggage, and dispersed. Jib settled his team in the freight car, and the other three men boarded a packed emigrant coach car, where baggage filled the aisle.

Fortunately, when Jib entrained, he was able to find a seat. The engine whistled, tooting the departure, the bell clanged, and the train jerked and started to move, slowly pulling away, leaving the depot behind. As it picked up speed, the car swayed, rocking back and forth. Jib, fitting his head against the back of the red-velvet-cushioned seat, sat at a window, an elbow resting on the sill, and watched the landscape slip by. After a while, the conductor entered the car, stopped at each seat, and took the tickets—and the train went on and on and on.

At North Platte, the wheels ground to a stop. A young lady, wearing a fashionable bonnet tied with a colorful ribbon under her chin and carrying a basket, jostled down the aisle searching for a place to sit. No one seemed interested in helping her find one. Jib could see her predicament and gave her a part of his seat.

He discovered she was a schoolteacher going to her first teaching post, and, to his delight, the hamper she carried was packed with food. Though it was a companionable trip, it was also uncomfortable because of the heat and crowdedness, and he repeatedly stifled his yawns. Even lulled by the rhythm of the rails and the swaying of the car, he was unable to doze much on the lengthy ride.

The train stopped several times throughout the trip, and, at each stop, there were the sounds of people boarding and debarking. Two days later, the iron horse chugged into the Sidney station, snorted and clanged, and ground to a hissing stop with a final jerk. Jib gathered his things together in readiness to leave, gingerly came to his feet, and steadied himself. He rubbed his sore neck, pressed a hand to his stiff back, grinned sheepishly at the woman, and said, "Git a twinge every once in a while. Lumbago most likely. Always knew I'd suffer with it. Runs in muh family."

He shuffled down the narrow aisle toward the exit and stepped to the crowded platform where people milled about. He took in a deep breath and rubbed his bristly chin. Then he and the three men made their way to the freight car to claim the mules and hack.

They discussed the fact that Curtis Knowles was not there to meet them.

Back at the depot Elf cupped one hand at the side of his face peering through a window of the waiting room. No people lounged on the benches inside. He went around to check the other side of the building but saw no one.

Frank stood outside the front door. "Got the fidgets or something?"

"Guess so," Elf said, shrugging.

Jib jammed his hands into his pockets. "Any sign of Mr. Knowles?" he asked.

The young man turned and peered up and down the main thoroughfare. "Nope," he said. "This pacin' and waitin' 'round fer 'im makes me uneasy. I jist wanna git goin'."

"So do we," James glanced at the others with impatience. "We'll get there, all right. Can't wait to be a rich man?"

"Ain't countin' on makin' no fortune. Jist wanna make enough tuh help muh ma."

Jib lifted his chin. "Is that why yuh signed on?"

Elf nodded.

"Why the rest of you fellas going to the Black Hills?" James surveyed each man.

Jib pulled a handkerchief out of his pocket, wiped his forehead, and mopped the back of his neck, "Reckon I'm jist wore out with muhself. Ain't never been there because I been here in Nebrasky. Got a hankerin' tuh git somewhere else."

"Yeah," Elf added. "Heerd it's a hard trip, though. I's worked with horses before . . . sometimes mules. Never been around oxens anytime. Frank here's said he's spent his life workin' with freightin' animals."

Curtis Knowles appeared right then, crossing the platform. "You boys're prompt. I like that and apologize for keeping you waiting. Let's eat some breakfast. My treat. We'll load up afterward. That job will take us till late in the afternoon to finish."

The task of assembling the supplies took the greater part of the day to sort and stow them.

James stopped carrying boxes long enough to scan the surroundings. "Sidney's a lively town!"

"Sure is." Curtis never looked at him as he spoke. "It's the principal outfitting point for the gold mines. Full of freighters and teams. Got to be careful, though, because there're plenty of unsavory characters filling the sidewalks and streets."

The men worked fast, grunting to the task of packing four sturdy wagons with mining gear like shovels, picks, pails, and rubber boots. Other equipment included a tent, a small iron stove with its necessary pipes, and a bundle of woolen blankets. They did their best distributing the items and packing them in securely. That done, they turned their attention to food and medicine.

"We can purchase army-style provisions that'll last several months for under twenty dollars. Anyone interested in doing that?" Curtis asked the men.

"Sounds like we might as well," James said. "Need to stock lard, flour, bacon, beans, sugar, coffee, and salt."

Curtis Knowles, standing at the side of a wagon, nodded in agreement. "When we get completely done, I'll make an inspection and if everything suits me, then we can go. It's still early enough we can easily make five or so miles. Like to leave Sidney for fear of having something stolen from us. If we stop not too far out, whatever we've overlooked, we can come back and buy. The bulls are out back in the pen."

Elf scratched his neck. "What's our wagon train goin' tuh be called?"

"We need a name?" Frank stroked his grizzled mustache.

"Shore." Elf folded his arms across his chest. "We kin paint it on the wagon sides."

Jib said nothing but removed his hat and ran a hand through his hair. He was more concerned about getting started.

Each man climbed to the seat of his wagon. Curtis was the lead teamster who raised his arm, popped his whip, and led off. Elf came next, then Jib, driving his hack and clucking to his mules. Frank and James brought up the last two wagons. In high spirits, they left the town behind, their wagons rolling in line.

The wagons creaked and jolted on the bumpy and rutted road, rumbling along until twilight when Knowles gave the signal to draw up close to one another and make a circle. It was a fine campsite with creek water and thick, high grass for the animals. Elf, Frank, and Curtis unyoked the oxen and drove them out to graze.

Jib unhitched his mules before he helped James pitch the tent, gather brush for kindling a fire, and heat some water to make coffee. "I'm starved. Ain't yuh fellas?" His stomach rumbled and ached, reminding him that it had been many hours since he had eaten. He knew his belly felt hollow and figured the others were in the same boat.

"Absolutely," they answered. Their hunger pangs reminded them they'd had nothing to eat since morning—not even so much as a drink of water. With cold rations and fresh-made coffee, they ate ravenously.

"Sleep tight, fellas. We're getting an early start tomorrow. We'll leave here no later than seven o'clock," Knowles said.

Jib toyed with the coffee cup handle. "Yuh givin' a wake-up call?"

"Sure."

It came at four-thirty the next morning. The men staggered out of their sleeping bags, stretched to work the soreness from their bones of yesterday's physical activity, and prepared for the day.

They stoked the fire to life and started coffee. They prepared breakfast, ate, and cleaned up. They rolled up their bedrolls, pulled the tent pegs, lowered the tentpoles, folded the tent, and repacked each wagon. That done, they drove the oxen into camp and yoked them.

Everything was ready. Everyone was too. Curtis Knowles raised his arm. Whips popped in the air. Oxen strained into the yokes and the wheels turned. The unnamed outfit rolled north.

Late morning, they came across six deserted Indian lodges. Curtis gave the signal to pull in for the noon rest. Jib climbed into the body of his hack and gathered camera equipment.

He took pictures of the lodges and the scenic area instead of eating. Meanwhile, a buffalo herd passed in the distance.

That night, they camped at Nine Mile Water Hole, which happened to be a stage stop, too.

After the evening meal, and it had grown dark, they sat around the campfire. Elf, swatting mosquitoes that left welts on his face and neck, stood and walked around the fire to stand downwind in the smoke.

"Daggone pests," he said. "I won't be able tuh git tuh sleep because of them bothersome skeeters. Jib, I wanna look through yer pi'tures yuh done took tuhday."

A mosquito buzzed Jib and he fanned it away from his ear. "Be glad tuh show yuh."

"How'd you get started into photography, anyway?" Frank asked.

Jib raised his eyebrows, ran a hand over his hair, and puffed out his cheeks. "It was durin' the War Between the States."

"Oh, yeah? Gotta be a story in there somewhere. Go on and tell us. Ain't got nothin' better tuh do."

He arranged his hands like a little tent, fingertip to fingertip. "I joined up after muh seventeenth birthday and marched tuh Fredericksburg. Somebody had tuh take pictures. Captain put his finger on me. Right off the bat, I seen the horrors of war." He paused and swallowed hard. "Prepared glass plates and developed 'em right then and there on the battlefield." He remained silent for a while. "Couple of months later we was at Gettysburg—absolute misery it was." He stopped short. "Livin' like dogs in a world of dyin'. Fightin' lasted three days and was the bloodiest thin' I ever wanna see. Jist awful. Moans and screams comin' from the wounded. Distorted bodies strowed about the ground. Destruction of life everywhere. After a while, everythin' quiet, even the birds not makin' sounds, only noise was all the buzzin' of flies on the blood. The stench of that stuck in muh nostrils forever." He shook his head. "Hope I never hafta witness war again. Don't even wanna fight Indians no how." He brushed his mouth with the back of his hand, as if to clean it, and looked around at the faces of the men. "Rains came, sweepin' across the battleground. Like God was cleanin' thin's up. Brought a fresh smell of damp grass and earth that, for a mite of time, stopped the stink of blood and gunpowder smoke . . . and death. That's the truth, men."

They nodded and fell quiet for a while, afraid to disturb the spell, and a solemn hush settled over the group. Silence reigned the rest of the night.

The next morning, Jib got up, yawned, and sucked in gusts of fresh air. In spite of his soreness from sleeping on the hard ground, he said to anyone who cared to listen, "Goin' tuh be a blessed day."

"Only if the wind'd blow a bit more so's tuh shoo off the skeeters," Elf said.

Curtis came around the wagon. "Today, we'll have the opportunity to see the Courthouse and Jail Rocks. Jib, if you want to take pictures, you'll have your chance. Need to warn you all, this'll be a tough trip the next several days because of the Sand Hills. You'll have a powerful amount of thinking time because of the slow travel. Will be that way until we reach the Niobrara River. Everyone ready?"

They signaled and got underway.

In time they reached the looming (and imposing) tower formations. Jib said, "Cain't wait tuh git some shots of the monuments."

The group set up camp and remained at Pumpkin Creek for two days giving the animals and the men time to rest up for the trip ahead. It turned out Curtis Knowles was right. The great sand bluffs were forty to sixty feet high. As the oxen dragged their wagon over the top of the loose sand, pushing hard into their wooden yoke, they had to stop from time to time, their heads drooping and their nostrils dilated. After resting a few minutes, their breathing slowed and they lifted their heads to go forward again. The men found that the dust coated their throats and gritted between their teeth. Jib complained about having to blow dust out of his nose and wipe his eyes.

After traveling four days, they came to Camp Clarke's Bridge over the North Platte River. Approaching, they joined up with several teams also bound for the Hills. Their outfit would be safer in the company of more bullwhackers and mule skinners.

At night, Jib's mind began to dwell on the Black Hills—particularly when he had nothing to do but think of the gold mines. Could he possibly strike it rich? Of course there was that possibility. But if he did, what would he do then—leave the Hills and settle down? Where should he go and with whom? Many times lately, without meaning to, the image of Addie Kate crossed his mind. It was her beautiful eyes he remembered best. Hah! Maybe he ought to go back to Kentucky and carry her out of that foolish sect—after he made his fortune, that is.

In only a few more days, barring any complications from the weather or animals or terrain, he would be at the mines. For hours at a stretch, he lived his imaginings.

On the eighth day, the bright sunshine in a cloudless blue sky gave way by midday to dark and ugly clouds, and, by early afternoon, Jib felt a drop of moisture on his face. He glanced up and watched a bolt of lightning streak down in the western sky just as another drop touched him. The intense crack and roll of thunder caused the hair on his arms to stand up. A slight drizzle developed into a steady light rain. The sharp zigzag lines of lightning flashed again and again in the west, and the deep roll of thunder grew louder.

The wind picked up and became fitful, gusting, making the sand swirl around. Curtis called for the men to stop. "Sounds like a storm's coming our way. Better put your slickers on. We'll go ahead and camp here."

He no sooner gave the warning than the rain began pelting down in sheets—blown this way and that by the wind. It was a warm rain, but once it had soaked their clothes and the wind had picked up, they shivered. It was not easy for them to set up the tent in the pouring rain.

The fierce lightning hit more than once close by—its swift, sword-like thrusts of blinding light stabbing deep into the earth. The thunder clapped and grumbled. The men, now cold and wet, were also tired, hungry, sore, and achy.

The weather forced the huddling together of several teams. Three freighters, headed back to Sidney for supplies, came from the Black Hills, and twelve wagons going to the Hills also pulled into the campsite. Altogether, those who hunkered down numbered twenty wagons, thirty-three men, and two women.

The "rise and shine" call for Jib and the others sounded early. The men worked fast, grunting as they completed their morning chores of rolling up their beds; striking, folding, and stowing away the tent; and packing the wagon. When they finished, they drove up the oxen and mules and hitched the teams to the wagons. The outfit soon headed out. Though the work of the days was the same, the weather and the scenery constantly changed.

Their travel through the Sand Hills proved to be difficult and tedious, and, toward the end of it, before they crossed the Niobrara River, it hailed. Jib had experienced fleeting hail squalls and knew they usually lasted only minutes.

The hailstones came thick and fast. At first, they plummeted small, the size of walnuts, but as they continued, they got larger by the minute, to that of a goose egg, dropping everywhere—on the wagons, the animals, and the men.

"What'll we do?" Elf asked. "Reckon we'll be beat tuh death?"

"Seek protection, men!" Curtis yelled over the racket. They followed his order.

Jib halted his hack, and he and Elf climbed down to huddle underneath it, watching the hailstones bounce on the ground. The others in the group followed suit and scrambled under theirs.

The men, protected from the battering, left the poor mules and oxen to absorb the pelting of the hailstones. When the storm passed, the men discovered the canvases covering their goods had been destroyed, shredded by the stones, soaking everything.

Several days later, they arrived at the Running Water stage stop. It was a relief to be done with the dirt and wind and rain and hard travel for a while. Here at the waystation, canvas covers would be repaired or replaced and the animals rested. The men sorted through their freight and laid the equipment and tools out to the sun and air, allowing for things to dry out. Jib took pictures of it all.

"In less than a week, we'll be in Dakota Territory," he kept telling himself. It was a prospect that brought him great relief.

* * *

The days at Pleasant Hill dragged by for Addie Kate—one by one, ever so slowly—getting up, airing the bedding, completing her assigned chores. She moved mechanically through each day, dutifully completing her assignments, afraid of any lax time that would give her an opportunity to think of Jib and what might have been if she'd gone with him.

Where was he? What was he doing? Was he all right? Would he ever come back for her? She pretended that at any minute he would appear. However, he didn't come. No one came.

She did not complain, but the truth of the matter was, it had been the most distressing almost two years now for her without any word from Jib. She had not forgotten him, had he forgotten *her*?

Chapter 13

July 25, 1878

*I*n the late afternoon of Thursday, July twenty-fifth, the Knowles's group—five wagons and drivers in all—traveled across the border into Dakota Territory and set up camp on the south side of the Cheyenne River. The men ambled along its grassy bank. "Be an easy crossing," James said. "Only about a hundred feet wide at this point. Quite fordable."

Jib stood in the shallows at the edge of the water. "Oh, yuh think?" he scoffed, winking at Elf and Frank. They snorted.

The group crossed over early the next morning and moved upstream to an open area that lay along the riverbank. It had been an unchallenged crossing.

The conversation around the campfire that night centered on the gold mines as if they were the place where the world ended. "Better get there first," said Curtis Knowles. "We've got to pass through the Red Canyon—that in itself will be a trial."

"What do you mean?" Frank demanded.

"We'll reach it about five miles beyond the Cheyenne. Trail is long and narrow. Rugged, ragged, jagged, and craggy. Walls tower over a thousand feet above the floor of it . . . it's a favorite place for road agents or Indians to ambush. We'll have to proceed with caution. Can't let our eyes get quiet. Got to keep 'em peeled for trouble lurking around. Best make plans for the next stage of our journey and be ready for anything."

"Soundin' like the valley of the shadow of death," Jib commented. "Wouldn't hurt none tuh pray tuh God Almighty and ask for protection before we set out tomorrow so we can git through the place safe and sound."

"Not a bad idea. Calling upon the help of the Lord is always a good plan. Sorry, Jib, but you won't be able to stop along the way to take pictures. Too dangerous. And it will be necessary to have our rifles loaded and handy. We'll have to be alert at all times for any problems."

In the gray of the early morning, Jib gathered up the reins and clucked to the mules. The others also made ready. They moved out, watching every ridge and cliff and crag—the walls rising almost sheer on both sides. It made a grim and forbidding trip.

* * *

Three days later, at midmorning, they pulled into Custer. The town was a spread-out community with log cabins, tents, and jerry-built houses and buildings, numbering about four hundred. It sat near French Creek, the minor tributary where the gold had been discovered fifteen years prior.

The Knowles party, on the trail twenty-four days, now tired and hungry, celebrated their arrival by eating a meal of slapjacks and bacon.

"Me and Elf are goin' tuh do our wash. Then we're takin' a look around town. We want tuh check out the sights," Jib said. "So far, I ain't likin' what I'm a hearin' about the mine situation. And I ain't impressed by the looks of the town. Me and Elf ain't meanin' tuh stay."

"So you're wanting to move on?" Curtis Knowles pressed.

Jib nodded. "Hopin' there's better prospects for gold up north. It'll probably take us a couple of days tuh git there."

"It's your call and your conveyance. This is as far as I'm going, though. Don't recommend you go on alone. You two ought to do some inquiring around about another caravan and join up with them," Curtis said.

"Right now, we gotta find the soapsuds row," Jib said.

Elf spit in the grass. "Ain't got money enough tuh have muh duds warshed by a laundress."

"Ain't hirin' nobody tuh do the job. Wantin' tuh borrow three of their washin' containers."

The two made arrangements to use their washtubs. They stretched a rope between the wagons, carried buckets of water from French Creek and heated the water, then grated soap into the water and rubbed and scrubbed and wrung out each item. They hung the clothes on the lines and watched as they flapped and fluttered in the breeze. Toward late afternoon, satisfied with finishing their laundry, they moseyed along the main street of the town and eventually found the General Store. They entered expecting to learn of an outfit looking to head to the northern hills. Three men were inside talking together in earnest about the prospecting possibilities.

After listening in on them, Jib cleared his throat and boldly interrupted, "Who's the biggest toad in the puddle here?"

"Why you asking?" The man stared at Jib with an unfriendly expression.

"Couldn't help overhearin' yer talk."

"What you wanting?"

"Me and muh friend here would like tuh git tuh Deadwood."

"I see. And who are you?"

"Name's Jib Claycomb." He pointed with his thumb, indicating the man who stood behind him. "This here's Elf Jackson."

The man glanced from Jib's face to Elf's. "You two bullwhackers or mule skinners?"

Jib laughed. Elf snorted.

"I'll take that as a no. Well, then, why you hankering to go prospecting?"

"We been lookin' tuh find an outfit headed there. Ain't too keen on a goin' on our own. Like to join up with you."

The man ran his hand along his jaw. "You got experience?"

"Not with prospectin'. But we're quick learners. Elf, here, can handle mules and oxen. I own muh own hack and mules. Got this far from Nebraska."

"Uh-huh. Tell you what. If the two men here with me give their consent, I will, too." He turned around to address them in a whispered consultation. They raised their eyebrows, quirked their mouths, glanced at one another, and nodded to him. "Guess that settles the matter. Welcome aboard." They all shook hands.

"When yuh plannin' tuh head out?" Elf asked.

"Tomorrow about ten o'clock. Meet right here."

"We'll see yuh in the mornin'," Jib said. "If we got a question, who do we ask for? We don't even know who yuh are."

"Name's Luther Tate."

He clapped Jib on the back and left.

* * *

It was dusk when Jib and Elf got back to their old campsite. Curtis looked up as they came in. "How'd it go? What's the verdict? Did you find a company to travel with?"

"Yep, shore did. We're joinin' with a party of prospectors. Leave tomorrow mornin'."

"Yeah? Who's the outfit's pilot?"

"Luther Tate's the name."

"Luther Tate!?"

Jib stepped back and wiped his forehead with a sleeve. "Yuh know him?"

"Heard of his reputation."

"Appeared tuh me tuh be a decent sort of man."

"He's a snake that gets tied up in knots trying to follow his own tracks. Watch out that he doesn't hornswoggle you."

"Yuh don't like him?"

"Oh, I like him the same way a Christian likes the devil."

Chapter 14

*T*he sun was just up and shining in all its glory when Jib, driving his hack, spotted three bull-oxen teams parked at the General Store and four men, standing out front, huddled together.

He pulled Hez and Kez over to the hitching rail and jumped down from the seat. He yanked off his Stetson, slapped it against his thigh, and acknowledged the men with a nod. He leaned against a wagon wheel fanning himself with the hat and took note of the activity in the town. "Busy place, tuhday," he said to them.

Luther Tate came out of the establishment and approached the group. "This all you got?" he addressed Jib and Elf. They turned their attention to the man. "Don't haul around much, do you?"

"For muhself, muh needs are simple and muh wants are simpler," Jib said matter-of-factly.

"I'll say. Listen, fellas, now that everything's loaded, we're ready to roll." He glanced around at their faces. "Two men to a rig. One'll drive and the other'll ride shotgun. We'll travel until noon and have a dry camp to rest the animals. Then we'll head out again and keep on the watch for a good spot to stop for the night. Be a long day, men."

He turned and climbed to the seat. The others acted on his lead. Jib and Elf hoisted themselves into the hack's front and waited for the signal to start, which came with a raised arm, a crack of a whip, and a loud haw spoken to the lumbering creatures. The wagon train crawled slowly up the dusty street and headed north, puffs of gritty powder rising under the animals' hooves.

"Glad we're finally leavin', ain't yuh, Jib?"

"Custer wasn't what I thought it'd be. I was sorely disappointed," Jib grumbled. "Too coarse for me. Shoulda knowed better. What with bullwhackers and mule skinners and gamblers and saloons. Here we come, Deadwood. This country is beautiful beyond description. Sure would like tuh take some pictures. What people call them and what they be are different things. Them're mountains, not hills."

"Best be the promise o'gold in 'em, too," added Elf, laughing.

Jib bobbed his head and smiled. "Yep, hope so anyway. Don't wanna be on a fool's errand. Cain't hardly wait tuh git there."

Little daylight remained when they reached Hill City. The village had been booming at one time. That was years ago, though, and since had gone bust. The Tate caravan stopped and made camp on Spring Creek. They drove the oxen and mules to grass, struck tent pegs, and lifted wooden chests of necessary items out of the wagons.

During their layover, the old-timers who had stayed in the area demonstrated for the novices the simplest way to extract the precious metal. "Yuh use a tin pan."

"Lookin' like a pie plate," Jib commented.

"Yep, now submerge the thing, scoop up a panful of gravel and swirl what's there in a circular motion, like this," he said, showing them the action, "so's that the lighter sand and pebbles fall out. Yer heavier gold'll be on bottom—more'n likely, jist flakes."

The two men followed the instructions, and, to their surprise, they panned a small amount of gold dust while there. Jib tied it in his handkerchief and stuffed it in his pocket.

Two days later they pulled into Deadwood—a lively town with the main street bustling with bull trains, miners with their pack mules, and cowboys in boots and overalls and broad-brimmed hats, all crowding into the thoroughfare.

The town, built on a narrow, steep-sided gorge enclosed by high pine-covered mountains, was the biggest, richest, and best-known city in the Hills. Whitewood Creek ran through it, the water running red from the washings of the sluice boxes. Deadwood consisted of false-fronted frame buildings, cabins, shanties, and tents scattered in the gulch, and, on the hillsides, flumes and sluice boxes perched everywhere. There were brick structures, churches, schoolhouses and the first-rate Welch House. Restaurants advertised meals for twenty-five cents and second-class hotels were numerous. Due to the scores of saloons, the air hung heavy with liquor's stale odor that issued from them.

The matter of a place with a bed had yet to be settled. "Let's explore to find an unused shanty," Luther said. "Save some money from hotel bills. If I remember right, I know where one is."

Well after nightfall, toward midnight, he found the cabin. It was small, tiny in fact, consisting of one room, one window, and one door, but it had a sizable fireplace and rough bunks built against two of the walls. He and Jib were the only ones who curled up and slept.

Jib had no idea how long he'd been sleeping but became mindful of movement around him, and when awakened enough, he was aware of someone filching his pockets. He pretended to be asleep because the darkness prevented him from identifying the person. He figured the thief belonged to a band of outlaws in the area. Where was Tate?

When Jib became fully awake, and his eyes began to focus, he stretched out and grabbed hold of the man, scuffling and grunting and snorting as he deposited the robber on the floor. It was then that he recognized the guilty party. He was Luther Tate!

I'll be daggone! Curtis Knowles was right. Luther Tate's a snake.

"What's this?" Jib shouted, and, intending to startle the man, he reared up and clutched the offender's throat, rolling him over. "Yuh ain't gonna git away with this!" he barked.

Luther thrashed around trying to wriggle free, but to no avail. He coughed and gasped. "I . . . can't . . . breathe," he whimpered.

Jib released some pressure only to feel an excruciating, stabbing pain in his left side and, reaching down, ran his hand against the blade of a sharp knife, severely cutting his hand.

Luther broke Jib's hold on him, scrambled to his feet, and darted for the door. Jib started after the rascal but, in the dark, couldn't determine which direction he went.

"What in the world is goin' on?" Elf asked as Jib came running down the path out of the cabin.

"Tate tried tuh steal from me and then kill me with his Arkansas toothpick. I'm a bleedin' bad."

"Whoa! *His* knife? That long thing? No tellin' what people'll do tuh git a little gold. Show me the damage what he done tuh yuh."

They moved inside and lit a candle. In the dim light, Elf could see the cut in the side was not deep, but the slash in Jib's hand was serious. His hand was drenched with blood.

"Looks bad tuh me."

"What kin I do?"

"Yuh better git tuh the town's doc."

"Naw. Don't wanna go now."

"Gotta do somethin'."

"Like what?"

"Ain't got no doctorin' supplies. Cain't do nothin' but bind it up." Elf sorted through their trunks looking for something to use as a bandage and found an old bed sheet that he tore into strips.

"Muh poor hand."

"If it ain't painin' too awful much, we'll prop it up for yuh so's yuh can try and git some sleep. We hafta try tuh find the scoundrel in the mornin'."

The next day, the two men prowled the streets hunting the doctor. Locating the small unpretentious office, they entered to find a middle-aged man with a barrel chest and weak eyes that blinked continuously behind the square lenses of his glasses. He cleaned the wound, stitched it up, and bandaged the hand—and told Jib how to care for it.

"Keep from using it as much as possible," he advised him. "Almost nigh to impossible for a miner, but try."

The two left the doctor's and continued to search for Tate but saw no sign of him. In their quest, they made the rounds inquiring about work. Sometimes, seeing Jib's wrapped hand, the prospector wouldn't talk to them. Other times, they expressed interest in the two but gave no definite answer. The pair also checked into town plots. Would they look for an unoccupied cabin, or would they pitch Jib's tent? In the outlying area, vacant lots were not only cheaper but situated in a quieter setting.

"Hain't figgered out yet if this here place is any less coarse than was Custer. Don't quite know what we're goin' tuh do. What d'yuh think?"

Elf never answered the question. Instead, he said, "Ever'thin' goes up and down here 'ceptin' whiskey and labor. Hard drink bein' at the top o' the ladder and drudgery at the bottom. Seems that's the way life is here. I figger we gotta stay till we make a fist."

"No longer than we hafta." Jib added. "Might's well make the best of thin's. One bein', we got a cozy little place with a fireplace. At least we kin sit by the fire and stay warm on the snowy days." The cabin they rented was dark and cramped but it was, at least, well located.

"We's knowed too long what 'tis tuh be broke an' hungry. We's got tuh fin' us a job, Jib."

Chapter 15

"Been difficult for us findin' a minin' job since we ain't got no experience," Jib said. Elf nodded. But both men got something of a surprise when they found a position at a deep placer mine. The two, hired to slog for a man who owned three mines and needed more laborers, had hoped that working for wages would pay better. However, they came to know their boss paid them more as they gained experience with the backbreaking tasks of cradling, panning, scraping, and digging.

"Whew!" Elf grumbled. "The job has proved tuh be more involved than we anticipated what with havin' tuh wear rubber hip boots and wool clothes. We're always wet from warshin' out the gold."

"One thin' we didn't know beforehand. On rainy or snowy or freezin' days, we cain't work at the claim." Jib shook his head. "We need somethin' that'll provide for us and make us more money."

Winters were uncomfortably cold, which meant that any toiling at the mines was sporadic. One such day, past the middle of November, Jib awakened later than usual, carried in wood for the morning, rekindled the fire in the fireplace, and put the pot of coffee on.

"Up already?" Elf pulled up the heavy blankets to his eyes and peered above the edge. "What're yuh a fixin' tuh do?"

Jib, bent over putting on thick socks, said, "Go huntin'."

"Alone?"

"Reckon so. Wanna come?"

"Nope. Too tuckered out. Best be careful if goin' by yerself."

"Don't worry about me." He put on a heavy outer garment, left the cabin, and closed the door. Jib trudged to the open-faced shed that only partially protected the animals from the elements. It was nothing more than a lean-to of logs roofed with poles that were thatched with spruce boughs and slough grass. He placed a saddle on Kez, cinched it tightly, set himself in it, and they pushed their way up a tree-covered slope from the gulch.

As he faced the biting cold, winter air, Jib tugged his coat more closely about him to protect against the chill. The knifing north wind whipped at the woolen scarf wrapped around his head and over his ears, blew straight into his face, tingling it, and made his eyes water. The temperature was below freezing and too uncomfortable to work in the sluice. Light snow began to fall, further obscuring the pale winter sun. He poked his prickling face to check for numbness, and spoke to Kez as she strained up the grade.

At a little clearing that was out of the wind, the mule stopped. After resting a few minutes, Jib flicked the reins and she lifted her head, ready to go on. He scanned the unfamiliar landscape and found an eagle feather lying on the ground. He slid out of the saddle and dropped the reins over Kez's head, knelt to pick up the feather, and twirled it between his finger and thumb. Standing, his breathing poured like white smoke into the crisp air.

He recognized the high-pitched shriek of the eagle. Tipping back his head, he watched the majestic bird swoop and dip, spiral down, and lift on the air currents. Finally, it settled into its aerie situated in a tall tree. Jib's gaze followed its movements as it raised its wings twice, then folded them down like a man closing his cape.

The hills, now with a skiff of snow on the pine-needle-carpeted ground, were amazingly quiet. About a hundred yards from him, Jib spied a bighorn sheep, took aim and shot, but because his fingers were so cold and stiff, he missed. He went on and got to the foot of a mountain wall. Pausing for a moment, he observed a seeping spring trickling a small runnel down the steep mountainside. It was no more than a thin trickle from a crack in a rock higher up, but he was thirsty. Was it drinkable? He would find out. He stopped and got off Kez, tied the reins to a low, scant bush, and made his way to the continuous flow, stamping his feet to warm them.

Jib cupped his hands to catch the water tumbling along its path. Though the stream appeared to be clear, it was muddy dribbling through his fingers. He gawked at the grit left on them. He stared. Yellow dust that glittered. Was what he saw the real thing? He fought to breathe. He had heard of stranger things. He had learned about tailings. He studied the precipice from whence the flow came. Whose land was he on? Was it already spoken for or had it previously been mined and then abandoned?

He thought of the backbreaking work the two had done for weeks, with little to show for their labors, and here he was, without any effort, discovering gold. Looking down, in a mound of dirt and gravel, lay a clump of something the size of a ripe, juicy blackberry. He stooped, plucked the lump, and turned it over in his hand. Jib drew a deliberate breath and raised his eyes to the sky. "Thank Yuh, Lord! Yuh've truly blessed us." He yelled the words and let them echo back.

His stiff fingers fumbled unbuttoning his coat. He slipped the nugget into his shirt's breast pocket and wiped his hands dry on his handkerchief. He mounted Kez, clucked his tongue, and let her lope along the trail to the cabin, thinking on the way how the miracle of the day would give rise to countless possibilities for their futures.

Kez quickened her steps the closer they got to the shelter. Jib dismounted and trailed her, her tail switching. He grabbed armfuls of hay from the stack outside the shed's opening and threw them in front of the mules. He lost no time in dragging the saddle off her, rubbing her down, and getting into the warmth of the cabin.

He opened the door, burst inside, and stopped to wipe his feet. "Elf!" he called.

The young man was kneeling before the hearth, stirring up the fire, turning embers into a roaring blaze. A little puff of gray smoke circled about him as he jumped up and faced Jib. "Yuh git somethin'? Needin' some help?" He moved to the table, raised his cup of coffee to his lips, and took a sip. "Yuh want a hot drink?"

Jib strolled over to him. "Got somethin' all right. Yuh ain't gonna believe what it is."

"Try me."

"Remember we said we oughtna do wishful thinkin' of gittin' rich?" Jib smiled, withdrew the gobbet, and held it out in the palm of his hand. "Well, look here!"

Elf said nothing as he set down the cup, stood silent, and removed the rock to examine it. He dropped onto a stool and stared at the sample, his eyebrows arched high. He slowly whistled. "It's the real thin', all right. Where'd yuh git it?" He looked up into Jib's face.

"The place I went tuh hunt. There was a rill runnin' down the mountain side. I stopped tuh take a drink. When I cupped muh hands tuh catch the water, they filled with some kinda sand. Wasn't that at all. It was gold. Sifted around through the pebbles what were there, when right at muh feet was this." He pointed.

"Amazin'!" Elf inspected the chunk again. "Too fantastical."

"It is. This here is our chance tuh become prosperous."

"Let me git this straight, yuh found this layin' on the ground?"

Jib bobbed his head. "Yep. Gold is close tuh the surface—the perfect poor man's diggin'."

"We're gonna make a fist, ain't we? This's what we've been hopin' fer."

"The Lord Almighty has given this tuh us. If this nugget's found so easily, then there's a lot more up there. We cain't tell anyone neither until we stake our claim and sign the papers with the district recorder tuh git the mine registered in our names. When we sell it, we'll git even richer. Then we go home. Yuh wanna help yer ma, and I aim tuh buy a farm and git a wife."

"Ha! In that order?"

"Hopin' so. Have a fancy tuh hear a woman's voice inside muh house."

"Yuh got a woman?"

"I do . . . cain't quite explain the fascination for her, but found her tuh be a delight tuh be with. Always cheery. Jist know she's tuh be a part of muh future." Jib had never been able to forget Addie Kate. In fact, he thought about her a lot.

"That's nice. Is she perty tuh look at?"

"Yep. She's got flaxen hair, pale-as-milk skin, and she has the most beautiful eyes—as green as the sea. She's a beauty from within, too, and that kind never fades." He had never gotten her face out of his dreams. "She's a good woman who wears her goodness."

"Well now, that's important fer a happy marriage. Glad yuh got that all settled."

The next day, the pair took their rifles on the ruse of hunting and searched out the source of the waterfall. They located the spring that had become covered with silt and fallen leaves and pine needles, and by hacking away the overgrowth, came upon a deep gravel bed. The job proved to be more arduous than anticipated, and, by the time they completed the work, they were breathless.

Had no one ever found this place? Did they have the fifteen-dollar-a-foot cash amount that was necessary to purchase the three hundred feet of a placer mine? The two kept hushed about the find as they investigated the answers to their questions.

At the District Recorder's Office, the partners discovered the property had been deserted. Could the two register their right to a claim? Yes. They filed a certificate, then filled out and signed the required forms.

"Some of the long-timer prospectors probably won't believe we'll find anythin' on that there prop'ty, Jib, but we'll show 'em 'tis a rich placer," Elf said.

The day the two prospectors took possession of their claim was cold, but no snow fell. New to the rigors of working for themselves, they scraped, dug, sorted, and panned in spite of the coldness. They determined to make a go of their time and celebrated that they took out a little over one hundred dollars' worth.

"For one day, we've done plumb good," Jib said, with a sense of accomplishment in his voice. "We oughta sleep tuhnight. What do yuh say we go tuh town and git a hot meal and plenty of coffee?"

The news of the two men striking gold had quickly spread throughout the town, and the partners were now regarded with some awe to a certain degree. They laughed as they walked down the wood plank sidewalks of Deadwood. Jib shoved his hat back on his head, his hair tousled on his forehead, and tucked his hands in his trouser pockets as they entered the restaurant. A waitress, the only one in the place, pointed to a table at the front window that had a view of the hills beyond. She handed them a menu card and stood silent, waiting for their order.

"I'm hungry," said Elf.

Jib agreed. "So'm I. What kinda fixin's are there quick like?"

"Soup," she said.

"Let's start with that—any kind."

"It's potato."

"I'll have the same thin'," said Elf. "What else yuh got?"

She told him with businesslike crispness.

"I'll take steak, no pink a showin', fried taters, and apple pie . . . and coffee."

"Same here," Jib said.

She scurried to the kitchen and was back in a few moments with bread and butter, bowls of steaming potato soup, and cups of coffee.

"How's the mining going?" she asked as she busied herself in attending to them.

She walked away abruptly and, after several minutes, came back carrying a tray of considerable size with two plates, both holding a sizzling, well-done steak, a heaped serving of fried potatoes, and a generous slice of apple pie. She arranged the dishes before the men.

"Cook's done a swell job," Jib said, taking a taste. Elf nodded.

The waitress left them and came back with more hot coffee.

Jib and Elf gobbled up the meat and potatoes but took their time in eating their celebratory dessert.

"The d'sert was the best as any I ever ate," said Elf.

That night, back at home, the two discussed the prospects of their property and their responsibilities. Jib said, "There's still a considerable amount of gold still in the ground. I figger it kin be worked for more years yet. But yuh know somethin', Elf? Actually, the thin' is, I've reached muh limit of toleratin' the Hills, and I ain't suited tuh this kind of life. I'm thinkin' that minin' don't agree with me an awful whole lot. Soon as I git what shows it was worth comin' here, I'm leavin'."

"Minin' don't agree with me neither, Jib. This sure ain't the way we thought it'd be. Before we got here, seemed like a easy way tuh make a bundle of money. I figgered when I got the amount I needed tuh help muh ma, I'd git outa here, too. Last summer I decided 'tis either the skeeters or me, and, I'm mostly sure, them pests ain't leavin'. It's gotta be me what skedaddles outta here. So, pert near time tuh sell, if yer askin' me."

Having settled the business affairs to their satisfaction, Jib went to bed well pleased.

* * *

Addie Kate stared at the calendar on the wall. The bold, black block numbers on the page read with unmistakable clarity: **1879**. Two and a half years had passed since Jib was at Pleasant Hill. She used to be able to recall his image clearly, but that was no longer true. Now there was no longer any earthly reason to think about him at all. In fact, she had made a firm decision to stop thinking of Jib. No use letting dreams torment her. However, her resolve to do so did not hold sway because she continued to hope that one day he would come back for her.

The January night was bitterly cold, frost lay icy on the ground, and the wind howled through the village. Addie Kate heard a noise. She reached into the blackness and called Jib's name. He came to her and put his mouth on hers, and she rested in his arms. But when she awakened, the space was empty. Had she said his name out aloud? She did not want to raise suspicion with the Sisters in the bedroom. She flipped her pillow and shut her eyes again.

Chapter 16

In December it snowed heavily in Deadwood—ten inches. No work at the mine had happened for several days and the conversations of Jib and Elf revolved around the snow.

The two pegged up Jib's tent at the claim and brought the little heater stove so they could have a place to warm up in inclement weather and sleep in some sort of comfort when they did not go back to the cabin. Their fortune grew as dust and flakes and nuggets were repeatedly found. Everyone in town was talking about their find and speculating on how much gold they would glean from their placer mine.

"I'm thinkin' it's time for me tuh sell muh share," Jib said one day to his partner. "People're interested in buyin' our mine, and I'm rich enough. And I'm tired of the back-breakin' work of the cradlin', the cold, and the damp of the pannin'. Yuh gonna stay?"

"No, sir. I'm disgusted with this kinda life, too. Everythin's supposed tuh git better, but it never does. We've got what we was wantin' and there's still a right smart amount still there. Someone else kin work the mine fer plenty more years. Weather here's terrible. Wind howls. Snow comes in great quantities. I'm ready tuh leave."

The primary issue for the two to settle was the selling price to put on their property. They knew more of the precious metal was deeper down, but they did not want to expend the effort and expense in sinking a deep shaft to retrieve it. They decided to sell for three thousand two hundred fifty dollars.

Living in Dakota Territory for eight months had seemed a lifetime to them. Content with the earnings from their mining experience, they sold out, made a sizable profit from the sale, and packed up.

They joined with freighters who had recently made the jaunt to the Hills with a load of supplies hauled to Deadwood. The teams would unload their cargo of bacon, beans, flour, matches, and tea and head back to either Sidney or Yankton. It was the freighters' practice to make the excursion every thirty to forty days.

The company they were with followed the trail from Deadwood to Fort Pierre, then down to Yankton on the Missouri River. The two would go on to Omaha on their own. How long would it take to reach their destination? They did not know, for they learned the sternwheelers were not on a dependable timetable.

* * *

The professional freight teams had loaded up and headed back for the Hills. But the two now-retired prospectors had to wait another couple weeks for the *Far West* paddle steamer to arrive at Fort Pierre.

Jib saw the sternwheeler approaching, its two tall smokestacks spewing black clouds. Where was Elf? He found the younger man napping and shook him awake.

"Boat's comin' in."

At that moment, the first blast of the steam whistle shattered the quiet, signaling its imminent arrival at the pier.

The pair opted to pay the deck passage rate—which meant no meals and no sleeping berth.

They boarded and lost no time in finding and marking their own space in the common lounge. They planned to make do by eating the deer jerky, hardtack, and cheese they'd brought along and by dozing as best they could on the uncomfortable wooden benches. The trip would take at least two and a half days. Jib was sure he, Elf, and the mules—now housed in the cargo deck—would be able to survive.

It was early evening when the gong sounded for departure. The two went out to the open deck and leaned against the rail. As the paddle steamer slid away from the wharf, they studied the paddle wheels that sent all smaller, frailer floating craft rocking to and fro at the pier. They endured the spray that kicked up into their faces and dampened their clothes as they took a last glimpse of the dock.

On the dockside, people were waving their hats or handkerchiefs, wiping their eyes, yelling their goodbyes. Jib removed his hat, signaling a farewell, while the wind ruffled his hair. The paddleboat, with a considerable tooting of its whistles, tootled away, beginning its journey down the Missouri River, headed for Yankton.

Elf shouted, "Ain't wishin' the town no harm, but jist a hopin' never tuh see it again."

Jib drew deep breaths of air. "Yuh shouldn't hafta unless yuh wanna mine some more."

* * *

The day they approached their destination, those on board surged out on deck and watched the townspeople gather on the shore.

"First sight of real civilization since we left Nebraska months ago. Downright excitin' tuh be closer tuh home, ain't it?" Jib playfully poked Elf in the ribs with his elbow. The two descended the ridged gangway and claimed the mules and hack.

"Wanna ramble around the place? I'm hungry. Let's eat."

And, on that note, they set out.

They inquired as to the location of an eating establishment, crossed the street, and walked a short distance until they found it, opened the door and entered, each taking a chair at one of the tables.

"What kinda fixin's yuh got tuhday?" Jib asked the waitress who came to their table.

"Fried chicken," she said, turning her attention to him. "Has a crispy, crackly crust. You'll find it's delicious."

"Four pieces, then. It don't matter what they are, neither. And plenty of coffee."

She nodded.

"What else yuh got?" It was Elf this time.

"Potatoes, cream gravy, and buttered turnips."

"Any d'sert?"

"Rhubarb pie."

Both ended up ordering the same. When the food came, they chowed down eagerly and talked of inconsequential matters. Finishing the meal, they wiped their mouths and hands on the cloth napkins, slapped down the payment on the table, and left.

"We've gotta see where the animals kin git a room and board," Jib said. Elf nodded. The two sought out the usual places where they could purchase grain and hay for the mules. They made the rounds of the town, finally locating a livery stable where Jib gave Hez and Kez into the care of the man who came forward. "Feed and water 'em, please," he said.

"By gosh, Jib, we's had tuh traipse all o'er this place tryin' tuh fin' a li'le oats fer them mules of yorn." He glanced over at his friend.

Jib removed his old piece of a hat and scratched the top of his head. He put the Stetson back on and tugged the brim down. "Yankton looks like a pretty fit town. I'm gittin' me a room at the hotel, takin' me a relaxin' bath, havin' a shave, and sleepin' in a honest-tuh-goodness bed. Got the mules took care of, so now it's muh turn. Tomorrow, I'm plannin' on buyin' some new duds before I hafta board another steamer and head for Omaha."

Chapter 17

April 29, 1879

After registering at Omaha's Douglas House Hotel, Jib located his assigned room on the second floor. It would suffice. He went back to the lobby, which was plush with thick rugs, and positioned himself in an overstuffed chair, bowed his head, and pressed his palms together at his lips. He had said his goodbyes to Elf and seen the young man off on the train to Columbus and now sat absorbed in meditation.

It had been less than a year ago the two met, both of them ready to embark on a new adventure. They formed a solid friendship and, even better, a partnership in the gold mining business. It was hard to say goodbye knowing they were not at all likely to encounter each other again.

"Lord, Yer Word says Yuh guide us every day. Thanks for bringin' Elf intuh muh life. I ask that Yuh bless him daily. I'm sad tuh part from muh friend and partner."

Jib thought of all the farewells he'd said: To his brothers, his father, his sisters, military buddies, and, of course, Addie Kate. He did not particularly want to bring his mind to her, but there she was. "If I'm figgerin' on gittin' me a wife, cain't be jist any woman. I ain't gonna settle. Gotta be Addie Kate. She'll make me a fine helpmate and hopefully beget me children." He considered her sense of decency, her purity, and her guileless manner.

"Sir?" a man's voice called.

Jib raised his head and turned his attention to the sound.

"Would you like to read the latest edition of the newspaper?" The man held it out.

Jib ran his tongue under his lower lip. "Anythin' worth readin' in it?"

"Yes, sir. A notable trial starts day after tomorrow right here in Omaha. Everyone's talking about it."

Jib hoisted himself up, walked over to the registration desk, and took it. "Really? What makes it so sensational?"

"Well, this is the first time an Indian is permitted to appear in a United States courtroom."

"Who is it?"

"He's Standing Bear, a Ponca chief."

"What'd he do?"

"Ran away from the Indian Territory with his son's dead body. The way I understand the case, it is to decide if he can be considered a person and has any rights as a citizen."

"Whadda yuh know about his story?"

"Just what I've read. The tribe was forcibly removed from their homeland in 1877 by federal treaty. All they could take with them was whatever they could carry. Many of them succumbed along the way. Government settled them in Indian Territory. Just this last January, Chief Standing Bear and twenty-nine other Poncas set out for Nebraska with the body of the chief's son who had died on their Trail of Tears. They were labeled renegades because Indians were not supposed to leave the reservation without permission. In March, they had reached the Omaha reservation where the Secretary of the

Interior ordered they be arrested by the Army. General George Crook then moved them to Fort Omaha. The Indian filed a lawsuit against the government."

Jib jerked his head. "Kin anyone go tuh follow the legal proceedin's?"

"Well, I suppose you can . . . it is open to the public."

"I'll plan tuh be there." Jib turned and started back to the chair with the paper.

* * *

On Thursday, the first of May, he made his way to the third floor of the federal courthouse on the corner of Fifteenth and Dodge streets in Omaha. He arrived at the place early, only to discover many others were already there. "Huh. Curiosity brought 'em here, too. Like me."

He discovered the seats in the courtroom were filled with clergy, women, lawyers, businessmen, Army officers, and Indians. Stragglers shouldered for room against one another and the back wall. Jib, working his way into a space close to the front, glanced around. The man sitting two rows from him was Thomas Henry Tibbles, the editor for the *Omaha Daily Herald* and an activist for Native Americans.

A man stepped before the people and bellowed, "All rise!"

The lively buzz of conversation suddenly died, and there was a rustling as everyone got to their feet. The judge entered and stood in his place behind the bench.

The bailiff again addressed the people. "The Federal Court in the State of Nebraska, the Honorable District Court Judge Elmer Dundy presiding, is now in session. Please be seated and come to order."

A wooden rail divided the gallery from the principals. In front of Jib, on the left of the room, sat the prominent defense attorneys, Andrew Jackson Poppleton and John Lee Webster.

Seated in their chairs at oak tables to the right of the room were the district attorney, Genio Lambertson, and Army General George

Crook. They all faced the judge with their backs to the observers. No jury had been called to hear the arguments and decide the verdict.

The courtroom's door swung open, and the one bringing the suit, a Ponca chief, came into the room. The man was tall, wearing a wide belt of beadwork circling his waist, deerskin moccasins, and holding about his shoulders the red council blanket trimmed with blue stripes he wore when he conducted official business for the Poncas. Around his neck hung a necklace made from the claws of a grizzly bear. The chief presented an impressive picture.

The eyes of those in the room followed him as he made his way down the center aisle to where his lawyers waited for him at the large table. Mr. Poppleton extended his arm in a welcoming gesture.

A wave of murmurs went through the room. Judge Dundy gaveled for order, and the trial of Chief Standing Bear versus George Crook was officially underway. In a rich voice, he said, "The underlying basis for this lawsuit is to determine if the Indian is a person and that being so is—as far as the Constitution is concerned—a citizen of the United States."

Jib muttered to himself, "We all are made in God's image. Psalm one three nine tells us the Lord Almighty knows everythin' about us and that we are wonderfully made. He knits us tuhgether in a secret place, and nothin' is hid from Him."

The judge asked, "Is the plaintiff ready to proceed?"

"Yes, Your Honor." The younger of Standing Bear's two attorneys, Mr. Webster, eased around the table and strolled toward the judge's bench and began. "Indians are people granted citizenship as well as equal protection and due process of the rules and regulations as understood by the Fourteenth Amendment," he declared.

Then the district attorney framed out the direction of the case for his client, General Crook, and, in effect, the government. He spoke for three hours before concluding, "As far as the law is concerned, the Indian is a savage and neither a person nor a citizen. Therefore, he has no rights and cannot bring a suit against the United States," he argued. With that, he walked back to his seat.

Jib winced at Mr. Lambertson's argument, shifted, and squirmed uncomfortably. *Rights come from God.*

A slight commotion like the buzzing of bees arose in the room, and Judge Dundy rapped the gavel and called for order. "We will break for lunch until two o'clock this afternoon."

"All rise," ordered the bailiff. The judge made his exit, and the crowd began to shuffle their way out of the room.

Jib breathed a sigh of relief and gritted his teeth. Would he have time to find a restaurant, then get back soon enough to keep his same spot? He decided not to eat but simply go outside for some fresh air.

* * *

When the litigation took up again, a respectful silence fell as Mr. Webster summoned the Indian as a witness. After a long and deliberate pause, the chief got up and took the stand.

"What was your reason for leaving the Indian Territory illegally?"

Glancing around, Standing Bear finally looked at the judge and, speaking with the aid of his interpreter, Bright Eyes, the daughter of the Omaha chief, said, "My people were told by your president the Ponca had to leave. It is our land. God gave it to us. We suffered the hardship of travel, illness, and lack of food in moving to a strange territory. Many members of the tribe perished, including my son, Bear Shield. My son, when he was dying, made me promise that if I ever went back to the homeland, I would take his bones and bury them in Mother Earth at the Niobrara River. That is why we left the Indian Territory."

He finished giving his testimony, his lawyers rested their case, and the district attorney called no witnesses. Though it had been a long day, the judge instructed the lawyers to begin their closing arguments. Mr. Webster started to summarize the important points on behalf of

Standing Bear and the Ponca Nation but soon stated he felt too poorly to continue.

The judge struck his gavel. "We will convene at ten o'clock tomorrow morning for the presentation of closing arguments. Court is now adjourned."

The principals sat at the tables while the courtroom emptied. Jib waited as the noisy crowd spilled out of the room. Then he slipped out alone and started for the hotel.

"Good evening, sir. Long day for you," the desk clerk said cheerfully.

Jib nodded but was not in the mood to chitchat and kept walking.

"How's it going?"

"Our government ain't treated the Indians fairly." He frowned, shook his head as he passed the man, climbed the stairs, and went to his room.

Jib sat on the side of his bed. "Holy God, the One and only true God. Yuh know what steps are planned for Chief Standing Bear's future. I ask that wisdom be given tuh the judge that he will decide this case according tuh Yer will. Amen."

He undressed, crawled into bed, and lay awake a long time.

* * *

The next morning, at the stated time, the courtroom came to order. Mr. Webster cleared his throat and began his concluding address. "Ponca Indians are not savages," he began, continuing his remarks at a leisurely pace, speaking for three and a half hours. He quoted from the Fourteenth Amendment that all persons born in the United States are citizens and cannot be deprived of life, liberty, or property without due process of law. "What are they?" he asked. "Are they wild animals?"

At three o'clock, District Attorney Lambertson stated his one major theme: "There's room for sentiment in this case for Standing Bear, but keep in mind the law says that as an Indian, he is neither a citizen nor a person. Since he is not a citizen, the court has no right to issue the writ of habeas corpus." He traced the arc of his mustache with his thumb and index finger and sank to his chair, yanking out a handkerchief to mop his forehead, cheeks, and neck. He completed his line of reasoning at six o'clock, having spoken for more than three hours.

The crowd released a collective breath. The judge ordered a dinner recess for one hour, and everyone left the room.

After the evening meal, the court convened once more, and Mr. Poppleton spoke for close to three hours as well. As he began to wind down, he challenged each of the government's indictments. "Is Standing Bear a person? To deny his legal right to the writ, the court will have to conclude that the Ponca are not people, that they are not human beings."

It had been a very long day. The proceedings had lasted almost twelve hours. Before the court dismissed, Judge Dundy said, "Please remain seated. Chief Standing Bear would like to speak as his own representative."

Jib peered at the man who rose slowly from his seat and walked to the open space between the principals' tables. The Indian stopped, and a significant silence fell upon the room. He faced the judge—and drew out his right hand. With Bright Eyes serving as his interpreter, he said, "My hand is not the color as yours, but if I pierce it, I shall feel pain. If you pierce your hand, you also feel pain. The blood that will flow from mine will be of the same color as yours. The same God made us both. I am a man."

Then he pivoted and scanned the people. "I have a vision of myself standing on a high bank of a great river, with my wife and little girl at my side," he said. "I cannot cross the river, and impassable cliffs rise behind me. I stand where no member of my race ever stood before. There is no tradition to guide me. I hear the noise of great waters and sense a flood coming. The waters rise to our feet and then to our knees. My little girl stretches her hands toward me and says, 'Save me.' In despair I look toward the cliffs behind me, and I glimpse a dim trail that may lead to safety. It looks to be impassable, but I make the attempt. I take my child by the hand, and my wife follows after me. Our hands and our feet are torn by the sharp rocks, and our trail is marked by our blood. Beyond the path I see green prairies."

Chief Standing Bear stopped and glanced around. There was complete silence in the courtroom. When he spoke again, his voice lowered. "In the middle of the path, there stands a man more powerful than I. Behind him, I see soldiers in great numbers like the leaves of the trees. They must obey the man's orders. I, too, must obey the man's orders. If that man gives me permission, I may pass on to the prairies, to life and liberty. If he refuses, I must go back and sink beneath the flood. We are weak and tired and cannot fight the man."

Standing Bear held the whole courtroom in his spell. He turned toward the bench, and with a sweep of his arm, his hand outstretched, he pointed at the judge and said, "You are that man."

Jib immediately thought of the Old Testament story in which the prophet Nathan confronted King David following his sin with Bathsheba. "You are that man," the prophet had said.

An awesome hush in the room reigned for several moments as the old chief sat down. General Crook, who had arrested Chief Standing Bear, leaned forward on the table and covered his face with his hands. A number of the ladies in the back of the room sobbed and pulled handkerchiefs out of their sleeves.

At once the people applauded, rose to their feet, and cheered. General Crook got up from his chair and went over to shake Standing Bear's hand. Mr. Tibbles was next. Before long, the crowd rushed to pump the chief's hand. Jib fought his way through the throng. He had to meet this Ponca and shake the chief's hand. Even the ladies flocked to him, and, for an hour, Standing Bear had a reception.

Finally, the bailiff cried out for order. When the courtroom grew quiet again, the judge said he would take the case under advisement and release his decision in a few days. "Court is now concluded," he said, tapping his gavel and exiting. It was shortly after ten o'clock on a warm evening on May the second, 1879.

Jib returned to the hotel. He would miss the announcement of the verdict because he was leaving Omaha the next day. He had stayed three more days than he had anticipated in the first place.

The sternwheeler was coming in and he couldn't wait to get to St. Louis and on with the next phase of his life—finding and buying a farm. Where, he was not that particular. He knew, though, he had to go to Addie Kate and convince her to marry him.

He made his way through the lobby, acknowledging guests with a nod, some sitting in the chairs, others standing around in small clusters, still others leaning against the walls. The hotel, packed to capacity, accommodated the reporters and spectators who came to Omaha for the famous trial.

* * *

After the paddlewheel boat docked at St. Louis, after Jib disembarked, and after he claimed his freight of Hcz and Kcz and the hack, he found the newspaper office to learn the verdict of Chief Standing Bear's trial. Jib read that on May the twelfth, Judge Elmer Dundy ruled in favor of Standing Bear, declaring that Indians were indeed persons under the law and had all the unalienable rights to "life, liberty, and the pursuit of happiness," which the Declaration of Independence said had been given to all humans by their Creator.

He also discovered that Standing Bear; the editor, Thomas Tibbles; and Bright Eyes went on a speaking tour of the eastern United States informing the public about the story of the Poncas.

Part 3

Chapter 18

September 12, 1879

*I*t was Friday, and excitement reigned in the area around Pleasant Hill. A railroad trestle at the village of Highbridge, constructed over the Kentucky River, was quite an engineering feat—two hundred seventy-five feet high and the first major cantilevered bridge built in the United States—and was being dedicated. An elaborate ceremony had been planned and advertised in honor of the occasion.

A light rain began well before dawn. Hardly more than a drizzle at first, it became a steady downpour and continued into the morning. At times the sun bordered on peeking out from the dark clouds, but it never quite did.

The inclement weather held the heavy scent of wild grapes and the cidery smell of fallen apples, but the wetness did not appear to deter a multitude from attending the festivities. Wagons, buggies, and buckboards were not so much parked as abandoned around the grounds. Addie Kate, along with Ella Beth and several of the Sisters, arrived late. The entire space crackled with enthusiastic zeal—throngs of people yelling and whooping in high spirits.

Distracted by the commotion, Addie Kate wandered away from the Shakers. She threaded her way through the bustle and clamor of the crowd to where she could watch the proceedings. The event was historic with a lot of hoopla. President Rutherford B. Hayes and two of his seven sons, Birchard and Rutherford, were to be in attendance at the jubilee. William T. Sherman, now the commanding general of the Army, was to be there as well. She strolled for some time through the throng of spectators and newspaper people.

It was a noisy morning. The crows were at it and the katydids and cicadas sang in muted debate. Grasshoppers leaped out of her way as she walked around.

Photographers set up their cameras all in a row facing the grandstand. She thought of Jib. Where was he now? Was he even alive? Had he married? Oh, probably. No, he said he wasn't the marrying kind. What was he doing? Would he have seen any publicity about this celebration? She glanced this way and that, searching for Ella Beth.

Addie Kate stopped short. She breathed hard through parted lips and her heart thundered in her chest as she focused on a man. For a long time, all she could do was stare at him.

"Jib," she said breathlessly.

Was it him? She thought so. Sure resembled him, anyway. She sucked in a deep breath and emptied her lungs in a slow stream, but it didn't help calm her. Her knees went weak. She flattened a hand against her churning stomach.

"It has to be him," she said out loud. The man was nicely tanned, had square shoulders and disheveled sun-bleached hair. "Oh!" She brought her hands to her head and her amazement morphed to eagerness and delight as she willed herself to walk normally toward him. "Jib, you did come back."

She broke into a run and ran across the grass, her feet pounding the ground. She jostled her way through the onlookers, tears rolling down her cheeks. "Why come back now, after three years?" But here he was, back in her life—her heart almost too full for bearing. Someone darted between her and Jib and she was no longer able to see him. Unable to breathe in a usual manner, she stopped. Where did he go? And then he withdrew from the black focusing cloth arranged over his camera.

She cupped her hands around her mouth and called out, "Jib! You're here!" She moved toward him, wishing she might fling her arms about his neck and cling to him.

Startled, he raised his head and wheeled around. He looked different yet still the same. Had he changed? Why shouldn't he? She supposed she had changed, too.

Standing a short distance apart, they gaped at each other. He gave a yawp of laughter, whipped off his hat, and struck a courtly bow. "Addie Kate!" he exclaimed, and promptly deposited the Stetson on his head.

She approached, he put his arms about her, and she clung to him. "Don't let go of me."

"No, I'll never let go of you again."

"Oh, Jib, I'm so glad you came."

"I had to."

"I thought you were going out West."

"Did."

She looked up into his face.

He smiled, crinkling up his eyes and pulling his lips against his teeth. "Now I'm here."

"I must say you look wonderful," she said, and she meant it.

"Yuh ain't forgot me, huh?"

She pulled away and shook her head slowly. "No," she said.

"That's nice because I'm aimin' tuh marry yuh." He swept her into his arms in a swift movement, swung her around, and kissed her flat on the mouth.

"Jib, put me down!" He did, setting her on her feet. "How did you know I would be here?"

"Dint for shore. Glad tuh see yuh." He slid his arm around her waist and held her tightly against his side as if he would never let her go, and she was holding on to him like she didn't want him to let her go. There they stood for everyone to see.

She did not rebel at his embrace but nuzzled against his shoulder. "I thought of you so often. This doesn't seem real." She drew away to arm's length.

"Yuh ain't been out of muh mind since I done went away." They stared at each other. "Came back tuh find yuh more splendid than yuh was before."

If any of the Eldresses witnessed their display of affection, there would be consequences. She was well aware of that, but she didn't concern herself about it at the moment.

He leaned his forehead against hers. "It's so good tuh see yuh, Addie Kate. Yuh's lookin' swell. Did yuh miss me?"

"I did. Only every day," she whispered. "I can't tell you how many times I thought of you. How have you been? Seeing you here is an answer to my prayers. When I saw you, I thought it was my imagination. It's marvelous to be talking with you again. I have waited for you three years. *Three years, Jib!* Seemed like a thousand to me. I'm so happy you are here!"

"So much's happened—a awful lot tuh tell yuh." He straightened his back and folded his arms across his chest. "I figgered goin' out West would git me cured."

"Of what?"

"Gittin' yuh outta muh mind . . . found out it never worked . . . missed yuh too much. I knew that without yuh, muh life would not be the same."

"I've made an awful mess of things," she said sorrowfully. "I never—" she stopped and stared off at the near distance.

"Go on," he prompted.

"I didn't think things out. I didn't understand what you meant to me, or the vows I had taken, or even what I myself meant. Looking back, it's impossible for me to say what I thought. But I never knew how much I'd miss you."

"I knowed it, though. Why do yuh think I pushed hard for yuh tuh go with me? We hafta go on from here."

"I would have written you, but I didn't know where to send the letter. You really came to this dedication today just to find me?"

"Uh-huh. Told muhself yuh's not as special as yuh are. I tried convincin' muhself there's gotta be other women like yuh . . . but there ain't. Ain't taken kindly tuh the idea of the lonely life. I hadda come back and find out if yer ready tuh go with me and be muh wife. Never been no woman that suits me but you, Addie Kate."

"I went all to pieces when you went away, Jib," she said, putting her hand over his. "I'm sorry. I was foolish not to leave with you when you asked me. I wish we had not lost all those years. I realize you were right."

"Then let's erase the past. We'll forget about it. Nothin' of benefit comes of thinkin' what might've been," he said as he waved his hand through the air.

"You're right, but I regret having taken so long to figure this out. I finally settled everything inside my mind and my heart. I'm older and wiser now and becoming the woman I always wanted to be."

"Meanin' yer what? Thirty?"

"Yes."

He tut-tutted. "Absolutely elderly." He stroked her cheek, brushing the edge of her lips. "Yuh'll come with me now?"

"I will go with you," Addie Kate said. "Seems only right that I do. We could have been together three years ago except for my stupid stubbornness. I thought you were going out to the Big Country."

"Did. Come back tuh take some pictures of this celebration. Camera's all ready." His thumb jabbed the air above his shoulder at the tripod draped with the black oiled cover. "This is a mighty feat.

Advertised everywhere. If the drizzle would ever stop, I could snap one or two. And . . ." he said, "I realized I was missin' somethin' important in muh life . . . a family. That's the real reason I come back is tuh git yuh, Addie Kate. Yuh had a powerful effect on me."

She stood for too long a moment looking at him. "What now?"

"I aim tuh git hitched."

"Oh? Are we going to be married?" she asked lightly.

"Yep." He put his arms around her. "I know we can do this, Addie Kate. I'm a wantin' tuh settle down. There's a right time for everythin'. Good Book says so. How about it? Are yuh ready tuh leave this place?"

She looked up into his face and nodded. "Yes. I never have felt like I fit in here." She swallowed hard. "I'm ready to leave with only the clothes I'm wearing."

Jib released his grasp about her and scratched his head. "So let's git outta here."

"Yes, let's!" She smiled and clasped her hands at her heart. "I am going to be married today," she heard herself say.

He grinned and ran his fingertip from beneath Addie Kate's ear all the way down along her jawline. "We'll git a license and find a church and stand before a preacher. Be all legal and proper. Decent folks do that."

"I promised myself a long time ago that if you ever came back and still wanted me as your wife, I would leave immediately, and I would do my best to make my husband happy."

He scooped her up in his arms again. "Gimme a few minutes. I need tuh pack up all muh equipment, then we'll jist ride off and disappear from the Shakers."

They glanced at each other, smiled, and nodded. He said, "We couldn't've asked for a nicer day, could we?"

She laughed. "This is perfect for making my escape. All the hubbub'll make it easy to slip away without detection. Mm-hmm. I'm ready to leave everything." She touched her white covering—the required cap. Getting rid of it sounded like freedom to her.

Were the Elders right when they branded those who left the community—those who "went to the flesh"—as embracing eternal damnation? At one time Addie Kate had been proud of being a Shaker—when she was a child and didn't know any better. But since Jib opened her eyes to the folly of the sect, she realized there was no future with them. What would her fate be with the man from the world? She had no idea now, but she anticipated it would be one that was free from stifling rules. Addie Kate stood straight, her chin high. She'd made her decision years ago. Now she would follow through with it.

She wanted to be done with Pleasant Hill, for sure, but she wouldn't desert the Shakers by darkness of night as so many others had. No, she would leave in broad daylight. And she didn't want to hurt Ella Beth by abandoning her. "While you're packing up your equipment, I'll go say goodbye to my sister."

Chapter 19

Ella Beth, standing in a group of Shakers, appeared as though she was enjoying their chitchat. Giving them several minutes together, Addie Kate walked up with the most casual air and caught her sister's arm to pull her aside. "Please come with me," she murmured. "I want to talk with you, even though I'm not for sure if it'd be wise of me to do so." She had already made up her mind she would tell her older sister.

"What is it?" Ella Beth yanked free of the grasp.

"Shh!" The younger woman held her finger to her lips signaling her sister to quiet down. She peeped over her shoulder as the two walked away from the others. "Just come."

"All right. What is this about?"

Addie Kate glanced cautiously about them and said in a low voice, "I'm leaving."

"You're returning to the village? Don't you want to stay for the dedication?"

"No, you misunderstand. I am going away from Pleasant Hill."

Ella Beth stopped. "You're joking! Why . . . what do you mean by doing a thing like that? How do you propose you'll be able to accomplish it?"

"Jib." She smiled without showing her teeth. "He's here."

For a full minute there was a strained silence. "Sorry, but I don't want to hear any more about that man. Let me go back to the others."

"No, don't go. Not yet anyway. *Promise* you won't tell a soul what I'm about to say . . . at least until tonight."

"How can I do that when I don't know what it is?"

"I won't tell you until you give me your word of honor." Addie Kate waited for some sign of agreement from her sibling as they moseyed along in the squishy grass, huddled under the same umbrella.

"All right. I give my pledge. So, what is this all about?"

Addie Kate drew in a humongous breath to calm her nerves, ran her tongue across her lips several times, and said, "Matrimony."

Ella Beth raised her eyebrows "You don't mean—you can't mean—that you're going to be married to him? When is this supposed to happen?"

"Today . . . in a few minutes."

"Why?" The older sister stared, her mouth agape. "Whatever possessed you to think of doing such a thing?" she screeched. "You can't leave—especially with him. If you are out in the world, your religion will be stripped away and you won't amount to a handful of beans. Don't do this. We need you here. What will we do without you?"

A crow banked past them, cawing to beat the band, flapping its wings. Addie Kate watched it till it perched in a tree at the edge of the grounds. She wagged her head but resisted rolling her eyes. "You'll manage."

"Adelaide Kathleen!"

"What?"

"Nothing but trouble will come to you by going with that man."

"You're demanding me to stay away from him?"

"Yes," Ella Beth countered angrily. "You have been too feisty since being around the man."

Addie Kate winced, wishing she'd kept her mouth shut about her plans. She shook her head. "I'm still going away with Jib."

"*What?*"

"Shh! People are married all the time."

"Not Believers. You're as crazy as a loon! You aren't listening to me!"

"I am too! I'm simply not agreeing with you." Addie Kate put her hands on her hips. "You can stop ordering me around. I'm thirty years old. I want to live my own life."

"Your age has nothing to do with it. I'm talking about madness. You don't know him."

"How can you say that? Of course I do." Actually, Ella Beth was right. But Addie Kate would admit that only to herself.

"You haven't even seen him for three years."

"True. Today something happened."

"Bang! Like that?"

Addie Kate nodded. "Yes, he's here to take me away. I'm weary of being spied on every minute and following rules that don't make sense to me. I want to dress as I like and come and go as I please." Leaving would guarantee that she would no longer need to cower in fear of Jerusha's threats ever again.

"You have lost your right mind! Be wedded to a man from the world? That's wicked." Ella Beth glared at her younger sister. "He will disappoint you," she asserted firmly.

Addie Kate flapped a hand in disgust. "No, he won't."

"He'll leave you high and dry out in the middle of nowhere," Ella Beth argued.

"Shame on you. Jib's a principled man," Addie Kate said calmly. "We belong together."

"Be realistic!"

"I am. I know what I'm doing."

"Apparently not. You don't realize what might happen. Be sensible. This could mean unhappiness for you, poverty . . . loneliness. I don't understand why you would ever want to go away from this place with its peace and security."

Addie Kate leaned forward. "Listen to me, then, and I'll tell you why. Shakers think we're so pious because we separate from the world. I think we're the stiff-necked ones with all our rules. I'm tired of this. I do not fit in here and you are well aware of that fact. I will never be a true Shaker because I cannot obey edicts which seem unreasonable to me." Her voice became raspy. "We're just like the Pharisees, walking around in our own pride, thanking God we are not like those of the world. We think we have all the answers to living a good life. We don't! I'm getting away from here in order to live the desires of my heart."

Ella Beth looked sadly at her younger sister. "You'll make a terrible mess of your life."

"I don't think so."

"You'll only see it in hindsight. You are saying that everything they've ever done for you—"

The crow came back, scolding loudly. They both glanced up at it.

"I do recognize what they have done for me, and I do appreciate it, too," Addie Kate said.

"Are you trying to hurt me then?"

"No. This is not about you. It is about me. I'm not you. I'm my own person. I need to go from here—more than anything."

"No, you don't. You only think you do."

"Why are you treating me like a child? Shouldn't people be allowed to achieve what they aspire to in life? I must live my life, not yours. I crave something more than what's here, and I want to be able to attain it."

"You sound childish and self-centered to me—and like you're using Jib to realize your own selfish desires. You surprise me."

"I amaze myself."

"You'll disgrace our family," Ella Beth said, shaking her head.

"How can I? Our brothers left years ago. Did you suffer dishonor then, too?"

"It is clever of Jib getting you to forsake us," Ella Beth continued. "If you'll remember, he showed you absolutely no consideration for three years, and has probably been with women from the world a number of times. He may even be a murderer! Don't be so gullible!"

Addie Kate laughed. "You're being ridiculous. Only you could believe the worst of him."

Ella Beth snapped. "So you are saying you'd rather be a person of the flesh than a Believer? You're willing to give up everything you have to go off with him?"

Addie Kate nodded. "Mm-hmm," she said quietly. "What is the 'everything' that is mine here? Tell me. The truth is that most of the time, I feel like a prisoner. I'm told what to do, what to wear, and what to eat. I'm sick and tired of bowing to Jerusha and doing the same things over and over. I know there are plenty of Shakers who don't mind dragging along day after day, working and eating and sleeping—but I'm not one of them. I don't hanker to come to the end of my life and regret that I didn't pursue my dreams. I prefer to love a man and covet his love for me. I yearn to birth a baby and own my home. Oh yes, I comprehend exactly what I'm doing."

Exasperated, Ella Beth said, "You're being difficult."

Addie Kate rolled her eyes. "Maybe so. But this is not an issue for you to decide what I do."

"What can you gain from going with him?"

"Huh-uh. The right question to ask is what can I give to him by doing this for me?" She would go with Jib. She *had* to.

"I think he's totally and completely hornswoggled you. What about the Sisters and Brethren? What are you going to say to them?"

"I'll tell them nothing. I'll just ride off."

"You're running away?"

"Yes."

"What will they think of you?"

"I don't care. I'm not giving up on what I want because of silly gossip. They are not my judge. It doesn't make any difference to me what the tongues will clatter."

"What if something goes wrong and things don't work out and you'll cry to come back?"

"When I let myself love a man, it will be forever, come trouble or sorrow or distress. I have made up my mind it is going to work out, so I can assure you I'll never return, no matter what."

"You say that now. You're so sure of things. I'll never see you again most likely. I do wonder why blood isn't thicker than water for you?"

"Please don't be bitter," Addie Kate pleaded.

They faced each other, tears sliding down Ella Beth's cheeks. She wrapped her arms about her younger sister and they hugged tightly for a long time. When the embrace ended, the siblings parted.

"I don't see any purpose in prolonging this. Goodbye, little sister," Ella Beth said. "I do hope all will be right for you."

Addie Kate nodded, kissed her sister on the cheek, and lifted a hand in farewell as she squared her shoulders, turned her back, and walked off to meet her waiting husband-to-be.

Chapter 20

*A*ddie Kate approached Jib as he finished packing up his camera equipment. "I'm back!" she announced.

He whipped around a quarter turn and smiled. "Ready? Come on, then," he said. "Let's git on our way."

He walked a few paces, turned and paused, and motioned her to come along. He grabbed her elbow to lead her. "Stay close tuh me."

She ignored the butterflies in her stomach as they threaded their way through the crowd. Apparently nobody noticed them or, if they did, thought nothing of it. Jib guided her through the obstacle course of chattering people to where he left his team. He reached under the front seat of the hack and pulled out a round box, presenting it with some flair. "Open it," he said, handing it to her.

"Oh my." She focused on it, looked up at him, and broke the ribbon that tied the package. Her hands trembled causing her to fumble with the brown wrapping paper. She removed the lid to find inside a fashionable straw poke bonnet lined with dark green velvet, its crown adorned with felt grapes and sprays of ivy leaves. She lifted it out and discovered that underneath lay a lavishly embroidered daffodil-yellow silk shawl with its fringe knotted in an intricate pattern.

Overcome by his generosity, she gaped at him in astonishment. "Mr. Claycomb, you've taken my breath away. They're exquisite! I've never had anything so stylish and elegant. You bought these? . . . For me?" She brushed her fingers over the fabric.

He put his hand on her shoulder and gave a gentle squeeze. "I did . . . planned it for when we made our get away. I figgered we needed tuh hide the Shaker garb as much as possible."

She pulled the mantelet out, held it at arm's length, and caught her breath. "Oh, I can't wear these."

"Why not?"

"They're too beautiful."

"Hogwash, put 'em on."

She yanked off her little white cap, settled the bonnet over her cropped hair, and tied the green ribbon into a bow under her chin, below her left ear. She then grasped the cape to her heart and beamed at him. "I feel special."

"Yuh are." He gently kissed her temple. "And I'm gonna give yuh lots of things."

"Won't the rain ruin these if I put them on?"

"Naw. Cain't." Jib said and smiled at her.

She draped the beautiful cloak over her bonneted head, spread it about her shoulders, and struck a pose.

"Yuh look right nice."

"How did you know that I'd be here today and that I would go with you?"

He pinched his lower lip. "I dint, but our heavenly Father did. He told me tuh come."

"Doesn't make any sense to me."

"That's all right. Does tuh me. Prayed about it a powerful lot because I feared there'd be some resentment toward me on account of all them silent years. But He assured me yuh'd be waitin'."

"God told you? How come He didn't tell me you were coming . . . so I could be ready?"

"I ain't doubtin' He did. Yuh weren't listenin'." He narrowed his eyes. "He knew yuh'd be too scared tuh go away on yer own. So He had me come."

"Oh," she said. It was true that if she did not seize this opportunity to leave, she would lose any chance to break off from Pleasant Hill. Her heart hammered with fearfulness as Jib gallantly helped her mount to the front seat. She straightened her spine and clutched the mantle closer to her chest. "I'm . . . I'm . . . running away."

"Runnin' away? Naw. We're simply leavin' here in order tuh git somewhere else." He hoisted himself up to sit beside her, took the reins, slapped them on the mules' flanks, and goaded the brace forward. "Yuh ready tuh git hitched?" He smiled at her. "We're goin' tuh Harrodsburg for that. The best of everythin' in life is ahead of us."

"It seems incredible to me," she said.

With a lurch, they were off, the wheels rasping through the high grass, the hack creaking and groaning as it jerked and jolted over the uneven trail. Neither Addie Kate nor Jib spoke as they pulled away from the Highbridge celebration, her sister, and from all the familiar sights and faces—everything she had ever known. She vowed to herself then and there that she would never come back. *Never!* She wanted to move on from the Shakers, find freedom, and enjoy what lay ahead for her and with her soon-to-be husband.

A little of her tension eased as they drove along, and her gripping of the seat was to avoid being sent sprawling to the ground by the unexpected jolts. She fell to happy thoughts centering on the constant companionship of couples, the intimacy of marriage, the miracle of motherhood, and the courage of putting her hand in Jib's and walking with him into the future.

He glanced at her. "Ain't it excitin' that we're actually doin' this? In a few hours we'll be married. I'mma goin' tuh be crazy about muh wife."

"Aren't you even a little apprehensive?" Her voice jumbled and bounced with the ruts.

"No, timin's right for us doin' this."

"Yes, of course." But she wished she was as courageous inside as her words to him conveyed. "I'm excited . . . and a bit nervous, too, both at the same time."

"Normal, I'd say. I'll always protect yuh, Addie Kate. We jist hafta make sure we're outta the county before the Elders realize you're gone."

Hearing that, Addie Kate's skin prickled and she wondered if his insides were stirring as much as hers were. "How much farther to Harrodsburg?" She was sure she could not breathe until she was well away from there, away from the strict regimentation and scrutinizing eyes of the Elders and Eldresses, to the dream she had held in her heart for twenty-some years: a husband, a home, and, hopefully, a family.

"Not too far. It's gonna be a whole new world openin' up tuh us."

"I know. I keep imagining what a wonderful helpmate I plan to be for you."

No one waved goodbye to her. No one but her sister knew she was gone. She and Jib stole away from a dedication to be married. *Eloping!* Husband and wife till death parted them.

Addie Kate sniggered. The Shaker community would be scandalized. She did not care. And no one traveling the road would think anything was out of the ordinary seeing a couple sitting together on the front seat.

They rode along for some time without speaking. "Yuh all right? Jib asked.

She nodded. "Yes, just too happy to talk."

She nestled next to him with her hands tightly clasped in her lap. She appreciated the silence he allowed her, for it gave her time to mull over her actions. She was doing the right thing, she was sure. Jib was the kind of man she had always wanted to marry, if that occasion ever came along. And now it had. She presumed their relationship would not be characterized as passionate, but, then again, passion fades in time, and companionship and compatibility take its place. They had those qualities already. A man wanted a woman to cook and clean for him and bear his children. A woman needed a man to provide for her, keep a roof overhead, and put bread on the table. She and Jib would be content with possessing a home and having a family. They would live the kind of life she had dreamed about for years. Now that it was about to become a reality, she wasn't going to give up on its fulfillment.

Ever since she started off with him, in a flutter of delight for herself, she was also conscious of heartache for Ella Beth. She found herself drifting into a nostalgic reverie. What was she doing now? She who was incapable of holding her tongue. Probably blabbing to everyone she could find that her sister had chosen to flesh off. Would the Elders do anything when they heard she had deserted them—gone to the ways of the world? She marveled how easy her escape had been, easier than she dared hope.

"Yoo-hoo, Addie Kate, come back tuh earth. Yer woolgatherin'. What're yuh thinkin' about?" Jib asked.

She came out of her daydream with a start to find him staring at her. She smiled sheepishly.

"Well . . ." he pressed.

"What? I . . . I was daydreaming."

"I saw that. Yer a brave little woman for makin' the bold move of leavin'. That took incredible courage. Don't worry none what the Sisters and Brethren is a doin' and sayin'."

"However did you sense I was thinking of them?" She asked, a hand splayed over her chest.

"Jist thought readin'. This is the right time for yuh tuh do this very thin'. Believe me. Yuh won't regret it," he assured her. "Trust me. I'll treat yuh like yuh should be treated. Yuh'll see."

"You've made a mighty sweet pledge." She mused how he was always certain about everything, sure of himself. "We have had what must be one of the most miraculous escapes possible."

"Yep," he said. "I was afraid Ella Beth'd talk yuh over." The corners of his eyes crinkled as he smiled at her.

"She tried, believe me. But you're an honorable man, Beckett Hollingsworth Claycomb. One of the most important things when a woman marries is to make sure her husband is her friend. You are that to me. I can't think of myself as married to anyone but you, Jib. I'll like being your wife. After all, I asked God for you . . . for a long time. I just never could figure out how in the world He would answer my prayers. Now I know."

Jib put his head back and laughed—a loud guffaw. "I do believe I'm goin' tuh like bein' yer husband."

"My wish is to make you the best wife any man ever had in the whole world."

"I'm lookin' forward tuh that," he said.

Chapter 21

*J*ib's mules slogged their way on the sloppy road to Harrodsburg, their heads bobbing in time with their steps, and the harness straps moving a little over their rumps and along their backs. The muted buzzing of the hidden cicadas hummed in the woods.

"Addie Kate, yuh asked me how I knowed tuh come on this day. Well, once I got tuh Indiana and down intuh Kentucky, there was signs everywhere—plastered on fences and propped up in shop windows—about the dedication of the Highbridge trestle what was tuhday. I knew they were the perfect cover for me tuh show up there. See how God works details out?"

"You think so?"

He nodded, spreading his thumb and forefinger across his upper lip. "Yep, I do. When I finally realized I was missin' out on somethin' important in life—a wife and family—came tuh git yuh. Dint want tuh spend another winter in Dakoty Territory. Colder than ice up there. Wind always blowin'. Tired of freezin' muh tail off . . . so tuh speak."

"Oh Jib."

"It's true. On muh way here, I seen a little interestin' sale bill advertisin' a auction. Farm, it said . . . tuh be sold for taxes owed settlin' up the affairs of an estate. Read and reread the words. Posters everywhere. Decided tuh check out the property. Once I seen the place and land, I reckoned it'd go for quite a penny, but bein' nosey, I stuck around tuh watch. Turned out bids was goin' low, so I bid on the tract with the dwellin'. Guess nobody was interested in that parcel since the house was in sad shape. Looks like it's been neglected for some time. But, the price bein' right, I snatched her up. Drawed as much tuh the outbuildin's as tuh the house. Cain't wait until yuh see the place. I'm warnin' yuh, it'll take some work. Called the Norbert Adams place."

"Our place now." Addie Kate imagined it, her eyes shut. "I'm living a wonderful story."

"There's Harrodsburg." Jib directed her attention to the jumble of buildings.

She glimpsed the settlement in the distance, noticing the spire of a church. Their journey had gone without incident, and they'd stayed on the wagon road, right out in the open.

As they reached the edge of town, Jib slowed Hez and Kez to a walk. "Yuh realize I'll hafta kiss yuh at the end of the ceremony . . . when he says we're husband and wife . . . in front of the preacher even. Can yuh manage that?"

She smiled and faintly shrugged. "I'll do the best I can," she mumbled.

Harrodsburg hummed with activity in spite of the drizzle and its resulting mud. Open wagons, buckboards, and buggies crowded the main street that widened out into a square, in the center of which stood the Mercer County Courthouse. It was a brick edifice with a big clock tower, framed by sidewalks and a variety of businesses scattered around—a bank, a hardware store, the post office, a blacksmith's shop, and a mercantile.

Jib pulled the team to a stop, vaulted off the high seat, and tied the reins to the hitching rail.

After he assisted Addie Kate down, the two entered the government building and met an older, stooped man with a drooping white mustache who directed them to the Clerk's Office.

"May I help you?"

They looked around to see who had spoken. A middle-aged man, clean-shaven, sat at a desk some four feet from a wide counter.

"Yes, sir," Jib said. "Me and muh lady aim tuh git a marriage license."

Addie Kate thought the man would say more, but his gaze merely went from Jib to her, then back to Jib.

He scooted his chair away from the desk and came forward, reached below the countertop to pull out a large, black bound book, and slapped it down on the work surface. He opened it, flipped forward a few pages, and read aloud. "To any Minister of the Gospel, or other person legally authorized to solemnize Matrimony. You are permitted to solemnize the Rites of Matrimony between . . ." He stopped reading and looked at them. "Names please."

"Beckett Hollin'sworth Claycomb," Jib said.

"Spell it, please," demanded the man. He wrote in a flowing script the letters as Jib said them. The man peeked at Addie Kate when Jib finished. "Your turn," he said, barely smiling.

"Adelaide Kathleen Flockhart." She spoke clearly and distinctly pronounced each letter.

She smiled at Jib after she signed the application. She hadn't put her name on anything for years.

No need to. The inked signature represented her, and, difficult though it was to accomplish, she was pleased with the way it looked.

The man never bothered to read anymore of the form. But he filled in the blank spaces as they responded to his questions and ended by scribbling the county, the date, and his name.

He handed them the marriage certificate to have the officiant complete the remaining blanks and sign the document. Jib paid the fee and the couple left the Clerk's Office.

Addie Kate's gaze went to Jib and she found him looking at her. "Now we've got tuh find a clergyman who'll pronounce the vows," Jib said as they climbed in the hack. He took hold of the reins, clucked to the mules, and soon turned them into the yard of a charming old house next to the Methodist Episcopal Church. He halted the brace, clambered down, tethered the team to the post, and came to help Addie Kate from the high seat. "Here we are."

"Good gracious, but my heart is bumping around in my chest. You'd think I had been climbing a steep hill."

He wrapped his arms around her. "I'm excited, too." He pulled away. "Ain't never been hitched before. We'll find a minister here, I reckon," he said.

They mounted the stone steps, worn away in the middle, and stepped on the porch where a bell hung with a rope. Jib pulled it and a hollow clanging followed. Soon a distinguished-looking man with white-streaked hair opened the door, thrusting his arm into a coat sleeve.

Addie Kate stood beside Jib as he told the man what they wanted and showed him the paperwork. "This way," the pastor said. They trailed him, splashing across the squishy grass, and went into the church—to the sanctuary. She and Jib answered the questions he asked regarding their intent.

"Where do you want us?" Addie Kate asked.

"The lady stands here." The preacher motioned her forward.

When she moved to the spot he had pointed to, she was so shaky she wondered if her legs would hold her up. She was actually getting married—the desire of her heart—a great moment of her life.

"The gentleman, this side. Now please join hands and face each other." They stood before the altar table and held tightly to each other's hands. The reverend opened his little book and at once decided he needed to blow his nose. Addie Kate and Jib stared at him while he fumbled for his handkerchief, shook it out of its folds, and trumpeted into it, first one nostril and then the other, and pushed the hankie back into his pocket. He cleared his throat and opened his book again.

"The woman makes her declaration first," he said. "Adelaide Kathleen Flockhart, will you have Beckett Hollingsworth Claycomb, to be your husband, to live together in holy marriage . . . and forsaking all others, be faithful to him as long as you both shall live?"

Clinging to Jib's hands, she raised her head, swallowed hard, and cleared her throat. "I will."

Then Jib took his turn repeating the words of the officiant. The couple promised to love, honor, and cherish each other, for better or worse, for richer or poorer, in sickness and in health, until death parted them. Then a blessing was given by the minister and Jib placed a gold band on the fourth finger of Addie Kate's left hand.

"And now, by the power vested in me by the State of Kentucky and the Methodist Episcopal Church, I pronounce you husband and wife." He closed his book, peeked at them, and declared to Jib, "You may kiss your wife now."

Jib leaned close to Addie Kate. "Hello, Mrs. Claycomb." His breath passed across her ear and he kissed her lightly on the lips.

The ceremony was brief, taking less than ten minutes from the time they roused the clergyman and his wife from the parsonage. Now she and Jib were united for life.

It was strange, but it was exciting, too, to wear a man's wedding band and his name and be alone with him without shame.

"This is right and good," she said with a flutter at her heart.

"Congratulations, Mr. and Mrs. Claycomb," he said as he pumped Jib's hand. "You have picked a prize." He paused and raised his eyebrows. "I can tell by her clothes that she's a Shaker. I wonder how in thunder you got her away from the village."

Addie Kate waited as Jib pressed an Indian Princess three-dollar gold piece into the man's palm. They thanked him and left.

"Gittin' married wasn't difficult at all. Matter of fact, it was downright simple. Now comes the hard part."

"What's that?"

"Bein' and stayin' married. I promise tuh do muh best tuh be a good husband tuh yuh."

She smiled and said, "And I will be a good wife to you with God's help."

The couple continued walking in silence across the lawn. Jib helped Addie Kate climb up into the hack. She settled herself on the high seat while Jib untied the mules and went around to the other side.

He hoisted himself up and twisted to face her. "Yuh feelin' happy?"

She laid her hands on his and said, "Oh, Jib, you just can't know. I am the happiest woman in the whole world."

"Think, Addie Kate, you've done escaped Pleasant Hill. Yuh's free now."

"Am I?" She shook her head slowly. "I don't think so. I'm married—to you. I'm Mrs. Beckett Hollingsworth Claycomb. Remember?"

Jib drew his fingers down his chin and pursed his lips. "I'm apt tuh remember. How do yuh feel . . . any different?"

For a few seconds they sat, looking at each other. "No," she said. "Not different . . . because being Mrs. Claycomb doesn't seem quite real to me yet." She held up her left hand, gazed at the golden ring, and twiddled it on her finger. She knew she would never again be who she was before—a celibate Shaker Sister. "We're husband and wife."

She tingled with delight in her new status and fought against the almost overwhelming urge to shout just to give sound to the relief she felt. She married him because she wanted to—possessing no pangs of regret or remorse. She realized he was not in love with her but that he merely wanted to rescue her from the religious sect.

He winked at her, tilted his head, and said, "Yep. Really and truly. We're Mr. and Mrs. Beckett Hollin'sworth Claycomb 'til death do us part."

She nodded, and, in an attempt to calm down, she took several deep breaths. "My heavenly Father has guided me over the years and blessed me richly. It's like a dream." Would she awaken and find everything shattered and she'd find herself back at Pleasant Hill—without Jib?

"Hey, now, Addie Kate. Was yuh a wonderin' if it could ever happen? Well, it did. Dreams do come true. I wanna be a part of makin' yer life happy and content."

"I know now that good things do come a person's way if they just wait long enough."

"Are yuh sayin' that most don't wanna wait?" Jib took up the reins. "Git up!" he shouted to the mules and flapped the straps.

The mules pricked their ears forward and pulled the hack out onto the road and out into the town square.

Chapter 22

*M*r. and Mrs. Beckett Claycomb stopped at the Harrodsburg Mercantile to stock up on food staples, some fresh produce, and the necessary supplies for their journey to Indiana. She bought two dresses—one a calico of green with yellow and red flowers, the other a gingham of blue and white checks. She also purchased ten yards of a delicate cream-colored cotton lawn and enough bleached muslin to make underwear and nightgowns. She would not need to dress in the Shaker garb ever again.

The couple loaded their packages into the hack and drove out of town making their way along the Chaplin River. "Wanna git intuh the next county before dark," Jib said. Addie Kate focused on the soothing drumming of the rain on the oiled top, the sucking noise of the mules' hooves, and the roll of the hack's wheels in the now muddy road.

The day had been dreary. Twilight would come early. "We better pull in at a likely lookin' spot and set up camp. Hopin' somethin' is in that stream we kin catch easy enough," he said.

Shortly, he guided the team into a copse and halted them in a tangle of undergrowth and briars where they would be almost hidden. A limestone outcropping provided them some shelter.

"This is like a secret place," Addie Kate said, looking around.

Jib unhitched Hez and Kez and led them down the sloping banks to the edge of the water for a drink, brought them back and hobbled them, and left them to feed on the long grass. He heaped dried leaves and dead twigs together under the overhang, lit a match, and applied it to the jumbled kindling. He trimmed off lower branches of some nearby trees and put them on the pile, sending sparks flying.

"Better be careful," he said. "Don't wanna get too sizable a fire goin' that'll attract attention—in case someone comes lookin' for yuh." He dusted his hands on his trouser legs.

A shiver passed down Addie Kate's spine at the thought. What could the Elders do to her anyway? She and Jib were legally married. Neither said a word for several minutes.

"Know somethin' . . . I seen plenty of the scarlet-purple sassafras. How'd yuh like me tuh dig up a few roots so we kin make some tea? We'll want a little warmin' up from all this wetness, won't we?"

Addie Kate nodded and clutched her shawl tighter around her. "I'll fetch some water." She went down to the stream and brought back a bucketful, filled the coffeepot, and placed it directly in the flames.

Jib pulled out his axe and a shovel, dug up a length of root, cleaned off the dirt, and scraped away the dark outer bark. He rinsed it off and dropped it in the kettle to brew.

He knelt, both knees to the ground, sat back, his hands on his thighs, and waited for the couple of logs he had just added to catch fire. When they flamed up, he tossed the shavings from the sassafras into the flames, the snippets emitting an aromatic fragrance. "We'll let the kettle come tuh a boil and wait fer a good bed of coals."

Addie Kate wiped off two large-sized russet potatoes, placed them in the Dutch oven, and buried it in the fire's hot embers. Jib went fishing and in no time caught two dinner-sized catfish.

While he gutted and skinned them, she melted lard in a black cast-iron skillet. She dredged the fish in cornmeal and dropped them side by side in the hot grease where they spattered and sizzled.

Jib got the thick and heavy Indian rubber sheet and spread it on the ground under the protection of the outcropping. "We're celebratin' our weddin' with a picnic dinner," he said.

Addie Kate lifted the skillet's lid and turned the fish carefully to brown on the opposite side.

"Smells powerful delicious, don't it?" Jib said while he raked aside the ashes and slag from around the Dutch oven to retrieve the potatoes.

She nodded and removed the crusty fish from the frying pan. She licked a thumb and forefinger as she handed him his plate.

Their meal consisted of the crispy pan-fried catfish and the baked potatoes—their brown skins crackly. She poked a fork into her potato to split it open—the mealy white heart mashing easily—and made it sweet with a lump of butter. To top off their supper, they would eat ripe wild pears they'd found along the way—and drink the hot tea.

They ate in silence until the end of the meal. Then Jib smoothed his tousled hair with both hands. "Mighty fine eatin', Mrs. Claycomb." They scrubbed the dishes, and he patted the space beside him with his hand and hitched himself over a bit. "Come, sit with me here by the fire."

She did as he directed. He put his arm around her and she rested her head against his shoulder. The roughness of his shirt brushed against her cheek when she snuggled into the curve of his arm.

"Yuh warm enough?" he whispered in her ear.

She nodded and stifled a yawn.

"Yer tired," he said, watching her.

"I must be a little bit." No, she was worn out.

"Me, too." Jib said. But they sat on lazily in the warmth of each other. From time to time, he gave the fire a prod with the toe of his boot.

"Tell me again about our farm."

"Got twenty acres. Four of 'em are cleared. Ain't bottom land, neither. Gotta sturdy barn. Rickety chicken house. Rock spring house. Cellar for canned goods. Some timber. Persimmon and apple trees, that I could see. Black walnut and honey locust. Blackberry thicket. Grape vines hangin' full of leaves. Never looked for the fruit. Space for a nice-sized garden. Shallow creek runs through the property. Pond. Farm will supply everything we need tuh live a fine life."

Addie Kate watched the smoke dance as the evening breeze stirred the embers, and she listened to Jib's quiet voice. She raised up and faced him. "What about the house?"

"Built by a wise and careful man." He picked up a stick and poked the fire again. Sparks flew out.

"Why do you say that?"

"Sits on a little rise. Musta had a family because there's plenty of room. Got covered porches on the front and back. Stone foundation with a outside entrance tuh the basement. Place needs whitewashed. Lots of work tuh be done on it."

She relaxed and settled down again next to him. "I'm not afraid of that."

"I knew yuh wouldn't be."

"It's a home in which life has already touched. How many rooms are there . . . altogether?"

"Hmm. Let's see." He stared off to the distance. "Eight."

"Is there any furniture?"

"Some. Not very much. It'll do us for a while."

"I can't wait to get there and see the place and love it into shape. It costs to go to auctions. They require payment at the time of sale. I'm curious as to the amount of mortgage we have?"

"Ain't got one. Money wasn't a problem. Place is ours, free and clear."

"I'm even more intrigued now. How did you finance it, then?"

"Black Hills."

"What do you mean?"

"Me and a partner owned a placer gold mine in Dakota Territory. Struck it rich. Besides what we mined, we sold the claim and made a sizable profit."

She raised up again and faced him. "You . . . prospected, Jib? Did you really? And you . . . discovered . . . gold?"

He nodded. "More true, though, tuh say it found me."

"My gracious, but you've had an exciting life."

"It's still a comin'. Our life together will be excitin', too . . . it's only jist beginnin'."

Addie Kate smothered a yawn. At that moment a branch broke in two and sent up a shower of sparks. "I'm envious of the freedom you enjoyed. You have been able to do as you pleased."

He bent back his head and chuckled. "Reckon I have lived as I pretty much wanted—travelin' and prospectin'. Confrontin' Indians, blizzards, and hailstorms. Takin' pictures, that sort of thin'. Saw the elephant, so tuh speak."

"I agree that you saw it all."

"No doubtin' about it." He got to his feet and looked into her face. "Now yuh best be gittin' tuh bed."

She gulped some air. "I've been thinking about it." But she never moved. "What about you?"

He rubbed a finger below his lower lip. "I'll jist stay out here for a while. Now, go on." He threaded his fingers through his hair. "Yuh done thinkin'?"

"Yes," she said. The dying fire sank to a bed of glowing and graying ashes.

He helped her to stand and waited while she brushed off the back of her skirt. He motioned toward the hack with the tilt of his head, and drawing her close to him, walked her to the opening. He took her face in his hands and kissed her flat on the mouth. "No regrets?"

"So far, not a single one." She thought it was wonderful to look into his eyes and not be ashamed.

With a chivalrous bow, he said, "Yer *boudoir* awaits, Mrs. Claycomb. It won't be a feather bed, but you'll be under a roof."

Addie Kate took a deep breath, pulled away from him, and climbed up into her bedroom, grateful for the privacy he afforded her on her first night away from the Shakers. She wriggled out of her garments and crawled between the sheets in her chemise, making the plump straw-stuffed mattress crackle with her movements. She stretched out on her back and fell into a reverie about the day's events—her escape from Pleasant Hill and her marriage. She fingered her wedding ring and whispered, "I am Addie Kate Claycomb now."

Her gaze focused on the oiled canvas roof as she listened to the pattering of the rain and thought about the man with whom she was now committed to spend the rest of her life.

Though there was no passion between them, there was strong respect and companionship because as far as she knew, he was not in love with her. So she kept to herself how much she cared for him. At least in this relationship, she'd have a home of her own and hopefully children to follow. A lump formed in her throat.

"Praise You, God, for giving me a good man for a husband. I do ask that You take care of us, knowing You'll be with us. May we glorify Your name by keeping our promise to You and to one another." She locked her hands under her head and crossed her ankles.

Falling asleep was the last thing possible for her she thought, but weariness swept through her. Settling into a comfortable position, she closed her eyes for a second, and, contrary to her expectations, she fell asleep and slept well. It was a deep slumber, the kind she hadn't had for a long time.

Chapter 23

"Addie Kate," Jib said. He had put off waking her until the last possible minute. Lifting the back flap on the hack, he reached in to gently touch her foot. She hadn't moved. He called her name again, this time more forcefully. "You awake?"

"Yes!" She rolled over and pressed her face into the pillow, yawned, and stretched. She blinked, clearing her eyes, and saw Jib looking at her. Disoriented by the edge of sleep, she bolted upright and let out a startled scream.

"Whoa! Nothin' tuh be scared about. Havin' a bad dream?"

"No," she said, shaking.

"What was it, then?"

"I forgot," she said.

"Yuh don't remember why yuh screamed?"

"No, I was fuddled and thought I was still at Pleasant Hill . . . and there you were standing in the opening. I didn't expect to hear a man's voice. I just reacted."

"Thought I'd let yuh sleep in some," Jib said when she jumped down out of the end of the hack. "It's time we were leavin'. Why don't yuh go tuh the creek and wash the eye sand away?"

She nodded. The sun by this time had risen. How could she have overslept?

"The rain clouds blew off durin' the night. It'll be a pleasurable day," he said.

Ashamed to have slept late, she ran to the privacy of the trees to attend to her personal needs and then down to the river where she splashed cold water on her face and smoothed her hair back with wet palms. She came back and slipped on a new dress she'd bought the previous day. When she joined Jib, she found he had prepared a breakfast of thick, crusty bread, yellow cheese, apple cider, and coffee.

"I'm sorry to've been such a sleepy head," she apologized.

"Yuh was tired out . . . needed the rest. Yuh look different," he said, his voice raspy.

"Has to be the clothes . . . and not having the head covering. I'll be able to let my hair grow now. I always wanted it to be long so that I could braid it. I guess I could wear a switch in the meantime."

"Yep, a hairpiece would do the trick. How yuh like bein' outta the Shaker Sister garb?"

"Heavenly, but it isn't proper to dress in worldly clothes."

"Fiddle-faddle, Addie Kate, yuh ain't one of 'em no more."

"You're right!" She smiled.

"Listen, I figger it might take us nine or ten more days tuh reach our home in Corydon. We won't be travelin' on Sunday because of it bein' the day of rest."

They rode in silence for much of the morning on their first full day as husband and wife. Finally, Addie Kate asked, "You told me how you got into photography, but what did you do after the war?"

"Hmm. That was a long time ago. Sixty-five was it? Fourteen years. Went home for a spell tuh show Ma I was alive and well. Caught the wanderlust, I reckon, as did many of the ex-soldiers. Most of us was young whippersnappers and unmarried. Knew I had tuh git busy at earnin' a livin', so I became a itinerate photographer. Hankered tuh see as much of the country as I could while I was able tuh do so.

Photography gave me that opportunity. Talk in all the years of the war was that the government was buildin' a transcontinental railroad. Wanted tuh be a part of recordin' history. So packed up the camera and made muh way by paddle steamer tuh St. Louis. Went on and landed in Omaha."

Jib stopped and glanced at her. She sat beside him and found herself looking at his mouth as though hypnotized. "Go on. I enjoy learning about your adventures."

He continued. "I call that territory out west the 'Big Country,' because it is. There's a lot of sky on the prairie. Took pictures of anyone and anythin' along the way tuh make some money. Seemed like everyone was interested in the layin' of the rails. Was a field photographer at times as well as workin' bein' one of the shovelers. We followed the surveyors and graders. Know this is true, the train tracks could notta been done without us ex-soldiers and our experience with locomotives. Many a time durin' the war, we hadda build our own lines movin' the troops and supplies. Took us and Irish immigrant men tuh git that done. Got pictures of what we were doin'. Winters were mighty cold. Winds didn't jist blow, they howled. And snow came blowin' in real quick like and in great quantities. Stayed with Union Pacific for . . . oh, let's see, nigh on tuh four years . . . until they finished the line in the spring of sixty-nine in Utah Territory. I'm talkin' way too much. Sorry. Bored yet?"

Addie Kate made a little face. "My gracious no. You can weave such exciting stories. They are quite fascinating." She meant what she said, for while he talked she had gone into a kind of dream—with images of the prairie and gold mines and grizzly bears flashing in and out of her mind.

* * *

At noon on Monday they stopped along the road to eat a cold meal. Jib led Hez and Kez down to the Birdtown Branch to drink and put them on picket lines to graze.

They were near Springfield, and that evening they stopped in the town and camped in a church's yard. It had a hand water pump beside a sycamore tree. The water was clear and ice cold and delicious to drink, and there was plenty of grass for Hez and Kez.

A shivering, brown-and-white puppy appeared from behind the church. He growled deep in his throat at them.

"Oh, the poor little thing," Addie Kate sympathized. "What kind of dog is it?"

"Let's see," said Jib. He checked. "The pup is a male."

"I meant the breed," she clarified.

"Oh, looks like he's half hound and the other half is . . . who knows what?" Jib laughed.

"Well, he's nothing but skin and bones. Come here, Poochie," she said, slapping her thighs.

The dog's ears pricked forward and he barked once, but he did not approach her.

"He's afraid of us. We've got to find where he belongs."

She and Jib walked to several houses close by to get some milk and to inquire about the dog, but nobody claimed him or knew where he belonged. When they went back to their camp site, they fed him. They placed a pan of rabbit gravy down for him, his small body quivering as he noisily lapped it up, and waited for him to finish eating.

"I guess he's ours now," Jib said.

"I've never had a pet before. What shall we name him? We can't call him 'Puppy.' And I don't want our dog's name to be 'Spot' or 'Brownie.'"

"Don't matter tuh me what yuh name him."

"*Me?* . . . What if we call him 'Kitty?'"

Jib laughed. "That might make him confused."

She turned to the puppy and said, "You will be called 'Kitty.' Think you can remember that?" He looked up at her, stopped trembling, and wagged his tail.

One morning, two days later, Jib said, "Could yuh stand tuh push a little harder on our way home? Maybe make our days longer?"

"Of course. That'd be fine with me. I can hardly wait to get there myself," she said.

For the next four days, the newlyweds put in an extra hour on their journey. They had decided to eat their main meal at noon when they stopped to rest the team. They would stop in the evening in semidarkness.

Kitty trotted beside them keeping pace, but there were times he disappeared in the bushes when he chased a rabbit that flashed across the trail and out of sight at the sound of the mules' hooves and the wagon wheels. After a while he'd come bounding back to them, his tongue lolling.

They had been traveling north through Kentucky. On a Friday morning, eight days after their marriage, Jib turned toward Brandenburg. "Three more nights and we'll be home." His hand came down on her own two hands clasped in her lap. "Why yuh smilin'?" he asked.

"Was I? I wasn't aware of it. I like being Mrs. Beckett Hollingsworth Claycomb. I now have almost everything I have ever wanted in the whole wide world and am pleased. I hope I'll always feel this way."

"That's yer choice, but yuh make a delightful bride, Addie Kate. Yer a sweet, patient woman who's always neat with what yuh's doin' and how yuh look." He turned his head and winked at her.

Her mouth was quiet, but her heart thumped against her ribs.

* * *

During the late afternoon of their last Saturday in Kentucky, they stopped on a rise overlooking the Ohio River. Its flow rippled below

201

and glittered with sun sparks. Across the watery expanse, the last of the evening sun gilded the trees' early tinges of scarlet and orange colors on the Indiana slopes. Jib and Addie Kate camped earlier than usual down among some cedar trees.

They would stay at that spot for two nights—through Sunday. After he staked out the mules for the night, he went to the hack, grabbed his fishing pole, dug a few worms, and hunted some grasshoppers. He made his way down to the river's edge with Addie Kate coming behind him and Kitty trailing dutifully. By the water, the air was cooler but smelled musty and fishy.

Jib fastened a grasshopper and cast out the line. Addie Kate didn't much care to fish because of removing the hook. So she turned back and climbed farther up the bank with Kitty where she enjoyed the peaceful sound of the shallow waves against the rocks, the sucking sounds of the river's current, and the droning of the cicadas hidden in the trees. She looked from time to time to see Jib standing on the flat rocky ledge. She wanted to be ready with a word of praise.

Relaxing under the towering trees, she absentmindedly fondled the dog's silky ears as her attention focused on a hawk flying overhead. A little bird flitted around the big bird as it banked, turned, rose, and fell. Was the bigger one harassing the littler one? She watched with interest as the hawk swooped under the small bird and lifted it up, then dove to a tree branch where the little bird dismounted. The hawk continued on, soaring higher than ever, and soon was out of her sight. The setting was so tranquil she wanted to hold time still for a long while.

"Got one!" Jib yelled as he hauled in a good-sized catfish. He unhooked it, knelt on one knee to rinse his hands in the water, and then dried them on his handkerchief. He ambled up, carrying the fish with his finger hooked through a gill. Addie Kate sat on a tree stump and watched him gut and clean the fish. The couple headed back to their campsite and prepared their supper. They roasted the fish over an open flame and ate ravenously. With their hunger satisfied, they fed

Kitty, then washed and put away the cooking equipment. They sat watching the dying flames as a breeze blew across the graying coals, reddening the ashes.

Addie Kate stared at the embers and sighed. "The piney scent makes everything smell so fresh here." She peeked at Jib. He had lowered himself to the needle-strewn ground around the cedars and sprawled full length on a blanket, his hands clasped under his head, his hat tipped forward, covering his eyes. A slight wind rustled through the trees' branches and shook a few needles down on him.

She smiled at the image. "I've truly enjoyed our travel and am almost sorry for it to soon be over, but I'm so excited about crossing into Indiana and leaving Kentucky forever. Aren't you?"

Chapter 24

*M*onday, September twenty-second, broke with a brilliant sun. Addie Kate jumped down out of her temporary bedroom into a golden glaze on everything and drew in deep breaths of the fresh air. "We couldn't ask for a more perfect day to go home," she said to Jib. She couldn't remember when she had awakened in the morning with such eagerness for what lie ahead.

"With a blue sky and warm sunshine, only good thin's happen with weather like this. Yuh ready?" he asked.

She nodded.

They came to Solomon Brandenburg's Landing and Ferry just as the ferrymen showed up to start the workday. Jib blew out a long breath between his lips and held the reins tightly as he drove the mules forward. They stepped gingerly onto the flat ferryboat that would convey them across to Indiana. Only two wagons could be transported at a time.

Addie Kate and Jib were silent as they sat on the front seat of the hack, Kitty between them. They made their way, the raft swaying away from the land of Kentucky and slowly crossing the Ohio River—a brown watery expanse a mile wide at that point. Addie Kate gnawed her lower lip as they crossed. They'd done it. They would shortly be in Indiana and, by the end of a long day, would arrive at their farm.

Jib led the team up the slippery bank. At the crest of the slope, they stopped and gazed back at Kentucky, enjoying the sight at how beautiful the valley was with the river winding through it, the water gleaming and shimmering through the trees. A breeze chilled her, making her cross her arms.

"We made it, didn't we?" she said, smiling at him. "God is gracious."

"I agree," Jib said.

In the early afternoon of their eleventh day, they proceeded into the county-seat town of Corydon, the mules' metal shoes raising dust on the trail and then thundering across the arched wooden bridge spanning Indian Creek. Jib had been talking and she had missed part of what he said, but she caught the word "Corydon" and straightened to attention.

"I'm shore we'll like livin' in this town," he was saying, holding the reins loosely and resting his elbows on his knees. "Jist so yuh know, most everybody calls our property 'the Norbert Adams place.' Imma thinkin' that next year we'll have a garden . . . and . . . a milk cow and some chickens."

A bubble rose in Addie Kate's throat. Her heart beat fast. "I can't wait to get there." She leaned forward on the seat trying to see everything as they continued through the area.

Corydon exemplified a picturesque community with its imposing houses and busy main street with stores and businesses about a town square. They rode out the west side a quarter of a mile past the city limits, the last of the dwellings thinning to a few and the countryside beginning.

Jib slowed the mules and guided them off the hard-packed road and onto the traces of an old path barely showing beneath encroaching grass. "Whoa," he crooned, pulling back on the reins. The sound of their hooves' plodding came to a stop before a two-storied, old-fashioned, wood-framed farmhouse. The silver-weathered wood and the overgrowth of weeds, along with the brush and matted leaves taking over the yard, contributed to the ramshackle appearance.

"This is our new home." Jib glanced at Addie Kate.

At the first sight of the house, she gasped and felt her stomach drop. "You're right about the looks of the place. It's been forsaken, losing its battle against the elements," she said, "but can still be made adorable. It just needs the eye of faith. Its bones say it is inviting and distinguished looking."

The house, shrouded in foliage, had a gray slate roof and gave glimpses of decorative scale trim and turned-wood brackets in the gables. The dirty windows were set in the traditional eight small panes to a sash.

"Makes my heart sick to see a house looking like this. What a shame to have allowed it to fall into such a decayed condition!" Addie Kate said. "Houses need to be lived in. They're sad when left empty."

Dismayed at what she saw, she evaluated the shabby-looking structure perched on a knoll about seventy feet from the roadway. Invading mulberry saplings, sumac scrub, creeping vines, and weeds had taken over and grown high enough to obscure the front porch and the foundation.

"The place passed down through the same family for many generations. But guessin' the younger folks give up on it because it has been abandoned for several years," Jib offered. "Taxes went unpaid. Debt added upon debt. Lookin' more than a might forlorn amidst the saplin's springin' up everywhere. But we'll change all that."

"Poor old house . . . neglected, for sure, left to the mercy of Mother Nature, and she has not been kind." She stared at the littered yard and shook her head. "Must have been an awful long time since any of the family's been here. We need to cheer her up and love her back to health."

Jib shoved his hat back with his index finger, gathered up the reins, clucked to the mules, and pulled the hack to the hitching post. He descended from his high seat and tethered the mules.

"Goin' tuh be a heap of work gittin' everythin' in shape, ain't it?"

Addie Kate climbed down without help and considered the house. She said, "Uh-huh. But this place—with shade trees and a barn and fences and sheds and a . . . a yard—will boast of beautiful flowers and birds and plenty of sunshine for our children so they'll grow up strong and healthy with bright eyes and rosy cheeks. Oh, Jib, we'll have everything necessary for a blessed life here."

"Yep," he said, putting a finger to the side of his nose. "We're gonna be happy here."

"Very much so. This will become a perfectly charming country home. This is all an unbelievable dream come true for me." She smiled at Jib and sighed with delight. "I want you to know how pleased I am. I'm tingling all over, because I'm happier than I've ever known."

"I somehow knew yuh'd be."

Her gaze panned the overgrown lawn—weeds, moldy piles of leaves, unpruned bushes, and trees. The deep-foliaged elms and sugar maples, now with tinges of red and orange and yellow colors, contrasted with the silvered outbuildings. An ancient oak tree spread its branches over the backyard, and, slightly beyond its shade, creeping vines of grapes twined themselves carelessly on a sagging fence. The pasture and the rolling hills contributed to the pastoral setting. Silence reigned after a slight breeze ruffled the withered vegetation.

He took off his hat and stood bareheaded, allowing the wind to tousle his hair. "When I bought the place, I seen in muh imagination what it could be, the wife I'd bring here, and the children we'll beget. I know this ain't in the best of shape now, but we're gonna breathe new life into it and make the place what we want it tuh be."

"Comfortable and homey," she said, smiling at him. "That was quite inadequate. I think it's a lovely house . . . maybe not right now . . . but it will be." With hands on her hips, she surveyed the outbuildings a long moment. "But the shame is, who would neglect such a fine house and leave it to rack and ruin this way?"

"Who knows? I agree, though, there is a welcomin' dignity tuh it. Farm sold in pieces at the auction. Figgered the house'd sell right off, it bein' so solid, but, nope, nobody else made a bid. The land was goin' so low, I snatched this parcel up. Drawn as much tuh the out-buildin's as tuh the house. Know they all need whitewashin', but they are in fair condition, exceptin' the chicken coop. Yuh really like the property?"

"I do. I like old things. Just think, long ago a family laughed with each other and loved one another right here. The house has seen better days, and there's a lot to do to it. But we'll bring her back to her true glory."

Jib clapped his hands and rubbed his palms together briskly. "What do yuh say we give our home a Claycomb inspection?" He motioned in the direction of the house.

She gripped his arm tightly with both her hands. "Yes, let's. I'll say this much, if the inside is half as delightful as the outside, I'll be enchanted."

"Come along with me, won't cha?" He took her hand. Neither spoke as they mounted the four steps. On the front porch they found carved posts, balusters, and brackets hidden behind creeping vines. Jib turned to Addie Kate and put his hand around her neck, drew her close, and kissed her with gentleness.

She laughed. "What's that for?"

"Because yer here with me," he said. He made a grand, sweeping wave toward the entry, produced from his pocket the skeleton key, fitted it into the iron hasp latch, and turned it. The lock clacked and the unoiled hinges groaned when Jib dramatically flung open the door with the gesture of a showman who is about to reveal his masterpiece. "Gotta be doin' this right." He swept her off her feet and carried her across the threshold into the front hall of the house that smelled of shut-in air, mice, and rot.

Once inside, Jib made no move to put her down and kicked the door closed behind him.

"We're here . . . in our own home." He pressed his lips to hers, then set her down gently. "What d'yuh think?"

She scanned the entry. Random-width wood floors. A pocket door to the room on the right. An open door to a room on the left at the foot of the stairway to the upper floor.

"Let's go tuh the right and look at that. I think it could be the parlor."

They embarked on a tour of inspection. Entering, she paused and let her gaze take in the faded wallpaper, hanging in long strips from the stained walls. Dingy and shredded Nottingham lace curtains hung at the windows, and dirty rag rugs were scattered about. There was also a separate front entry to the room.

"The floor's dusty, but I believe it wouldn't take too much effort to revitalize it," Addie Kate said.

"Probably." He stood with his legs braced apart, his hands clasped behind his back.

"My eyes and nose tell me that spiders and mice've taken over," she reflected. On further checking, dead flies and wasps cluttered the windowsills.

She touched the few pieces of furniture—a lackluster collection, consisting of two chairs, a scarred dresser with several drawers and a tall mirror above it, a square table with legs splayed out at sharp angles and clutching glass balls in their claw feet. The fireplace, with an ornately hand-carved mantel, still possessed a glossy sheen from a long-ago lacquered finish. Everything in sight was in need of vigorous cleaning—dust and cobwebs were aplenty.

She glanced over at Jib. "An impressive fireplace. I love the tile surround. I wasn't counting on so much furniture still here. Ours?"

"Reckon so. Guessin' the family members took what thin's they wanted and left what they dint want. It is worn, but will do for a while, don't yuh think?"

She nodded. "What's here is salvageable. We don't need much. Aren't we lucky to have such simple needs?"

"Come and see the scenery," he said, pulling aside the curtain panel filtering the light streaming through the glass.

"Sittin' on this rise, we've got a view that takes in the whole valley."

She stepped to the window, looked up the road and across the field and saw the forest of oaks, maples, and honey locusts dappled with shadows and wearing their fall tinges. "Breathtaking, isn't it? I see we have neighbors. Do we know who they are?"

"Not yet, anyways."

"This is a magnificent old place and there are fine trees and a wonderful location. What's in here?"

She moved into the next room divided by an opened pocket door and marveled at the ample dining room space. At the triple windows, water-stained muslin curtains hung limp. The floors in this room were the same pine, covered in some places by thick, grimy handmade rugs.

The scratched-and-stained round oak table was fitted with a pedestal base and sat in front of a built-in china cupboard. The chairs encircling the table were mismatched.

"What's in here?" Addie Kate pointed to a door.

"Well, let's take a gander."

She moved only her eyes as she absorbed the details of a room with three windows. "What a pleasant surprise. This is the most attractive kitchen I've ever seen. The best part is the marvelous field of vision. We face the east and can see the back yard and pasture."

A narrow stairway steeply angled up from one corner to the floor above. The plain planked floors, worn and sloped almost imperceptibly, were maple with old, dirty braided rugs scattered about. The dark slate-colored soapstone sink supported a hand pump with its iron handle cocked like a flamingo's leg. A rusty cast-iron kitchen cookstove with nickel trimmings stood out away from the wall. A round pipe ran from its back to where it connected to the chimney. Its copper-lined reservoir, now a blue-green color, sat on the right of it. The firebox was on the left. The ceiling above the cookstove was

211

discolored with soot and obviously in much need of washing. A dusty bureau with brass handles and a scarred surface had apparently done duty as a preparation table for the previous owners.

"This is an exquisite piece," she said, running her hand over the top.

Addie Kate liked what she saw and smiled her approval at Jib. "Where does this door lead?"

"Open it and find out."

She did and found a ladder leading to the cellar. "I'll check about that later."

They went out of the kitchen into a smaller room that had two sash windows on one wall, a window facing onto the front porch with a magnificent country view, a door that opened into a closet built under the entry stairway, and a door that led back out to the entry hall. On an inside wall, nestled in a corner, stood an ornate, round-bellied cast-iron stove on four claws, its small door made of isinglass, standing ajar. The couple had made a complete circle of the downstairs.

"What a delightful room—an excellent place to sit in and think your own thoughts. Do you suppose this was either a music room or a library? There are shelves in that closet." She pinched her lower lip and studied the arrangement. "Actually, it would be perfect for you to use as your photography studio. Plenty of light that'd be just right for taking photographs. A storage area for your camera equipment."

"I agree. People comin' in for pictures won't hafta go traipsin' through the house."

Addie Kate nodded. She wandered around the lower rooms of the house again, imagining the people who had lived there, and wondering why the family never paid the taxes that necessitated their property being divided up and sold as separate parcels at a public auction.

"What's the upstairs like?"

"Wanna go and investigate?" he asked.

Chapter 25

*T*he couple climbed the stairs with Addie Kate leading the way. "This staircase is in excellent condition," she said, running her fingers lightly over the handrail. "Feel the smoothness of the wood."

"Yep. Walnut."

"With a light sanding and some polish and elbow grease, it will be beautiful. The carved newel post is an impressive piece of woodworking."

The treads creaked as they ascended to the hall above. They reached a rectangular landing with five doors. Jib pushed open the nearest one to a room at the front of the house. Faded floral wallpaper fell in graceful curls from plastered walls, and in the space against one wall stood a pencil-post bed with a stained, beautifully-pieced quilt folded on the ropes. Shoved opposite was an armoire, and in the middle of the room were two spindle-legged chairs. A door at the very front opened to a small balcony which overlooked the yard.

"I didn't know this was here. I never noticed it from the outside. Must have been hidden by the vines and trees."

"Why don't this be yer bedroom?" Jib said.

She wrinkled her brow and, looking at him, frowned. "Then where will yours be?"

He shrugged. "Don't know yet. Hafta decide."

Her hand on one of the bed posters, Addie Kate said, "Isn't it a little strange to be married and keep separate bedrooms?"

"No, not necessarily."

"I know I've been sheltered all my life, but I have heard the practice was for a husband and wife to sleep in the same bed."

Jib rubbed his jaw and cleared his throat. "I gotta admit I won't mind that arrangement if that's what yuh want."

Suddenly he was beside her and took her hand in his. Together they crossed the space and went out to the balcony, looking down upon the valley. He put an arm about her shoulder, and, without turning to look at him, she leaned against him, resting her head on his shoulder. For a long while they did not speak. Finally, he whispered, "Addie Kate?"

"Uh-huh?" She turned her attention his way.

He started to say something but stopped, swallowed, then put his index finger under her chin and tipped her face up to him. He took a deep breath and said, "I'm a simple man. I ain't a man of romance. But muh life's so much better now that yuh's with me. I'm hopin' yuh'll come tuh love me."

She waited to hear him say that he loved her. But no words from him to that effect came. She looked into his eyes and said, "I'll be a good wife to you, Jib." She wanted to say she'd fallen in love with him already, but she couldn't because his lips were on hers.

"It's gonna work out for us, ain't it? We're goin' tuh be very happy."

She clasped her hands at her chest. "Yes. We're going to live a wonderful, blessed life."

He flashed a broad grin and nodded. "Ready tuh inspect the rest of the upstairs?"

"I am."

"Yuh go on and lead the way. I'm wantin' tuh see the outbuildin's before it gits too dark."

Addie Kate entered the hallway and peered into a small and undistinguished room. "Hmm. What do you suppose this space was used for?" She glanced at Jib. "The door is narrow and different from the other doors. No fancy carved woodwork. Makes me wonder about it. You think it was for storage?" She stood in the opened doorway. "Here're some glass coal oil lamps." Picking one up she gave another to him to carry. "These'll come in handy tonight to give us the light we'll need to set up the bed."

Three other rooms completed the second-floor space. From the back, Addie Kate and Jib paused at a window and directed their attention to a perfect spot for a garden. "God has given us everythin' we need with what we kin make or grow right here on this farm," Jib pronounced.

"I agree," she said. "This is a marvelous place . . . a charming home for any woman to call her own. Eight rooms—ones that have heard laughter and love . . . anger and tears."

The Claycombs passed through the upper floor scouting every nook and cranny. The tour of inspection over, they descended the narrow, steeply-pitched stairway to the kitchen. Jib led the way with Addie Kate following, both gripping the handrail tightly as they went down. Again, she walked slowly throughout the downstairs before coming back to where Jib stood peering into the confines of the cookstove.

"I need tuh git a fire started because it'll be chilly this evenin'. Gotta make sure this range ain't choked with ashes. Hopin' the chimney ain't clogged up neither."

Addie Kate watched him twist a plunger hidden at the side of the stove pipe. "Hafta git the damper opened up when startin' a fire. It's gotta allow the firebox tuh draw the air," he said.

She nodded. "I'm trying to figure out what arrangements we need to make for tonight. I suggest we use the parlor. We can open a window or two and freshen the room. I'll sweep the floor before we lay down the mattress tick. How does that sound?"

"Fine. We'll jist make do tuhnight. I'll go git it from the hack." He spoke as he went out.

"I'll go with you to get the broom," she said, trailing him.

When they went outside to the back porch, Addie Kate held out one hand and Kitty dashed straight for her. He stood on his hind legs and pawed her skirt. She bent to pat the dog's head as he now waited at her feet, his tail thumping against the floor.

Jib's arm came around his wife's waist, drawing her closer. He kissed her on her hair and asked, "What's yer verdict?"

She drew back to face him. "You mean the house? I haven't words to say how much I like it and everything about it. This is going to be the happiest home in the world. May God bless us with many happy years. The peacefulness and the privacy are heavenly."

"I agree," he said. "But I wanted tuh know what yuh thought because a discontented wife kin ruin a man mighty quick. Now, let's git goin' on gittin' the bed in the parlor. I want time tuh explore the ole farm buildin's afore darkness comes."

Addie Kate opened a couple of windows in the parlor. The curtains moved to and fro across the sill—the air scented with the aroma of fall.

After she swept the floor, Jib placed the mattress. She spread a sheet over it and plumped the feather pillows. Their accommodations for the night were ready.

"Now let's go take a look around outside," he said.

"All right."

They left again by way of the kitchen. The sinking sun of the September afternoon touched everything in sight with gold. On the back porch Kitty raised his head, thumped his tail, and joined them as they walked by an old grape arbor that ran across the back. He sniffed around the twining vines and then went about his own business.

Ironweed, with its clusters of blooms now turned brown, had encroached on the premises.

At the boundary of the property, a tall persimmon tree had dropped its bright orange fruit to the ground. Jib gathered several and bit into one. He pointed at Addie Kate with half of it eaten.

"Umm, yummy. Not pithy at all. Must be the kind that don't need a frost tuh be juicy."

The barn, gambrel roofed with a hay mow, silvered by age and the weather, loomed a short distance from the house—wild morning glory vines softening its appearance, the tendrils attaching themselves to the facade. Jib put his hand on the smaller door's simple iron latch. The door with its unoiled hinges squeaked and groaned as he swung it open.

He stepped aside, gesturing for Addie Kate to enter the cavernous building. It was empty, its air smelling of rotted manure and old straw. "I generally love the odor of a barn," he said as he stood looking up at the high rafters across which chinks of dim sunlight filtered through. "This's been sittin' a little too long, I believe. Ain't had no animals in it recently, but they've been here, all right. Barn's done past the ripeness stage. Before we leave, I want you tuh appreciate the hand-hewed poplar beams. Forty feet long and a foot thick. 'Tis a sturdy buildin'."

He moved toward the opening. "We've stayed long enough." They went out, closed the door, and Jib put a stick through the hasp. Beyond the barn stood a windmill and its water tank. The stillness of the early evening left its flanges motionless.

The couple strolled to the very back of the yard and surveyed the summer kitchen, a long clapboard shed with its own rusty cookstove and a questionable chicken house. Both the structures needed to be painted.

"Be busy clearin' weeds and brush and gittin' thin's back in shape, won't I? I seen gaps in the fence, too. That'll take some time gittin' mended. We'll git us a milk cow an' some chickens soon."

Going on, they discovered a clothesline. "Oh, great," Addie Kate said. "I love to hang out the wash. The fragrance of the sun stays with the clothes."

Farther on, they located steep steps that dipped down to a springhouse, the walls dug out of a rocky hillside. "Shore hopin' the water ain't been contaminated with animals pilferin' around since the old door looks rotten and collapsin', hangin' halfway. I'll hafta take care of that, quick like." Jib pulled the handle of it with little effort, hesitated in the cool, dark stone depths, and listened as the cold water ran through a stone trough.

Beyond a huge oak tree, grapes grew scrappy and unruly, twining themselves on an old fence. The vines, loaded with leaves, held few purple globes. "They need tuh be pruned for fruitfulness," Jib said. "Next year we'll have more fruit."

Addie Kate tilted her head back and squinted at the heavens— the sky now a pale turquoise in the west. "Praise Thee, O God, from Whom all blessings flow," she shouted and twirled about as she held her arms out at her sides. "Jib, there is more calmness in my heart than I can ever remember having, and that is a new feeling for me. We're *home.*"

Back in the kitchen, Jib clanked a dust-coated burner plate out of its place and crammed twigs and chunks of branches inside the firebox before replacing the lid. Soon there was a snap and then a crackle and a half-hearted spurt of flame—and more warmth.

"Now that we've got the fire goin'," he said, "how about enjoyin' a cup of tea?"

"I'll hunt out the cups," Addie Kate volunteered.

Jib straightened, brushed his hands together, and put the kettle on to boil. Jerking in doing so, he splashed water on the hot metal, making steam rise in a cloud with a sizzle.

* * *

Darkness arrived and Jib filled one of the lamps with coal oil, trimmed the wick, lit it, and placed it in the center of the table. There was no glass chimney to protect the flame, so the lamp sent odd shadows flickering and wheeling in the semidarkness as they moved about.

"We've done all we can," Addie Kate said, yawning. "I'm tired. It will be so good to crawl in bed."

That night, their first in Corydon, Indiana, contentment reigned in the old run-down Norbert Adams house. As the couple lay on the comfortable hay-filled mattress with fresh sheets and soft pillows, they were steeped in peace, and they slept soundly until morning.

Chapter 26

The pearly morning came, breezy and cool. Addie Kate awoke with a pleasurable sense of happiness and lay on her back on the mattress tick. She yawned and stretched, extending her arms out of the top sheet into the coolness of the room. She crossed her ankles, locked her hands behind her head, and listened to Jib's movements as he went about, whistling softly, going back and forth in the kitchen. From the sounds, she pictured him in her mind laying the kindling and starting the fire for breakfast. Presently, there was the crackle of wood and the clanking of the cookstove's heavy iron burner plate being set in place.

Fully awake, she remembered the day was a Tuesday. She was at her home and with her husband. She smiled and breathed thankfulness for her new life—and her newfound freedom.

All those years at Pleasant Hill, she had become numbed to independence. Addie Kate was now free from the restrictions of the Shaker way—rules learned and practiced her whole life—a woman able to control her own destiny. In this new world of hers, no Elders or Eldresses would spy on her or sneak up on her. She could decide what she wanted to do each day. What would it be today? Well, after breakfast, that is. What if she prepared fried pies using the wild red-dish-purple plums she and Jib found along the river? The fruit was sweet and ripe. Why not serve salt pork and, of course, coffee? The idea she could choose was liberating.

When the house grew quiet, she got up and, still in her nightgown, went through the dining room and kitchen to step out on the porch in her bare feet. She found Jib in the back yard.

He stood poised at his camera, all set up, and was taking pictures of the house, the sun peeking over the treetops and casting a pinkish glow on the place. He glanced at her, shaded his eyes with one hand, squinted, and grinned. "Mornin', Mrs. Claycomb. Yuh slept well, I hope. Glad yer awake! I've done built a fire in the cookstove for yuh. Probably ready. I've got quite an appetite."

She waved and hurried back inside. She returned to the parlor, pulled her nightie off, and slipped the calico dress over her head. Addie Kate smiled as she thought that in the days since their marriage, she had grown used to the noises and some of the habits of Jib. She considered it a strange and exciting thing to be married. "I have never known such contentment," she said, speaking the words to give sound to her thoughts.

In the kitchen, she shook the kettle left sitting out on the wood range from last night, peered in, and smiled. Jib had already filled it with water. Embers glowed and ticked in the firebox.

How early did he get up, anyway? Next, Addie Kate unlatched and opened the wooden chest that held the pots and eating utensils. She hummed a Shaker tune under her breath as she sliced the salt pork and let it sizzle in the cast-iron skillet. Soon enough, the room was scented with the tantalizing aroma of rich coffee.

Jib brought in an armload of firewood, dropped it into the woodbox, making a clamorous clattering sound, and brushed off his arms. He washed his face in preparation for breakfast, then turned to Addie Kate, the towel held in his hand and water still trickling down his face.

He came to stand beside her. "Whatcha cookin'? Smells mighty good."

Addie Kate dumped sugar into a pan. "Plum filling and salt pork."

He sat at the table. She placed a cup before him, and in the act of pouring coffee into it, stopped with arrested arm to ask, "What do you propose to accomplish today?"

"Wanna take some more pictures of the place, then figgered tuh start clearin' out the trash. Yard's a disaster."

Addie Kate mixed the pie dough, rolled it out, and arranged the pastries in the hot grease. While they sizzled, she put a large tub of water on the cookstove to heat. "I've decided to scour this room. I'd rather cook and eat in a clean kitchen than in a dingy one. I'll get to the bedroom tomorrow. Surely we can sleep on the floor another night."

Jib nodded. "Heap of work tuh do here."

She brought the food to the table and sat. "Shall we ask for God's blessing before we eat?"

He lowered his coffee cup to the table and bowed his head. "Lord, we ask a blessin' on this meal. We ask Yuh tuh give us the strength we need for what is necessary tuh do tuhday. Amen." He fixed his gaze on Addie Kate. "Got the axe all sharpened tuh commence muh work. Sun's a shinin', very little breeze a movin'. Perfect day for burnin' the no-account stuff."

After they ate and the dishes were done, Addie Kate stood in the middle of the room, studied the situation, and made the decision as to where she'd begin attacking the dirt and grime. She covered her hair by taking a triangle of cloth, wrapping it around her head, and tying it over her forehead. With it knotted, she began her assault by sweeping the gritty floor as carefully as she could. She gathered a rag and a pail of hot water, swished a lump of lye soap about in it, and scrubbed the woodwork. She then got down on her knees and crawled about the baseboards, washing the grit from them.

"Whew!" she gasped when finished. She leaned back on her heels, perspiration beading her face, her cheeks hot, and pushed the damp bangs back from her brow. She straightened slowly, knuckling the ache in her back. She shined the kitchen's windows, polished the rusty cookstove with beeswax, and scoured the stained soapstone sink. Lastly came the scrubbing of the maple floor and the rinsing, which she did twice.

The room smelled of cleanliness. Addie Kate stood in the doorway, surveyed the space, and was satisfied with her work.

* * *

Jib regarded the front yard and the disorder caused by the matted leaves and the overgrowth of wild morning glory tendrils and scrub trees. He pushed back his hat and rolled up his sleeves, seized upon the vines first and then hacked away at several mulberry saplings that had apparently been planted by the birds. Clearing the small piece of land required digging up roots of old bushes or at least trimming back the overgrown ones. He whistled away as he dragged and piled the debris for a brush fire.

Feeding the flames from time to time, listening to the snapping and crackling, he watched the bonfire smoke spiral into the still morning air like gray plumes, carrying a suffocating odor. He slogged on into the morning as the sun grew warmer.

By midafternoon Jib had toiled almost without pause, steadily enlarging the cleared area and adding to the pile of refuse. Had Addie Kate stopped for a noon break? Had she worked this whole time, too? He took out his handkerchief to swipe it across his forehead and dab at his neck when he caught sight of two people walking on the road in his direction. He leaned on his rake handle with crossed arms and kept his gaze on them, and, sure enough, they turned in and approached him.

Jib, his face streaked with sweat and dirt, his fingers stiff and scratched, his clothes odorous of ashes, greeted them, "Howdy!" He jerked off his hat and raked a hand through his hair.

Kitty rose suddenly and growled at the couple.

"Settle down," Jib scolded. But the dog took no notice of his master and raced toward the strangers, barking.

"Dog friendly?" The man asked and stooped to pat Kitty and touched a forefinger to his Stetson in greeting. "Hullo, there," he called to Jib.

The man was moderately tall and dressed in his Sunday-go-to-meeting clothes. He presented a fine picture. "Me and the woman here live jist down the road. Come tuh pay a neighborly visit. Name's Rigton Farnsley. People in these here parts call me Bassie 'cause muh middle name is Sebastian. This here's Nova Blanche." He pointed to her behind him. She stood quietly, smiling. "We wanted tuh come and welcome yuh tuh the neighborhood."

The woman was small in stature, with dark hair done in a soft coil at the base of her neck. Her face was plain with a short, pert nose. "We brung some fried chicken and three pawpaws and a punkin pie," she said. "Baked it off yesterday after we seed yuh pull in. We grow our own punkins."

"Mighty nice of yuh. It's a pleasure tuh make yer acquaintance. I'm Jib and muh wife is Addie Kate. We're the Claycombs." He glanced from one to the other. "Got our work cut out fer us here, don' cha think?"

"Been a frightful place goin' on years now," Bassie said. "Ain't no body wanted tuh mess with fixin' it up. Glad tuh see yuh take a interest in it. Resurrect it, so tuh speak."

* * *

Addie Kate pressed her palms against the kitchen windowsill. She observed Jib talking with a couple. Who were they and what did they want? She stepped out to the porch to pour the bucket of rinse water on the ground and found out who the visitors were as Jib called to her.

"Come over and greet our neighbors."

She left the house and walked toward them, feeling shy. "This here is Bassie and Nova Blanche," he said.

"Hello," Addie Kate said.

Bassie touched his hat's brim and nodded. "Howdy, ma'am," he said.

Nova Blanche smiled. "Ever'one has always called me Bunny ever since I kin 'member."

"Look see, they brung us a supper of fried chicken, pawpaws, and a punkin pie. Ain't that somethin'?"

"How thoughtful," Addie Kate said. "To tell the truth, we've been working all day and have not stopped for any dinner. Come in, and we'll eat now. I'll put some water on for coffee. You'll join us, won't you?"

"I'll be a comin' in a while," Jib said. "Best not go off and leave these coals a glowin' tuh send up sparks and catch the house on fire."

Addie Kate led the way up the back steps and opened the door—delighted to show off her shiny and orderly kitchen—and stepped back to let them enter. "Do you live in the big farmhouse down the way?"

"My gracious!" Nova Blanche remarked upon entering the room. "It's suh clean in here! Tuh answer yer question, though, cain't see our place from here. We live back yonder, a ways off the road, hidden by the trees and briars."

"Oh," Addie Kate said while lifting out the round burner plate, stirring up the fire, and putting in some kindling. She situated the coffeepot down into the blaze so that it'd get hot more quickly. She brought out the tinware, set out four plates and cups, and hunted some forks and spoons for everyone.

"I kin tell yuh ever'thing what's happened in Corydon and share stories about ever'body who lives here since I been borned."

"You were born here?" Addie Kate asked, intrigued.

"Uh-huh. Both of us." offered Bassie. "We got memories of the same people."

"I'm envious of that."

"Yuh moved a lot?"

"Actually, no. But I never knew my parents. They died when I was a tiny baby. I have three brothers and a sister. Shakers raised us. They never talked about our families."

"Some folks stay put and some wanna move on. Takes all kinds what makes life interestin', don't it?" Nova Blanche commented. "Yuh'll like Corydon. Fine country here. Kind and helpful people and we got a friendly church, called Pennington Chapel. We got a prayer meetin' every Wednesday evenin'. Hope yuh'll want tuh go. That is after yuh git settled and the place begins tuh feel like home." She kept her gaze on Addie Kate as she said this.

"I'm bursting with curiosity about this house, Bunny. Since you're from here, you no doubt know all about the family who'd lived on this place. Please tell me what you know."

Bunny nodded and quirked her mouth. "'Tis interestin'. Name was Adams. The father of the clan what builded the house was Albin Charles. This was years and years ago. He married young to Valinda Jane Bryant. They beget eleven children—ten boys and one girl. The poor little girl was borned last. Can yuh imagine havin' ten older brothers? Anyhow's, the name's famous in this county. But pro'bly what made 'em most important is this house were a part of the unnerground railroad. The old man Albin dint believe in slavery. He helped freedom seekers on their journey so this house was a 'station' fer the runaways. He was, I heerd tell, a right smart 'conductor.' Yuh got a square gold-and-green colored glass winder, don' cha? That's the marker what the fugitives knowed where tuh stop. And don't yuh have a strange, little no-count room upstairs? That's where the runaways hid. A hole in the wall of a bedroom was how they crawled intuh the secret place. It has a different kinda door tuh it, too, don' it? That door use tuh not be there. The son what owned this house last was Norbert. Yuh pro'bly heerd this's his house. He meant tuh live here. Anyhows, he married a gal what never would hear of it. Guess they did fer a few years, but they abandoned everything and it's been empty ever since—nigh onto five years now. Nobody's wanted tuh buy the place with suh few acres, and the land itself bein' eroded and run down."

Addie Kate said, "You are right—that the story is interesting."

The food was delicious and Jib got to come inside after a while, once the fire dwindled. The Farnsley's were a friendly, sociable couple who stayed on and on. Addie Kate liked Nova Blanche immediately and found the two neighbors delightful and did not want them to leave.

But, finally, around dusk, Bassie brushed crumbs off his mouth with his sleeve, wiped his fingers on his pants, then jumped up, "Zookers! We best go home, woman! We left our chil'ren and besides, we need tuh take care of the animals. Never planned on bein' gone this long."

"How many children do you have?"

"We got three boys and two girls—good kids, too. Doubt they got intuh too much trouble."

Chapter 27

*T*he first Monday in November was a most disagreeable day, dawning dark and dreary. And yet, Mondays were always the days to do the laundry. Was the day of the week cast in stone? And what about the chore itself? Yes, nothing could change either. Addie Kate still adhered to the Shaker pattern. She put the copper boiler tub of water on to heat while she cooked breakfast for her and Jib. The cookstove, now stoked up, warmed the kitchen.

The outer door opened on a gust of wind and Jib came in, blown and cold. "Pretty crisp out there," he said, rubbing his hands together. "Better bundle up if yuh's gonna hang the wash out."

Halfway through the sausage patties and fried eggs, Addie Kate got up to pour coffee for both of them and slapped a wedge of apple pie on her and Jib's plates.

"Winter is a knockin' at our door. Small birds done gone tuh warmer places. Leaves has dropped and piled up, soggy and rottin'. Days is gittin' shorter. Nights is comin' earlier. Afraid snow'll be flyin' before tuhday's gone. We're overdue about settin' up the stovepipes. Reckon we kin git that completed before Bassie gits here? I'm tuh help him ring the noses of their little pigs."

"I had hoped to get the washing done early. Can we wait until I finish with that?"

He cocked his head and sat with his lower lip drawn over his upper. Then he said, "Yuh know, the wet clothes don't hafta be on the washin' line by eight in the mornin'."

While the wash water heated on the range, they spent some time struggling with fitting the pipes into the potbellied stove. They had one problem after another. Bassie came as they were grappling with them.

"Let me do that fer yuh," he said. "I's Johnny-on-the-spot when it comes tuh puttin' up stovepipes."

Sure enough, he was right. He got everything properly set up and the pipes attached in no time. Jib then put on his coat, kissed Addie Kate goodbye, and left with Bassie.

She was finally able to fill a pan with warm water from the cookstove's reservoir to do the dishes. With the kitchen straightened, she grated a bar of brown soap into the washtub. She had bought the soap in Harrodsburg after the saleslady said she added castor oil to the recipe to enable suds to form.

Addie Kate doused the dirty clothes, pushed the articles of clothing up and down vigorously against the ridges of the washboard, then scuffed them between her knuckles. For the heavier items, she slapped them against the slanted washboard. She wrung them out as best she could. From time to time, she would flick the water from her hands and brush a little wisp of hair out of her eyes. Washing clothes was hard work, but it was a pleasant chore for her.

The house soon smelled of cleanness. When each article was washed, rinsed, and wrung out, she tossed it into a wicker basket.

Wearing her shawl and pinning it under her chin, she hefted the heavy basket up onto her hip, left the house, and went out to the clothesline. She could see her breath as she stooped and stretched pinning up each item and was grateful for the white, woolen gloves she had made for herself.

The dishcloths smelled the clean scent of lye. The sheets, folded in half with corners matching, snapped and flapped as she hung them. The bath towels, pinned up next, and the washcloths were sized as she went down the line, and the clothing, harmonized by color, had to be hung just so, neatly and in orderly fashion. That had been the Shaker way drilled into her. Though she was not at Pleasant Hill, at times she felt Sister Jerusha was still peeking over her shoulder. More than once Addie Kate made changes of the items on the clothesline to satisfy the Eldress—who obviously wasn't even around. For some reason she found it hard to forget the expression on Jerusha's face when the wash was not hung just so. *I had always disappointed her in some way*, she thought.

While she was in the midst of her task, the sky darkened more and the air became blustery as a western wind picked up. During the time she worked her way down the clothesline, the feathery touch of a starry snowflake grazed her face, then a few more. By the time she pegged the last shirt, the flakes were larger and fell in earnest, and whiteness silently filled the land, and the articles froze in place.

It snowed the rest of the day, covering everything. Bunny came and helped Addie Kate gather the frozen-stiff clothes off the line. A little later, in the kitchen, Addie Kate asked, "Want something hot to drink to thaw out?"

"Sounds wonderful."

Clattering cups and saucers, Addie Kate poured a cup of coffee and held it out to her.

"Thanks," the neighbor said, accepting the steaming drink.

Addie Kate sat with her friend at the table, and, as she visited, she peeled potatoes for a supper of potato soup, letting the long brown curls fall from her hand.

Bunny finished her visit and said, "I better be gittin' back home. Reason I came by was tuh ask what yuh and Jib's doin' fer Thanksgivin'."

"I expect it'll be like most other days for us."

"Yer not celebratin'?"

"I doubt it."

"If it is jist Jib and yuh, come on over and spend the day with us. Hard fixin' a holiday feast when only two people's goin' tuh eat it. Thanksgivin' means gittin' tuhgether and givin' thanks and sharin' God's bounty. We might be raucous, but I love company. I'm partial tuh noisy, joyous gatherin's. We asked Aint Bea tuh come, too."

Addie Kate cocked her head and arched her brows. "You have an aunt who lives nearby?"

"Aint Bea ain't really muh relative. Everybody in these here parts calls her Aint. She's a widder whose husband done long been dead. She's the one in this here community we all call when a sickness comes tuh a family or when a new baby's arrivin'. Yuh'll find she's got definite opinions about thin's, but ever'one loves her dearly."

"I'll be sure to talk with Jib about it. Thank you for the invitation to celebrate with you."

After supper, with the kitchen cleaned and everything put away, she occupied herself by darning a hole in the heel of Jib's wool stocking.

Settled in the sitting room near the fire in the potbellied stove, she glanced up to catch his gaze upon her. He was doing nothing more than observing her. "What's going on?" she asked.

"Nothin'. Jist had a marvelous idea."

She smiled. "Tell me."

"How about we move our mattress off the bed and toss it tuh the floor before the opened balcony door so we kin watch the snowflakes come down? What d'yuh say?"

"Hmm." She raised her eyebrows. "Why Jib, how romantic, we may get pneumonia. But, no matter, let's do it!" She stuck the needle in the sock, laid the mending aside, and rose.

They went to their bedroom and opened the balcony door all the way to the evening air. They dragged the mattress tick off the bed to the floor, smoothed the blankets and put down pillows and, after getting into their nighties, blew out the lamp to be mesmerized by the white fluttering flakes, steadily falling.

"Ain't this the quietest thin' in all the world? Reckon when the snow stops fallin' and the moon comes up, the night'll be sparklin' clear and everything'll be so beautiful."

Addie Kate, lying beside Jib and resting her head against his shoulder, said, "You know what?"

"Huh-uh."

"I'm so happy my throat aches. My heart is overflowing, and my soul is at peace. As I swept the house today, I thought how I was a nobody at Pleasant Hill. No clothes I could choose. No possessions of my own. No independence, no nothing. Now, I'm living in a world that I previously could only wonder about. I'm hoping I'm fitting in all right."

"Yer doin' a fine job. This is yer world now."

* * *

Thanksgiving Day arrived. Jib and Addie Kate walked over to the Farnsley's house. They found the place was a quarter mile off the road and down a winding lane. The home was plain, two storied, and surrounded by a wooden fence.

Bunny led Addie Kate on a tour of the four spacious rooms downstairs where colorful hand-hooked or crocheted rugs lay scattered on some of the floors.

"They're works of art," Addie Kate said, admiring the workmanship.

"Thank yuh. I use whate'er rags are available. Old skirts, coats, or blouses. Come and see the needlework I done. I relax by usin' muh hands." Nova Blanche took her guest to the sitting room to show her the doilies, full and ruffly, starched to stiffness.

"I wanna show yuh the covers I made the boys." The two women climbed the enclosed stairway situated in the sitting room to two full-sized bedrooms on the second level. Nova Blanche steered Addie Kate into the boys' room. The walls were papered with newspapers, and the three beds were made up with beautifully crafted log-cabin design pieced quilts.

"They gotta pick out the colors they wanted. That far one belongs tuh David Arnold," she said, pointing, "because he's the oldest, bein' ten. Middle bed is Herbert Cleon's. He's eight, and the closest one tuh the door is Charles Maynard's. He's six years."

Addie Kate inspected the room. "This is a perfect space for them," she said. "I imagine they like sleeping here. Your whole house is so welcoming and comfortable."

"Thank yuh." She clutched Addie Kate's arm. "Now . . . let's go tuh the girls' room. Althea Marydelle is four and Jessie Louise is two years. I wanna show yuh their counterpanes I tatted. Then, we'll go down and add the final touches tuh the dinner."

When Addie Kate entered the dining room and saw the table festively decorated with an orange tablecloth, red corn, and green squash, she sucked in her breath, amazed by how impressive things looked. The lady of the house set about methodically lighting candles spaced along the table's center. "I know it's old-fashioned," she said, "but I love all the fussiness."

"This is absolutely stunning," Addie Kate whispered. "What can I help you with?" She circled the table, marveling over everything.

"Nothin', yuh and Jib are the guests. Most ever'thin's done, anyways. We'll carry the food in here and call ever'body to come." She meant what she said, and when the food was on the table, she herded everyone in.

The Farnsley's Thanksgiving menu consisted of roasted wild turkey, aromatic, crusty and brown; braised rabbit with creamy gravy; mashed potatoes; sage-flavored stuffing; buttered turnips and carrots; crunchy candied pickles; baking powder biscuits; plum butter; ripe Kieffer pears; and pumpkin and blackberry pies.

"So much food, we'll hardly have room on our plates for it all," Addie Kate commented.

Ten people gathered in the dining room. Bassie said, "Before we sit tuh partake this here delicious banquet, jine hands and say a word tuh our heavenly Father a thankin' Him fer His goodness tuh us. Aint Bea, would yuh like tuh start us off?"

Addie Kate peered over at the big-boned woman who appeared to be very capable of handling whatever came her way. She was plump and bosomy with gray hair that was pulled back severely and piled on top of her head in a round bun. The woman had rosy cheeks—and was toothless. Addie Kate guessed she was in her sixties and liked the new acquaintance at first sight.

Bea smiled at the group, cleared her throat, and licked her lips before she said her piece. "I value muh friends here and that we're all in fine fettle. We have been blessed beyond all rhyme and reason and want tuh give thanks fer God Almighty's goodness. Looks like there's plenty of food, so we all better have big appetites."

Everyone snickered, and Bassie asked, "Addie Kate, would yuh want tuh say next?"

"Yes," she said. "I'm almost overwhelmed with gratitude for freedom and health which enrich my life. I treasure my faith in Jesus Christ and love my husband, who is a very special companion." She did not glance his way to see his reaction to her comment. "I adore the twinkle in his eyes and his sense of humor, which means we can laugh together. I've come to acknowledge that being married is the best way of life. I cherish love, which is as basic and necessary as nourishment, rest, and breath. I'm beholden to my neighbors. I praise my heavenly Father for His care and blessings, for I am a happy woman. Happiness, I believe, is something that we can never have too much of and something we all deserve."

Each one expressed thanks—with the older children joining in giving honor to God.

Bassie offered up a prayer, and, immediately after, they all sat, passed the food, consumed the delicious dinner—the stuffing full of herbs and the pies with flakey crusts—and enjoyed the camaraderie around the table. Jib and Addie Kate stayed on and on, not wanting to go home. It was an enjoyable time.

"I have never eaten so much, talked so much, laughed so much, and had such fun," said Addie Kate as she and Jib made the trek home.

That night, after they completed the chores, the couple ate sandwiches of thickly sliced cold turkey and thin slices of stuffing and sweet pickles—leftovers that Nova Blanche sent with them.

The next morning, before the darkness lifted, Addie Kate crept as quietly as she could down the creaking steps to the kitchen. She took care laying the kindling in the cookstove and, satisfied, struck a match to it. When it had a burning start, she added a stick of wood, listened for it to crackle and purr, and flung her wrap about her shoulders. She walked out to the porch. All the familiar landmarks—the grape arbor, the woodpile, the maple trees stripped bare of their leaves—were still engulfed in the night's blackness. Addie Kate breathed in deeply the fresh air, crisp and cool, took delight in the quietness and peacefulness of the day, and turned toward the door, shivering. It was too cold to linger any longer. The room would be warmed up, making it the coziest in the whole house.

She knew that in a matter of days, she would have her answer to the question on her mind. Her thoughts spun in joy. What would she tell Jib?

Chapter 28

$\mathcal{D}$ecember arrived, cold and bleak. Jib's thoughts turned to the twenty-fifth. He brought the issue to Addie Kate's attention one night at the supper table in the middle of the month. "What we goin' tuh do for Christmas? It's only a couple weeks off now. We hafta make some plans."

She cleared the plates away, poured herself a cup of coffee, and sat. "Like what? What do we need to plan?"

"What did yuh usually do at the holiday time?"

She shook her head. "Shakers never did anything."

"Well, we're gonna do somethin'. First, we'll see what kinda decorations we kin find in town. We'll pop lotsa corn and string the kernels on some thread and make long strands."

"Never heard of doing that," she said.

"Second, we gotta git a tree off our farmland. Sharpened the axe yesterday. I always thought that gittin' one was the most excitin' thin'. We'll wait until Christmas Eve tuh find one."

"Do I need to go with you?" Why did she ask that, for there was no sensible reason she should not go along and help him pick one out.

"Don't yuh wanna go together?" He gave her hand a little squeeze.

"I have no idea what to do."

"Then go with me tuh learn the ways of the people in the world."

She laughed. She got the impression he was testing her with "rules" she wasn't yet all that familiar with.

In the afternoon of Christmas Eve, Jib and Addie Kate traipsed through the woods looking for a suitable fir. They began the ordeal of making a choice—hard to do because he was particular. But, then again, she was too. They studied each tree from every angle.

"We'll find the right one . . . eventually. We jist ain't seen it yet. How do yuh like this one?"

"Too short," she answered back, quickly. "Too crooked," she said of another.

At the edge of the grove was a five-foot pine with full boughs. He said, "What do yuh say about this one?"

She suddenly stopped. "It's perfect. That tree will look absolutely awesome with the popcorn garland we've made."

By the time they chopped the tree down, dragged it to the wagon, and crammed it in, the daylight was fading. They got it home without breaking any of the limbs, hauled it to the parlor, and stood the cut end in a pail of water.

"I'll add a cupful of blackstrap molasses tuh the water . . . keeps the needles fresh so they stay on the branches a longer time."

As they draped the chains about the pine's circumference, Addie Kate commented on the evenings they had spent popping and stringing the kernels. "We ate as much as we strung," she said. "We took forever to get the garland long enough because we had to stop and pop more batches. Remember?" she turned to him.

He nodded and chuckled.

She smiled about that as well as recalling the day she and Jib purchased the fragile glass balls and the small wooden nativity figures. She had carefully positioned on the mantel the three kings, a camel, an ox, a donkey, three shepherds, two angels, and, of course, Mary, Joseph, and baby Jesus.

At last, Addie Kate clamped tiny red wax candles in small tin holders to several branches. She spread a white sheet around the bucket, glanced over at him, and caught his gaze upon her. "We've created something magical," she said, not expecting a response. She took a deep breath through her nose. "Smell the fragrance." A sweet piney scent filled the room. "What a beautiful practice you have."

"Yuh ain't never done anythin' like this before?" Jib sounded surprised.

She shook her head. "Never. And this is so enjoyable."

"This'll give me a place tuh put muh present," Jib said, jerking his head in her direction.

"I don't understand what you mean."

"I put muh gift tuh yuh under here," he said, pointing. "On Christmas I pull it out and give it tuh yuh."

"Oh, but I won't be able to put anything there for you."

Jib peered straight into her green eyes. "Yuh sayin' I'm gittin' nothin'? That I been such a bad person I ain't gittin' a gift?"

She couldn't help shaking her head and pressing the air with both hands. "No! I'm not saying that at all. What I've planned to give you is . . . something . . . that can't be wrapped."

"Now yuh've got me wonderin'. Somethin' mysterious?"

Addie Kate nodded.

After their evening meal, Jib said, "Dishes and chores're done. Once we git cleaned up for church, let's open our gifts. Cain't wait no longer. Like a little kid, ain't I?"

She smiled, a tingling sensation running through her. She raced upstairs, dressed, and came back downstairs to light the little candles using a taper. Jib joined her.

With the last one lit, they stood back to admire the shimmering effect. Addie Kate watched with a lump in her throat, her hands clasped at her chest. "This is so lovely," she whispered. She went to the fireplace, now ablaze, and turned to face him, grinning widely. She looked at him long and hard. "My gift to you is simply wonderful."

Jib didn't say anything as he crossed the room until he got to her. "What is it?"

"You might want to sit down."

He stared intently at her. "Did somethin' happen?"

"Yes."

"What?"

"I . . . I'm growing a baby, Jib."

He gaped at her, his mouth open, with no words coming out.

She reached out a finger and pushed his chin up. "Did you hear me?" she asked. "Say something."

He smacked his hands together. "Incredible! Nothin' would make me happier. I'm gonna be a pa!" He embraced her and his lips were on hers. He lifted her off her feet and swung her around.

"Merry Christmas!" she said, laughing. "Isn't it exciting? . . . You can put me down."

Jib set her on the floor gently and released her. "Us with a little one. Ooh boy!" He rubbed his palms together. "When's the arrivin' time?"

"August."

"*August?* Hah! Yuh always said that month's got nothin' special. Won't be no more when our baby's here."

"I'm very happy about it." She was *pregnant*. Pleasure and joy surged through her. She and Jib would beget a son or daughter.

"You know that for years, before we met, I allowed myself only to wonder what life would be like to be married and birth a child. Then I felt guilty for having those worldly notions. But now I know what freedom from the Shaker way of thinking feels like. I can tell you that I am filled with wonder and amazement that our offspring is living within me." Her heart thumped.

"Our own offsprin'! I'm the happiest man in the world."

For a long time, they stood locked in each other's arms. The room glowed with light from the fireplace, the coal oil lamp, and the candles on the tree. And the couple completely forgot about the Christmas Eve service at the church.

Chapter 29

*L*ow-hanging clouds made New Year's Day dreary and depressing. Snow began falling in the late morning, pelting down in great flakes by midafternoon and keeping at it until after dark

That night, Addie Kate, in bed but sleepless, snug under the eiderdown comforter, listened to the whistling of the wind buffeting the old house. She ran her hand over her belly, still flat. "Lord, You alone know this little one who is being wonderfully knitted together in what Your Word says is the secret place."

Jib came upstairs, undressed, and sat on the side of the bed causing a rustle in the mattress. Sliding beneath the quilt, he whispered, "Yuh awake?"

"Yes."

"Was yuh asleep?"

"No, what is it?"

"I was lookin' out the kitchen window before comin' up. Ain't there somethin' jist wonderful seein' the moonlight on the white blanketin'? This here's the first of the new year."

"Uh-huh," she mumbled.

He kissed the top of her head, said goodnight, and shut his eyes. Shortly, the sound of his rhythmic, deep breathing said he was sound asleep.

The next morning, eight inches of whiteness covered the ground and the gray sky promised more. But, instead, sleet fell in a rasping swish against the windows. For three days they dwelled in a wonderland of glass-like splendor—beautiful to see, dangerous to walk on. The fourth day, the sun came out with such brightness—dazzlingly, in fact—making everything glisten.

Addie Kate, going downstairs later than usual, had made coffee by the time Jib came in from completing the morning chores.

He stopped inside the kitchen doorway. "Somethin' smells mighty good. What we havin'?" he asked. "Muh innards are growlin'."

She glanced over her shoulder. "I made a favorite. Fried mush and salt pork."

"I'm feelin' favored."

After he ate, he licked his fork, put it down, and said, "Come on, let's git the dishes done."

She slipped the plates into the water-filled dishpan that had been heating on the range and swished a lump of brown soap about in it. He got a dishtowel out of the old dresser. "I'll dry. Wanna hurry and go out and see the wonder of the outdoors." Addie Kate washed, he dried.

"I'm proud of yuh," he said, drying a cup and hanging it on a hook in the nearby cabinet.

She spun around on her heel to regard him. "Of me? For what?"

"Not gittin' sick at yer belly when yuh eat. I always thought most women did when they were growin' a baby." He wiped each plate before nesting it in place.

Addie Kate's gaze fastened on Jib for a few seconds. Tremendous pride as well as pleasure surged through her. "I guess I never thought about that," she said.

She had been fortunate that she never suffered from morning sickness. Her stomach roiled and heaved at times, but she'd simply stop, take several deep breaths through her opened mouth, and calm down until the nausea subsided.

He hung up the dishtowel. "Yuh ready tuh go see the sparkly outside since we're finished here?"

She nodded and fetched her shawl, and the two walked out to the porch, careful to check for slipperiness. Though the sun was bright, the cold was piercing. Jib put two fingers in his mouth, whistled a shrill blast for Kitty, and the three strolled toward the pond back of the barn, the icy crust crunching and squeaking under their booted feet. All around the sloping bank of the hollow, ice sparkled like diamonds in the sunlight, for a hidden spring seeped there, never stopping, but never producing much more than a trickle of water. They stood together. Then . . .

"Look!" Addie Kate said, pointing. "There's Hewitt. What's he doing out here?"

"Probably been tuh his ma's place, readin' I reckon." He waved to the man.

The man was all bundled up. His mother's house sat back from the road, secluded among trees and briars. The Claycombs had met him on previous occasions, though he chose to live a very private life. He did not much want people around him—his garden, his home, and his books were his life—for he apparently thrived on isolation. He would go to his mother's to read so he wouldn't be interrupted by his wife's opinion that he ought to be doing something productive. Hewitt had married Maizie Hughes later in life. She didn't like seclusion, and she insisted on living close to others.

He was not a tall man but average in height, slow-moving and slow speaking— though never having much to say—who farmed with a couple of thin old horses that appeared no more enthusiastic about farming than he did. He had a habit of ending all his sentences with "'don' cha know.'"

"He's a curious fellow, isn't he?" Addie Kate spoke softly, since Hewitt was coming their way. He had once told Addie Kate that reading was a worthwhile thing to do—don' cha know.

* * *

The conclusion of winter was near. Spring sweetness spread through the air, and the breeze brought faint odors of new grass and wet earth. The nights continued to be below freezing while the daytime temperatures, with the warm sunshine, were balmy with puffy white clouds scudding across the sky. The musty smell of the new-life season wafted in the air.

"The calendar says this is the month of spring. Thank goodness. I'm glad for cold weather to be over," Addie Kate said to Jib one morning.

He sat at a corner of the kitchen table with a pile of elderberry stalks before him. "This here month's always sugarin' time. Bassie says the sap's runnin' now. He's asked me tuh help git thin's goin'." With his penknife, Jib carefully whittled the spiles from the reeds. He laid each one when completed in a pyramid-like heap on the table.

Addie Kate stepped out the door, the early March wind whooshing into the room, setting the window curtains flying. She hugged her wrap around her to cut the chill of the blustery breeze, and stared off to the distance. "Come quick!" she yelled.

Coming out to join her, he bent to pat the dog on the head. "What yuh want?"

She pointed. The sky was black from a huge flock of starlings zigzagging across the heavens. Addie Kate watched, mesmerized by the birds flying off in one direction and then quite suddenly darting off in another, swooping here and there and back in a frenzy, staying together like one united family.

Jib stood a moment with his lower lip drawn over his upper. Finally, he said, "Ain't nothin' flatterin' we kin say about them."

"Well, they feast on insects."

"But they're noisy and disrespectful."

They observed the flight as the sky's rosiness faded and sunshine came to the farm. It was at that time Bassie Farnsley made his appearance.

"Mornin'," he called and saluted as he walked up. "Lookin' like this be a fine day fer openin' the sugar camp. Bitter cold's ended. Gittin' tuh be perfect timin' fer makin' surp."

"Come on in," Jib greeted his neighbor. "Had breakfast yet?"

"Not much of one," he said, entering the Claycomb's kitchen.

Addie Kate screwed up her face. She turned to the man, "You'll need something to give you strength and energy for today. Go ahead, sit."

She lifted a stove lid, roused the fire, and poked in a stick of wood. She waited until flames blazed anew in the cookstove before she soaped and rinsed her hands to mix the quick bread. Kneading the pliable dough and rolling it out, she addressed Bassie, "How would you like your eggs? Hard, over easy, or scrambled?" She smeared her palms on her apron and put the pan of biscuits in the oven.

"Runny yolks suits me," he said.

Addie Kate grabbed six, cracked the shells against the edge of a cast-iron skillet, and dropped their contents into hot grease. While they sizzled, she poured a cup of coffee for the man. She flipped the eggs, paused a minute, and took them up, offering a filled platter to both Jib and Bassie. "Would you like some buttermilk?" she asked, turning to the neighbor.

"Shore."

She dipped it from a pail to fill a cup and then checked the biscuits in the oven. "Umm. They're about ready," she announced and set the buttermilk before him.

"Thank yuh, ma'am." Bassie slipped three eggs off the platter onto his plate, chopped up the yolk with the white, and shoveled forkfuls into his mouth, consuming half his plateful as the biscuits came out. Slathering butter over one he cut in two, he picked up the earlier conversation.

"Lissen Jib, after me and yuh's ate our breakfast, we'll go down tuh the meadow." He munched away. "The first thing's we gotta do is scrub and scald the buckets. Got 'em hunted out already. Then after they're all cleaned, they hafta be hauled tuh the grove. Next, we hammer in the spiles. Yuh done a fine job whittlin' 'em. If yuh'd help me with all that, I'd be appreciatin' it. We got prob'ly sixty trees tuh tap." He reached for another biscuit and generously loaded on some red plum jelly.

"More trees'n that in yer grove," Jib said.

"Yer right, but they hafta be at least a foot in diameter before we drill intuh 'em. We got lots of mature maples, but many more younguns, too. Lucky fer us the days and nights're still perty cool. Sun's out tuhday . . . that helps. I plan tuh begin tomorry mornin'. Lots of work tuh makin' maple surp."

Jib swiped a chunk of biscuit across his plate, sopping up the yolk. "Busy time has come. I kin help until plantin' time for muh peas . . . on the seventeenth—Saint Patrick's Day. I cain't help that day."

"No problem. Shucks, the whole spell of sugarin' lasts only a couple of weeks, four bein' the mostest. Once the nighttime ain't freezin' up, season's over."

* * *

The next day, with the sun shining and warming everything, the men began tapping the trees. Bassie used a hatchet to smooth off the rough bark before boring into each tree with a brace and bit. "Gotta be on the side of the tree what gits the mostest sunlight, and it's gotta be at a angle fer the sap tuh drain out."

Jib followed him, hammering a spile into the drilled hole to act as a trough for the sap to flow through. He suspended a galvanized bucket under each spile to catch the sugar water.

"Yuh's gotta cover the bucket yuh hung tuh keep out rain an' dirt an' bugs . . . an' nosey critters," Bassie said, laughing.

The two worked until noon, broke for lunch, and finished up late that afternoon.

Bassie scrubbed two huge metal pans. "Years ago I built this shed and the fireplaces fer the boilin' of the sap. First step tuh makin' surp is tuh boil the sap over a blazin' fire. Gradually, as the water cooks off, the thickenin' liquid gits poured into the second pan where it's heated tuh surp stage."

They made the rounds of the trees twice a day, pouring the liquid from the buckets into wooden barrels which they then emptied into the first pan to cook down. On the days the sun shone brightly, from sunup to sunset the men collected over six barrels of sap and "stirred off" as much as four to five gallons of syrup.

By the time the syrup making ended and the camp closed, they had canned sixty quarts of maple syrup in Mason jars. It had taken a lot of work to get that sap from the trees and made into syrup, but it was worth it.

* * *

Before dawn on Sunday, March twenty-eighth, while still relatively dark, Addie Kate threw her shawl around her shoulders and went out to the back porch. It was Easter, and she thought of the women in the gospel accounts going to the sepulcher to anoint Jesus's body. She said out loud to no one but herself, she supposed, "How awesome for Mary Magdalene on that morning."

"What's that yer a jabberin' about? Kin I git in on the conversation?" Jib had come to the kitchen door and stood in its threshold.

She wheeled around, surprised he was there. "I was admiring the sky all powdered with stars and trying to decide which was the North Star. All of them are so bright, there is no distinguishing any special one. Come and see." He joined her, and together they went out into the yard and stared up at the heavens. "It is amazing, isn't it? No wonder the sunrise service starts at daybreak. Day always breaks, regardless if the sun shines or not. In the Bible, the women went to the tomb at daybreak—meaning, it was still somewhat dark."

"Uh-huh. I'm thinkin' we better wrap up real good when we go tuh the sunrise service. It's downright chilly. I'm shiverin' jist standin' here." He patted her shoulder. "Got the coffee a goin'?"

"I do. Shh. Listen. Hear the noise of the new day? I've never been to church at such an early time of morning—or in a graveyard, for that matter. It'll be interesting to say the least."

They went inside and huddled around the cookstove's warmth. Addie Kate got their cups down and filled them with the hot coffee which they drank before going to dress.

* * *

The couple arrived early at Pennington Chapel. The white clapboard church sat on a hill out in the country. The graveyard's grass was soft and green and dotted with dandelions. Lit lanterns marked the way to the place for the service. It was a beautiful scene, and with the birds twittering, it was most pleasant.

The people gathered, shivering and talking quietly, waiting. The minister had arrived. The instrumentalists had not, though.

The horizon grew lighter with a pink ribbon as the attendance increased. A man with a guitar and a woman with a violin appeared at sunrise. The preacher offered a prayer and the ceremony began. A young woman, dressed as Mary Magdalene might have been on that first Easter, stepped before everyone and read Mark's gospel account of the meeting in the Garden of Gethsemane. Those gathered sang "Christ the Lord Is Risen Today" and "Up from the Grave He Arose," and they heard a short homily. A man and woman performed a duet. His voice was deep and hers was a sweet soprano. When the man reached a high note, he would raise himself on his tiptoes. Addie

Kate thought it somewhat amusing. Then the people sang "The Day of Resurrection" and the preacher closed with a prayer—a simple service but reverent—a new and memorable experience for Addie Kate.

Chapter 30

*A*pril came—wet.

"Smell of spring is in the air, all right. Yesterday seemed right for mushroomin'—warm and moist, but don't think they're ready yet. Ground hasta warm up some more," Jib commented early one morning. "Ain't seen any May apples bloomin."

"Surely they are somewhere," Addie Kate said. "I have been hearing the fluting of the peepers, and the birds are definitely singing now, too, instead of just twittering as they do in winter."

"Hmm, they all announce the new season. Been checkin' on the dandelion greens seein' if it's time tuh dig 'em . . . cain't wait tuh boil some with a hunk of pork, cook up a kettle of beans, and bake some cornbread. Mmm-mmm. That there'll cure whatever ails a body. Mighty fine eatin', especially with a slab of apple pie."

For two weeks, their talk at mealtime included mushroom hunting. Jib came in for supper on a Monday evening in the second week of April—the twelfth. When they finished their meal and remained at the table lingering over coffee, he said, "Yesterday's jist right tuh go 'shroomin'. Was a mild day. Tuhday's even better. Wanna traipse in the woods tomorrow tuh see what we kin find?"

She brightened. "I would like that." She got up and stacked the dishes.

The next day they started out soon after the morning chores were completed. The dog went with them on their hunt. The couple right away found nine huge morels near a tree whose bark, now laying on the ground, had been stripped by lightning. Addie Kate pounced with cries of delight when they came upon another patch of the sponge-textured toadstools. Excited about their serendipity in finding so many, they headed home.

At the back porch, Addie Kate sat on a step and scraped mud from the side of her shoe with a stick. Kitty leaped up and planted his muddy paws on her shoulders. "Down!" she ordered. The dog dropped to all fours, came around, and swiped his tongue across her chin. "No!" she commanded. She wiped her face with her sleeve.

Poor Kitty. He was just letting her know he had enjoyed his frolic with them.

After painstakingly picking burrs from the eye-lacings of her high shoes, Addie Kate went inside and put their bounty in salt water to soak the little bugs out. When dinnertime came, she floured them and fried them crisp.

"These are the preferred eating of all the other kinds of mushrooms," she said, as she speared one, held up her fork, and admired the fruit of their adventure.

Two weeks later, on the twenty-sixth, Addie Kate awoke to find thick fog engulfing the area. She pattered downstairs to rouse the fire in the cookstove and got busy preparing a special breakfast for Jib, but she barely got started before he appeared.

"Happy Birthday!" she sing-songed. "Feel any older today?"

"Naw. Jist stiffer. Whatcha fixin'?"

"Chocolate gravy and biscuits.

"Whoa! Muh favorite. Cain't wait tuh see what yuh's cookin' fer dinner."

"I think I'll kill a big, fat hen. We'll have fried chicken and plenty of creamy gravy with crispy bits of crust left in from the frying, mashed potatoes, and pickings of wild asparagus. There's a bed of it along the road. How's that sound?"

"Like a meal fit for a king."

"That's what you are . . . for a day, anyway. I've a treat for you, too . . . after you've eaten."

After breakfast and while he remained seated in his chair, she sat on his lap, took his hand in her own and guided it to her thickening waist. Then she laid it flat against her belly. "Feel anything?" she asked.

"Umm, a tiny thump-thump," he said.

She gazed into his eyes. "Our little one."

Jib's eyes widened, his smile grew, and his face beamed. "Our baby," he repeated. "Hard tuh believe," he said under his breath.

* * *

May arrived with a gentle rain, and, in no time, the pink and white blossoms on the apple trees were in full bloom.

"This is pure ecstasy," Addie Kate said about their beauty and aroma. "Isn't it marvelous how the earth wakes up? April is a delicate green, but this month is dazzling sweetness."

A few weeks later, the honey locust trees—loaded with cream-colored flowers—emitted the sweet fragrance that wafted heavy all over the farm. "I could live forever with the scent of them and still love it," she declared. "I even cut off a branch and brought it inside for its perfume to permeate the whole house. It's the strongest in the late afternoon and early evening."

* * *

All too quickly July arrived with the heat bearing down on them. It was finally summer in Corydon. Thank goodness Addie Kate had finished the polishing, waxing, washing, and cleaning of the entire house. Now she walked through each room admiring the results of her work. She smiled as she went out to the back porch, plopped into the rocking chair, leaned back, and drew a deep breath. Jib joined her, and they sat in silence for some time tolerating the air's supersaturation, for it had been an extremely sweltering day. They watched the golden sunset and the moon climbing in the sky. Addie Kate—eight months pregnant, bulky and awkward with twenty extra pounds, and terribly uncomfortable—slowly rocked.

Jib gently rubbed his thumb back and forth against the top of her hand. After some time, he asked, "What yuh doin'?"

"Counting my blessings . . . naming them one by one. Every day is new, filled with simple adventures of living in the country," she said. "My only complaint today is the humidity that makes everything feel clammy. Otherwise, I love July."

"Stands tuh reason since yuh was borned in this month."

"Umm. Our country's, too . . . with the Fourth," she added.

On Wednesday the fifteenth, Jib asked her. "What're yuh plannin' for yer birthday dinner? Ain't it only two days away?"

She nodded. "Fresh-picked green beans cooked with pork, crisply fried potatoes, a slice of onion, slices of garden-grown tomatoes, and cucumbers in vinegar. For dessert, blackberry cobbler. Makes my mouth water just talking about it."

"Sounds good tuh me, too. Would yuh mind mixin' some cornbread?"

"I can."

* * *

August came with a muggy haze of hot weather. Addie Kate was miserable—barely able to do the things she thought she must. It was a busy time for her—hemming flannel cloth for diapers, stitching blankets, and embroidering sacques—understandable, since there was much to do the last days before the birth of her first child.

On Monday evening, the twenty-first, a day so hot and still the birds had stopped singing, Jib circled his wife's immense waist before he left to do the evening chores. "Yuh reckon I oughta bring Aint Bea or Bunny for yuh? Yuh're as round as a punkin. I'm afraid yer goin' tuh pop."

"I think you could wait until later. I have been having a dull ache all day long in my lower back that is not going away. Haven't paid too much attention to the pains."

But it was that very night that Addie Kate awakened with a gasp. Her eyes flew open at a spiked pain and she sat up at the edge of the bed, panting. A second contraction, stronger than the last, caused her to suck in her breath and grit her teeth. She woke Jib, her face sweaty and her hair wet. "I think this is it," she said. "Better bring Bunny or Aunt Bea or both of them."

He sprang out of bed and dressed in a hurry. "Yuh gonna be all right while I'm gone?"

She nodded. "Don't dilly-dally." There was a catch in her breath. "It's more than I expected—"

Jib swallowed hard. "I won't take long."

When the two women showed up at the Claycomb house, they took over. They tacked together old newspapers and spread them out on the mattress and covered them with clean, worn muslin sheets. They collected the necessary equipment, washed each piece carefully, and bathed Addie Kate. They were now ready for the delivery.

* * *

It was Tuesday morning. Jib lazed in the rocker, leaning back against the headrest. It was the sensible thing for him to do in such heat while he waited for Addie Kate to deliver their offspring. He rocked for a while, his legs keeping a steady rhythm, drifting in his thoughts and smiling to himself. They had made a baby and would soon be parents.

The remnant of last winter's logs was next to the steps. Jib thought he saw a three-foot snake slither out of the pile. He stopped rocking and straightened, his heart racing. Were his eyes playing tricks on him? He had no regard for reptiles. It probably was not poisonous, but he knew Addie Kate didn't like them near the house, and neither did he.

He cautiously approached the woodpile, caught sight of a timber rattler, and thwacked it with a handy split log, killing it. He went toward the barn to grab a shovel to bury the carcass, and passing by the grape arbor, glimpsed another rattler curled up around the trunk of a grapevine. It was about the same size as the first one. The dog, now whistled up, came over to him, growled around, and latched on to the reptile, shaking it violently.

Back at the porch with the shovel, Jib found that the first snake— the one he thought he had killed with the firewood—was gone. Dismayed at not finding it, he decided he'd not done it in after all.

He stomped into the house to get his hands on his rifle, came outside and poked around, but he could not locate the varmint. He presumed it had crawled away to a cooler spot. So Jib gave up trying to find that one and went to carry off the one the dog had done in at the arbor. Between there and the house, he met a third rattler and shot its head off. There was no doubt that one was dead.

Had there been three snakes in the yard on that sultry afternoon? Apparently. He went back to the stack and took it apart stick by stick, looking for the other two. And then . . . epiphany struck him. No, there had been only one snake that he had spotted three times. And the last time he saw it, he severed its head leaving the remains plainly in sight. Jib chuckled at himself and breathed a sigh of relief. While burying it, he discovered the reptile was full of eggs. He didn't want to think what might have happened if that mother-to-be had hatched her babies near the house. Jib shook his head, wiped his brow with the back of his hand, went back to the rocker, and sat. It had been a thrilling afternoon, almost as exciting as what was about to come. He quieted as Kitty came up to him, nuzzled his master's hand, and put his head on Jib's knee.

* * *

Jib puttered around in the kitchen. Done with the evening chores, he made a pot of coffee and sat at the table with a cup to his lips when the sound of a baby's cry reached him. He had been so tense that when he heard the squall, he wanted to shout.

"Yuh gots a beaut'ful li'le girl, Jib," Bunny hollered down to him.

He jumped up and went to stand at the foot of the stairs, hanging on to the carved newel post. "How's the two a doin'?"

"Jist fine. I'll let yuh know when tuh come on up. I'll git both cleaned up first."

"Nothin's sweeter than a baby girl," he murmured, then he smacked his hands together and whooped, "A daughter! Thank Yuh, Lord.!" He went back to the kitchen, paced back and forth, his head held high, his hands behind his back, waiting for his summons to come upstairs.

* * *

Exhausted, but immensely proud of herself, Addie Kate lay in bed, propped against her pillows, at last out of discomfort, the ordeal over.

"Yuh gots a darlin' little one," Bea said, bringing the infant to the new mother. "She's a dandy lookin' girl."

Addie Kate's heartbeat quickened. "Holding her in my arms takes my breath away," she said. She caressed the cheek of her daughter and smiled at the touch.

"Yuh'll be gettin' used tuh her. Want somethin' tuh eat or drink now?"

The newborn lay nestled in the curve of her mother's arm. "I'd like some hot tea, please—with milk and sugar."

"Sure thin'. Jib's done been called." Bea pulled a chair over to the bed for him. "He'll be here directly," she said, and left the room.

He came and stood in the doorway. "Yuh ready tuh see me?"

Her gaze made contact with his. "Yes, absolutely. I have been waiting for you to come." She flashed a beaming smile to him and waved her hand, beckoning him to come closer. "You better watch out, Mr. Claycomb, because I'm so happy my heart is about to explode. Come see our daughter. She's got white-gold fuzz hair, long eyelashes, and rosy, round cheeks. She's beautiful."

He tiptoed over, his hands together behind his back, bent over to kiss Addie Kate's forehead, and peered at the little life. "I ain't ever seen such a tiny one before up close, but I'm a thinkin' she's perfect," he mumbled.

"Are you disappointed even a little bit she isn't a boy?"

"Naw. I like girls jist as much." He caressed the baby's smooth cheek tenderly with the back of his index finger.

"I do so want to be a good mother to her."

"Fiddle, woman, yuh don't hafta worry none. Yuh'll be a wonderful momma," he said.

Bea came back in the room carrying a tray with a cup. She placed it on the chair seat and slipped the baby from Addie Kate's arms into her own and left the room.

"Oh, Jib, praise God the baby's healthy and has come fully equipped." She sat up, took up the cup, and sipped the drink. "Ahh," she said, before taking another sip and putting the cup back down.

"Yuh done real good, Addie Kate."

She nodded with a smile. "Here." She patted the bed and moved her legs to make room for him. "Sit."

He did and took her hand, held it a moment, and noticed its roughness. He closed his other hand over hers and glanced up to meet her gaze. "Anythin' I kin git yuh?"

"You already have given me everything I have ever wanted."

"What yuh wanna name her? Gotta be a strong one. I know we talked about several but never settled on one because we dint know whether our baby was gonna be a boy or girl."

"How would you like for her to be called Phoebe?"

He gave her hand a squeeze. "Muh ma's name."

"Um-hmm, it means radiant or shining one. Is that all right with you?"

He nodded. "Why wouldn't it be all right? What yuh thinkin' for her middle name?"

She looked straight at him. "How about Darlene? That was the name of my Shaker caretaker when I was growing up. Phoebe Darlene suits her quite well, don't you think?"

"Shore do," Jib said.

"I'm worn out completely, but she was worth all the effort. You being here with me helps. I am simply too excited to sleep."

"Yuh needs tuh rest though."

She smiled at him and shut her eyes. He got up to leave and, on the way to the door, met Bea coming in carrying the baby. He stopped and peeked at his daughter tucked snuggly in a cotton blanket. At the threshold, he came face to face with Althea, Jessie, and their mother.

Bea positioned the little bundle next to Addie Kate and shushed the visitors. "Shh. Only a quick peek, now. And don't climb on the bed."

Addie Kate opened her eyes. "Come see, girls."

They rushed in, shouting their excitement. They came to the bedside and hung over the baby, studying her.

"Her's wittle," Jessie said as she reached out to touch the baby's closed fist.

"How'd her git here?" asked Althea.

"She came from inside my belly," Addie Kate answered, matter-of-factly.

Five-year-old Althea argued, "No, her dint."

"Oh?" Addie Kate glanced at Bunny hoping for some help in explaining the matter.

"Who tol' yuh that yuh was gonna git a baby?"

This time Bunny hurriedly said, "God let 'er know."

Other than the times Addie Kate was nursing Phoebe, she slept most of that day. But she got up for a few hours the next day and ambled about the bedroom.

When Nova Blanche came into the room and found her out of bed, she chastised the new mother. "Here, here! What're yuh a doin'? Yer not s'posed tuh be up an' about, yet. Yuh gotta spend at least ten days in bed tuh give the innards 'nough time tuh git back in place."

"I can't stay the convalescent for too long or I'll grow weak. And I want to be fit enough to take care of the little life I just birthed," Addie Kate said.

She immersed herself in her daughter, falling in love with her. Being a mother was what she had wanted for as long as she could remember anything, and she had always thought of herself as being maternal. She wanted to prove it.

Chapter 31

*I*n the days that followed Phoebe's birth, her parents, captivated by their little daughter, asked on almost a daily basis, "Isn't she wonderful?" and "Aren't you thrilled over her?" Of course they always answered in the affirmative.

Jib snapped pictures of his baby girl frequently. She was, after all, his most accessible subject. Neighbors and friends said he acted like a foolish man over her. For the times she cried in hiccupping spurts, he would pick her up and put her in her mother's arms.

Addie Kate would hug her daughter for a time to calm her, her cheek against the downy head. Nova Blanche chastised the new mother by saying, "You shouldn't do that. She won't learn tuh soothe herself." Addie Kate replied, "I don't care. I don't like to hear her cry."

All too quickly Phoebe was a month old, then three months, squealing and holding up her arms to Jib. Every time he lifted her, her knees pumped against his chest and thrashed the air.

At six months she sat up. She learned to chew soft foods. She stood at seven months, toddled and tumbled down at nine months. Her baby teeth appeared.

Her parents marveled at her progress every minute. They watched her grow, slumber, play, and eat. Jib took photographs of Phoebe doing her thing, definitely not posed, and laughed when he found the right study of her. She would sprawl on the floor smacking blocks together. Sometimes he plopped down in front of her and stacked them for her to strike them down—and laugh.

Then . . .

Before Phoebe turned one year old, Addie Kate knew without a doubt she was expecting a second child. "God is gracious. Thank you, Lord, for blessing us again. My heart is full to overflowing."

Six months later, on February twenty-sixth, 1882, a delicate and tiny baby girl arrived in the Claycomb family. Again, Bunny and Bea attended to the birthing.

Addie Kate experienced a fleeting disappointment when the second daughter was born. "She should have been a splendid boy for you, Jib. Praise God she is healthy and lively. So what do you think of our little girl?" she asked him as he came to see her.

He knelt and tucked the edge of the flannel blanket away from the infant's chin for a better view of her. Nestled in her mother's arms, he looked at her sleeping so peacefully. "She's a pretty one, all right. . . . What we gonna name her?"

"How about 'Ruth'? That might be a good name to give her. It's strong . . . a Bible name."

He pursed his lips out and rubbed his fingers along his jaw looking thoughtful. "How's that?"

"Well, the book of Ruth in the Old Testament actually sounds similar to me—a foreigner in a new adopted land. She married a wealthy farmer and she had a baby."

"A lot like yer story, but it ain't this little one's. If that's what yuh wanna call her though, I'll agree to it, and what'll be her second name?"

"How about 'Arlene'?"

"Who do yuh know has got that name?"

"No one. I just thought it fit well with Ruth, and it rhymes with Darlene."

Althea and Jessie barged into the bedroom at that time, each holding Phoebe's hand. "We wanna see the new baby," they announced.

"Come and look," Addie Kate said.

"Now don't bounce on the bed," Nova Blanche cautioned.

The two Farnsleys stopped at the bedside, but Phoebe, confident in the way small children are of knowing they are absolutely right about everything, climbed up with her mother, put her arm around her mother's neck to brace herself, leaned over, peered at the newborn, and studied her new sister.

Ruth made a face and hiccupped, and the girls giggled.

Phoebe scooted to the floor, and the three young ones drifted away. Jib bent to kiss his wife on her temple. "I'll be back after I complete the evening chores."

Addie Kate was happy. She had wanted two things in her life. She had them now: a kind husband and children. She lay quietly in bed, closed her eyes, and ran her tongue across her lips. Her failure to produce a male concerned her, though. "Bunny, do you think Jib is disappointed the baby wasn't a boy?"

The woman took her friend's hand and gently squeezed it inside her own. "No! Ever'one's seen how he 'dores his chil'ren. I think he's proud tuh uh fathered two beaut'ful babies."

Addie Kate nodded and smiled. She thought her girls were cute as could be, and she vowed to spoil them. She recalled how Jib proved he was a loving father. She was well pleased with how he stepped into his role as father. He always took pleasure romping with Phoebe. When he entered a room, the little girl, fascinated with him, likely stopped whatever she was doing and followed him around.

* * *

The days began to wheel by, melting into each other. The Claycomb family relished the happy and cozy home that Addie Kate created and had longed for her whole existence. She loved her husband and her girls and having them around the house. She told anyone who would listen that she had two daughters and a husband whom most people thought was either a saint or a fool. To that she followed with the comment, "I think he's a little of both. For myself, you behold a contented woman who hopes to live to be one hundred years."

She kept an eye on her offspring as they played together, talking all the time, moving their little dolls in and out of the open-back dollhouse that Jib made for them. They were noisy at times, but they brought humor into Addie Kate's life.

Jib delighted in riding his daughters hither and yon on his shoulders. He flew kites with them and taught them how to care for the animals and how to trap and fish and garden. He adored them, and they idolized their father.

In the same way that Phoebe shadowed her father, Ruth trailed her older sister. At one point, Addie Kate had to take her younger child on her lap and tell her that she shouldn't do all Phoebe ordered her to do.

Phoebe, from a very young age, showed signs of an overbearing personality. Ruth, on the other hand, displayed a tenderhearted and happy-go-lucky nature. She didn't express anger often. She didn't need to.

* * *

Five weeks after Ruth turned three, it was Easter. Phoebe was four and would be five in August.

The Tuesday before the holiday, Jib said to Addie Kate, "We've got plenty of eggs, whaddya think about dyeing some of 'em so I kin hide 'em for the girls tuh find?"

"Phoebe has participated in egg hunts at church, but I've never dyed eggs before. Beets give a red color, but what do I do for other colors? I'll ask Bunny."

Addie Kate cooked the eggs on Friday and kept them in the spring house. On Saturday, she boiled red cabbage off during the day and added baking soda for a blue color. Turmeric yielded yellow and boiled dried blackberries gave purple. She and Jib worked together dying three dozen eggs after their daughters went to sleep that night.

After they accomplished the decorating, Addie Kate dumped all the dyes together into a pitcher and flung its contents out on the ground behind the springhouse. Unfortunately, the dog was lying down at the very spot the liquid landed, and because of the darkness, she did not see him. Kitty became multicolored as a result.

Easter morning arrived with rain. Jib waited for it to stop before he hid the eggs, but the hour grew later than he had hoped for the task to be completed.

The girls awakened and ran to the window. They spied their father with a basket. What was he doing? Was he hunting their eggs? Phoebe complained. "Pa's out there before we even get a chance to find any. Make him stop!" Fuming, she glared at her mother, her brow furrowed.

Addie Kate plastered a distressed expression on her face, went to the back porch, and yelled out to Jib in a gruff tone, "Now you put every egg right back where you found it. The girls are upset that you're out here when they haven't had their time at it yet."

Jib nodded, finished hiding the ones left in the basket, and came in the house looking as ashamed as he could muster. The sisters flashed to their room, dressed lickety-split, and scurried to go on their own search. They found not only colored eggs but that Kitty was also pastel-colored. "How did that happen?" they asked.

Addie Kate explained their discovery away by saying the Easter bunny must have tripped over their pet and spilled the dye on him. The reason apparently made sense to Phoebe and Ruth.

* * *

Addie Kate admitted to herself that the hours and the days with the girls seemed long sometimes, but the years went by rapidly. On a dreary Tuesday afternoon three weeks before Christmas, she sat at her kitchen table listening to the rain while it slapped against the windows, rapped on the metal back porch roof, and gurgled in the gutters. She held a sense of peace and contentment as the fire crackled in the cookstove, and coffee scented the air.

Phoebe, now nine years old, and Ruth, almost eight, were serving tea and toast to each other in the dining room. It was good to hear their happy little voices. In the midst of the chaotic weather, there was peace in the house. Jib would presently come in from the evening chores and want a cup of something hot to drink.

A knock at the front door interrupted her thoughts and the tea party. *Who in the world would come out on a day like today if they didn't have to?* Addie Kate wondered. Answering the door, she welcomed in a woman from the church who carried two boxes. They disappeared into the kitchen talking in hushed tones the whole way. The sisters grew curious and tiptoed to the door opening and flattened themselves against the wall. Phoebe swung around and shushed Ruth with a finger to her lips and strained to hear what the women were saying. Were the two siblings getting something special this year?

They became more intrigued when as soon as Mrs. Ames left, their mother went upstairs, taking the mysterious packages with her. Would they ever be able to snoop? Their opportunity came the following Monday when their mother hung out the wash.

In the little no-account room, they found what they were searching for and jumped up and down in excitement. Ever so carefully they opened the boxes' lids to find the prettiest dolls they had ever seen—each china head with painted pink cheeks, curly brown hair, blue eyes, and a red mouth. Neither girl could say a word. Holding them, they didn't want to put them back, and every night after that, they talked of their good fortune.

Christmas morning came. The girls expected to see the boxes they had scouted out, but none of the packages under the tree looked their size. What happened? Where were they?

The last gifts they unwrapped were dolls—homemade from feed sacks—with embroidered faces and yarn hair.

Ruth clutched her ragdoll to her chest as she divulged to her mother how they'd sneaked around and found the boxes with dolls. Addie Kate's eyes filled with tears. "Those weren't for you, girls. I was keeping them for Mrs. Ames. She was afraid Marcella and Marvella would snoop and find them at her house."

Phoebe turned her back and marched out of the room. One day, soon after the holiday, she stashed the ragdoll beneath the bed's mattress.

While Ruth enjoyed playing with hers, Phoebe sulked and grumbled about having them made of rags. After days of pouting and grousing, hardly speaking and eating, she pulled her doll out from its hiding place, only to find it somewhat mashed down and lopsided.

* * *

Addie Kate was on the back porch and leaned back in the rocker. She had just shared a bit of news with Jib.

"Jumpin' Jehoshaphat, will wonders never cease?" he exclaimed. "We've gotta tell the girls."

She nodded. "Yes, but they'll be so embarrassed," she said, and tears came to her eyes.

Jib found his daughters together—Phoebe, busy working on some project, and Ruth chattering away as she gave attention to her sister's work. He approached them. "Girls, come here."

They stopped all action, obeyed, and came close to him. "How'd yuh like it if there was a little baby comin' intuh the family?"

"Whose baby is coming?" Phoebe asked dourly.

"Well now, yer ma is goin' tuh git a baby in a few more months."

The sisters were stunned. "Oh, Pa, no!" they finally chorused. "Everyone's going to know."

"Well, yep, that's true," he said.

Several nights later, Jib caught them tittering and whispering when they should have been sleeping. He situated himself in the threshold admonishing them to settle down. "Now girls, what's goin' on? What do yuh find tuh talk so much about? I'd think yuh'd have enough time durin' the day. Close them eyes, now," he commanded.

After a momentary silence, Phoebe blurted out, "A girl from school, Christabelle Carmichael, who thinks she knows everything, has accused Ma of something awful."

Jib raised his eyebrows. "Is that so? What's she sayin'?"

"She said our ma was pregnant."

"Oh? What did yuh say?"

"I told her in no uncertain terms that my mother was not! 'She is not!' I said. 'And you better mind what you're reporting about her!' And Christabelle argued with me. She said, 'Your mother is gettin' a baby.'

"I said, 'She is gonna get a baby, but she ain't pregnant.' We figure you ought to know what people is telling about her, but, Pa, let's not mention any of this to Ma. She'll get all worried up."

Jib slowly nodded. "We mustn't do anythin' that might trouble her." Quite amused, he shared the story with Addie Kate. She moaned, "What a poor excuse for a mother I've been to our girls for not explaining things of life."

On July 23, 1894, another girl was born into the Claycomb family. She was given the name of Sarah Charlene.

Chapter 32

"Since the weather's turned off fine and dry, a bunch of us is goin' tuh help Hewitt dig a cistern. Shouldn't take but a couple of days," Jib told Addie Kate at breakfast one morning in the middle of April. He continued, "Ole Hewitt's been packin' their water from his ma's place, back in the woods somewheres. Carryin' it fer years—long before we came."

"We've been here sixteen years. After all that time, how come he wants a well now? His mother's spring has never dried up even in the hottest and driest weather," she commented as she poured another cup of coffee for them.

"He's been talkin' a powerful amount of time that somethin' ough-ta be done about a well because he's gettin' older and slower and they need tuh have a handier water supply than goin' off tuh his ma's every day. Don' cha know?"

She smiled at that last statement. So like Hewitt.

Over the years, she and Jib had spent much of their time improving their property. They upgraded and modernized the house and barn, now fit for the coming decade since he piped water from a higher spring down to those buildings. They planned and worked

271

for a productive life and had become successful fruit, chicken, and Christmas-tree farmers on their little farm.

"So today's the day you start, huh? Who's helping with the project?"

Jib finished his bacon and eggs and mopped up the grease on his plate with a biscuit. He folded a lump of butter into another one and ate it in one bite. "Bassie and his three boys . . . and me. That'll be six. Plenty of help."

The Farnsley men showed up at that time since they wanted to get an early start.

Jib went out to greet them. Addie Kate followed him out as far as the porch to wave them off. "You all be careful, you hear?"

"Always am," he said and kissed her before he bounded off the steps.

"I don't want to learn of anyone getting hurt—especially you, mister. Remember there's a little one now to raise."

Shortly after the men left, Nova Blanche and Jessie Louise walked over to the Claycomb home to bring the garments they had sewed for baby Sarah Charlene. They oohed and ahhed over the little clothes.

Addie Kate went to Sarah's cradle and stood looking down at her sweetness in sleep—her cheeks pink, her eye lashes bronze. She was beautiful.

* * *

Jessie Farnsley, now eighteen years old, raised up when she heard horse's hooves becoming louder, coming closer at a fast clip. "Why's Charlie comin' back . . . on Hewitt's old horse, too?"

"He's ridin' awful hard. Somethin' must be wrong," Nova Blanche said as she stood at the window, shaded her eyes, and stared into the near distance.

The women watched him as he pulled to a stop trailing a wild plume of dust and jumped down—the animal heaving and sweating—and ran up the back porch steps to the kitchen.

"What is it, son?" his mother asked.

He did not answer her, but walked directly to Addie Kate, jerked off his hat, and looked at her with a sober face.

"Something's happened," she whispered, laying a fist on her breast. He nodded.

"What is it?" she demanded.

"It's Jib," Charlie's voice quavered.

She gripped his arm and stared straight into his eyes. "How bad is it?" She did not move, nor did she lessen her grip.

His mouth quivered like a baby's and tears filled his eyes. "He's . . . dead."

Her heart stood still. She choked. "No! Not Jib! Oh, Charlie, not Jib! I don't understand! How could he be? Only this morning he—" Her words broke off. Her lips trembled.

"I'm horrible sorry."

"How did it come about? Tell me." She listened to his painful words.

"Acts'dent. He was diggin' the trench. Caved in on him. We all dug tryin' tuh save him. But it wharn't tuh be. I hate havin' tuh tell yuh, ma'am. This's the hardest thin' I ever had tuh do. The men'll be a carryin' him here in a little while."

Addie Kate's face crumpled. "It can't be true! He had so much to live for." Her hand covered her mouth, stifling a sob. "Sarah's not yet a year old. She'll never know her pa."

Nova Blanche reached out, pulled her friend into her arms, and rocked her as though she were a little child. "I'm so sorry," she said.

"I don't want him to be gone," Addie Kate wailed. She blinked hard as tears started up again. "Oh, why did it have to happen? Jib loved life so. It's unbearable to think of him not being close by. Oh, my heart hurts. What am I going to do without him? Who will take care of us?"

"Shh, Addie Kate. Yuh gotta push yerself through the days ahead. Yuh'll hafta make yer way past yer sorrow."

Later that day, numbed by the suddenness of her loss, Addie Kate sat at the sitting room's front window of her country home, her elbows planted on the sill, her chin resting in her upturned palms. She stared out at the valley with eyes that saw nothing of it, her mind racing with thoughts of her husband. He had been her man—he'd said time after time, "I'll love you until I die."

Remembering his promise, a warm feeling came over her, and she smiled. But it was little consolation. It was dreadful to think of him and not be able to touch him. He was a gentle-mannered person, well respected in the community. Had it really been sixteen years since they married and came to Indiana? It seemed like only a few years ago, certainly not as many as it actually was.

Her concentration drifted to the past, to forgotten occasions now brought to the forefront—being at Pleasant Hill and saying goodbye to her sister and that way of life. She cleared the memories of those days and focused on more recent recollections—of marrying Jib— the love of her life. How grateful she was that he came for her. For all these years, she hadn't regretted her choices, not for one single second. She brushed at her eyes, thankful that she hadn't missed out on this blessed life by staying with the Shakers. God broke through her thinking and gave her a wonderful husband and three babies. It was more than she deserved she decided—blessings freely given by a gracious heavenly Father.

Why, just that very morning, Jib sat in his usual place at the table—talking with Phoebe and Ruth and laughing with them. He was alive. "Now, he's dead," she mumbled without realizing she said the words.

Death was a terrible reality. Her lips trembled. An accident—horrible and tragic, so unexpected that she could not yet comprehend clearly what had happened.

Sitting there she wondered how her daughters were going to come to terms with the agonizing cold fact that their father was deceased.

Sarah Charlene would never know her father except through the witnessing from others. Passing away was so final.

Addie Kate stood and walked slowly over to a shelf where Jib had stacked several of his pictures. She picked up one sepia-toned photograph of Phoebe, before she turned one year old, clasping her rattle. In another, Ruth, barely able to sit up, sat posed naked in a washbowl; yet in another, it showed both girls hosting a tea party using an old crate as the table, a dishtowel as the "fancy" tablecloth, chipped old dishes as the "china," and Kitty as their guest. She smiled and shuffled through other prints that showed an afternoon of creek-side fishing and picnicking; the girls dressed in their Sunday best holding a pose for their father; and baby Sarah, just days old. Sadness struck her as she realized Sarah would never be photographed throughout her childhood by a loving father.

Addie Kate did not turn when light footsteps approached behind her. "Want some company?"

She glanced at Bunny, standing beside her, shrugged, then nodded. "I don't know what I am going to do. Without Jib, it is the end of my life."

Bunny put her arm about the grieving woman. "Yuh gotta live fer yer girls, now," she said. "Somethin' fine went out of the world tuhday," she added softly.

Addie Kate pointed a finger at her. "Have you ever experienced loss like this?"

"No," the friend admitted. "I'mma askin' God tuh give yuh some peace and comfort . . . hate to bother yuh, but yuh got any idees how yuh wanna dress him?"

Addie Kate shook her head.

"Sorry I hafta bother about that, but there ain't never a good time tuh ask it."

"It's all right."

"Time's a pushin.'"

Addie Kate nodded and returned to her chair at the window.

Jib's body came to the house in midafternoon. Bunny and Bea washed him, cut and combed his hair, dressed him in his best shirt and trousers, and laid him out for viewing.

The casket, placed in front of the fireplace, rested on a mortuary stand that was draped in crushed purple velvet. Candles burned steadily at the four corners. From where she sat, Addie Kate could see through the open door across the entry hall to where his body was.

Bea approached the grieving woman. "Yuh wanna come and see him?" She bent her head toward the parlor.

Addie Kate nodded, but she didn't move. An overwhelming weariness possessed her. She didn't want to get up and face the reality of his death just yet.

Her girls waited patiently and respectfully. Phoebe Darlene was almost fifteen years old. She was serious, like her father, in copying his way of wrinkling his brows. She'd been his fishing companion. The two would dig a can of worms and walk down to Raccoon Branch. Of the three, she was the only one who inherited her father's stocky build and facial features, but she was pale in color and short like her mother, too. Phoebe, with a take-charge personality, seldom displayed finesse in hiding her opinions.

Ruth Arlene, towheaded and blue-eyed, was small-boned, good-natured, and gentler than her sister. She turned thirteen years old in February.

Sarah Charlene, a mere eight months of age, would never experience her father's love for her, his helpfulness, or his delight in her. She awoke and gave out a hearty wail.

Addie Kate swung around to her youngest, now restless in the cradle. She reached over, scooped the baby into her arms, and cuddled her. Sarah had been a surprise, quite the blessing though, born to forty-five-year-old Addie Kate. Friends and neighbors surmised she was conceived when her mother was going through "the change." Sarah, with large green-colored eyes and thick lashes, possessed the

Claycomb golden fuzz for hair. Addie Kate vowed that Sarah would become familiar with her father's gifts and grace.

A momentary silence slipped by and Phoebe asked, "Shall we go see him?" She tilted her head toward the parlor.

Addie Kate pasted a smile on her face for her two older daughters and nodded. Still she did not get up. She continued to stare forlornly into space and did not speak.

"We need to go," Ruth urged. "People are starting to come."

Addie Kate stood and, carrying her baby, walked slowly out of the sitting room. Phoebe and Ruth escorted them. The women fell silent, nodded to them, and stepped aside as Addie Kate and the girls entered.

Bunny came forward to take Sarah Charlene from her mother's arms. The baby passed amiably to her neighbor, ducked her head, and pressed her face into the woman's shoulder.

"Take however much time yuh need now, but afterward, yuh come and eat," Bea ordered. "Yuh gotta keep yer strength up."

The news of the tragedy had traveled throughout the area and people came and spoke quietly to pay their respects. They brought food—meat, bread, and pies—and made coffee.

Addie Kate listened to their comments. "I feel so sorry for her," one said in an almost whisper. Another said, "Yes. She relied on him more'n I think even she realized. They was quite devoted tuh each other." Yet another interjected, "What'll she do?"

She inched toward the bier, shut her eyes, then opened them. She looked down upon the quiet face of her beloved for a long moment— her heart fluttering, her grief enormous. "Oh, Jib," she moaned. "I don't want this to be true. In all our years, you never failed me . . . whatever came our way. We had each other. In the midst of life is death. I fully understand now that our existence on this earth is as brief as a dream."

Her gaze moved from his face to his hands, one lying on the other, at his midsection. His old slouch hat rested in the hinge part of the casket where Phoebe and Ruth also laid a small bouquet of spring flowers tied with a lavender ribbon. It would be seen by everyone who came to look for one last time at Beckett Hollingsworth Claycomb. She hesitated a minute, not touching him but wanting to, and then she took her time in gently placing her hand on his and kissing his forehead. She knew she wouldn't see him anymore—other than in her mind. For her, no person in the world could be better company. He'd shared her bed and been a good husband in every way. "I will always and forever be yours," she muttered.

Earlier that day he had been full of life; now he lay dead. She felt the swelling in her throat. Then turning around to the women and stepping away, she said in a soft voice, "Thank you. He looks real nice . . . like he's asleep."

"Yer friends and neighbors has brung food fer yuh and the girls. Yuh need tuh go eat now."

Addie Kate nodded. As she moved out of the room, she overheard the whispers. "They was so happy together. What on earth will she do now?" And "She'll miss him a awful lot. Truly, he'll be missed by us all. Everybody knowed him."

Samuel Byrne, a man from the church, came up to her. "He was a fine gentleman, Addie Kate. What he left to you is greater than riches."

"Thank you. Everyone has been so kind."

He went on. "It has been a fine thing for me to be acquainted with Jib. I appreciated his patience and strength and sunny smile. He will be remembered for his honesty and common sense as well as his goodness. It so happened I was going by when the accident that killed him occurred. Something came over me, a deep sorrow, to learn that a man so well liked was so abruptly gone. Is there anything I can do for you, ma'am?"

Addie Kate shook her head. "Thank you. I appreciate your kind words, though. I've loved him for years. I'll love him forever. He was the one who gave me the desires of my heart."

Epilogue

$\mathcal{A}$ddie Kate never married again after Jib's untimely death. It was simply too much for her to lose him. For an extended period, she did nothing, her grief being enormous. Without him, her constant companion for sixteen years, she complained about being so lonesome she could hardly bear it. "He was always with me," she would say, "day in and day out." She said more than once that the homeplace was full of his memory, and that everywhere she went, she sensed his presence. Though Jib had been a photographer and taken pictures of anything and anyone, it was not easy to find many of him because he was always the one behind the camera. She possessed only one picture of him—with her. She ran her finger over the photograph touching his image every day.

For the rest of her life, she remained on the land the two worked hard to improve. Jib firmly believed that a farmer should leave his farm in better condition than he'd found it. Proud she could help him with the work, she blushed when he bragged to others that she had "made a hand" with the crosscut saw.

Addie Kate Claycomb entered her eternal home in February 1912 at the age of sixty-two years and five months. Family and friends maintained she died of a broken heart, never recovering from Jib's passing.

Phoebe Darlene, almost fifteen at the time of her father's death, stayed with her mother and sisters. She became a fine nurserywoman—her apples and grapes highly prized in the area—experimenting with grafts on the fruit trees. Never marrying and being the oldest of the three daughters, she felt responsible for everyone and took her position as the head of the family after their mother's death. At age thirty-two, the opportunity provided itself for her to purchase a small orchard in a nearby village, and she jumped at it. After almost thirty-three years, the Claycomb farm sold at auction.

Phoebe's new property lay at the edge of Bradford, less than twenty miles away from the old homeplace, and consisted of forty acres planted in apples, pears, and grapes. A frame three-room house sat on the place near a hard-packed dirt road—just the right size.

In June of 1901, at the age of nineteen, Ruth Arlene united in wedlock with a handsome young man called Columbus Deveraux Tilson, a farmer and carpenter from Byrneville. The town folk attended the simple wedding and came to congratulate the couple—and shivaree them. Though the Tilson's were married for seventeen years, no babies came their way. The two said the reason for that was Columbus's contracting the mumps while a teenager. When the Spanish Influenza pandemic struck in 1918, he succumbed to it, and Ruth went to live with her sisters, remained a widow, and became the keeper of a bee apiary, raised chickens, and tended a vegetable garden. She hunted and trapped for meat, and, when necessary, she displayed carpentry skills learned from her husband.

Sarah Charlene was a petite woman, attractive with a clear complexion, light hair, and green eyes. She was very domestic, possessed a knack for making something out of nothing, and played the piano quite well. She moved in with Phoebe accepting the responsibilities for the cooking of the meals and the cleaning of the house. In March 1913, a tornado ripped through Terre Haute, and, in a matter of days, the city suffered a massive flood. Appeals went through the entire state of Indiana for volunteers to come help with the cleanup. Sarah answered the call and left Bradford. She would be nineteen in July.

In Terre Haute, she met a young law student called Landon Joseph Matthews, also a volunteer. They fell in love, and by November Sarah realized she was pregnant and unmarried. By Thanksgiving, she had returned to the safety of Phoebe's home. As far as the community knew, she had wed but lost her husband to the mysterious and frightful disease called sugar diabetes. She assumed his surname, and, on May 20, 1914, she gave birth to a daughter whom she named Joselene—combining the first four letters of his middle name and the last four letters of her middle name.

Sarah tended flower and herb gardens as well as handling the house duties. She took ill, suffering with cancer for years, and died on September 8, 1934.

Author's Notes

The seed for *The Desires of My Heart* was planted years ago when my sisters and I vacationed in the Berkshires where we spent two days at the Hancock Shaker Village in Pittsfield, Massachusetts. Touring the living history museum and listening to the interpreters tell the Shakers' story, I gained a sympathetic interest in the strange religious sect that sought perfection in their lives, intending to create heaven on earth.

The Shakers, a humble and hardworking people, stressed simplicity and grace of style and function in buildings, furniture, tools, clothing and household accessories. They were separatists, removing themselves from the rest of the world because of its cares and vices.

Intrigued by their foundational beliefs of cleanliness, order, simple living habits, and, curiously, celibacy, I pondered soberly how this conviction must have grieved many young women. What choices could they make if brought to the village as children, and whose dreams from childhood featured marriage and family? What possibilities for a future were there for a woman when she turned "of age" and her religion forbid matrimony?

I could not give up my fascination with the community of people who chose to live a chaste life, who worked hard at ordinary jobs, who loved God and life so much they wanted to make their own lives reflect the perfection of God's Heaven separate from the world. To learn more about their way of life, my sisters and I visited the Pleasant Hill Shaker Village near Harrodsburg, Kentucky, staying a few days on the premises where the once-planted seed of a story about a Shaker woman and a non-Shaker man grew and took shape.

The Desires of My Heart is not a documentary or biography; it's fiction. In writing this novel, I grafted a made-up plot into historical facts—or maybe it was the other way around, inserting truth into a fairy tale. For the most part, the characters and events in the story are a work of my imagination, but other characters and events are based on fact. Any errors in getting the history of the times correct remain all mine.

I am not aware of any historical evidence that suggests the Shakers would admit non-Believers to infirmary care. I have read that the doctors of a Shaker village did call in doctors from "the world" when it became evident their patient's health was not improving. And since Shakers welcomed visitors to their worship meetings, and children from the world (not in Shaker care) attended their schools, I took the liberty to admit a non-Shaker to the infirmary. The devastating fire mentioned in the prologue actually happened on the very date as written. The story line necessitated a crisis that would bring Addie Kate and Jib Claycomb together.

Pleasant Hill and Its Shakers by Thomas D. Clark and F. Gerald Ham and *The Shaker Adventure* by Marguerite Fellows Melcher provided key information about the Shakers—their doctrine and their way of life. *The Shaker Communities of Kentucky: Pleasant Hill and South Union* by James W. Hooper and *Old Shakertown and the Shakers* by Daniel Mac-Hir Hutton contributed valuable material as well.

To gain knowledge of the amazing innovations and the clever inventions of the Pleasant Hill Shakers, I came across June Sprigg's

By Shaker Hands; Simple Beauty by William C. Ketchum, Jr.; *The Kentucky Shakers* by Julia Neal; and *Work and Worship Among the Shakers* by Edward Deming Andrews and Faith Andrews.

To get a sense of the texture and details for living on the prairie in a dugout or soddy, I tracked down *It Happened In Nebraska* by Tammy Partsch and *Man of the Plains*, edited by Donald F. Danker. *Happy As A Big Sunflower* by Rolf Johnson provided details about life on the prairie as well as in the Dakota Territory.

For working in the gold mines as depicted in part 2, two valuable resources included *An Illinois Gold Hunter in the Black Hills: The Diary of Jerry Bryan, March 13 to August 20, 1876,* and *Gold in the Black Hills* by Watson Parker.

The Trial of Standing Bear by Frank Keating supplied the facts of the lawsuit. Standing Bear was an amazing figure in history. The litigation was a landmark civil rights case. He was a Ponca chief and I wrote his character to reflect his courage and toughness.

His court case in Omaha, Nebraska, in May 1879, is portrayed as I understood the proceedings recorded for posterity, and his famous statement is quoted. All principals involved are called by their real names. Jib's reference to King David and the prophet Nathan is found in 2 Samuel 12:7.

In part 3, the dedication of the Highbridge trestle did occur on the date mentioned in the story, and President Hayes and two of his seven sons attended. The town of Corydon is in southern Indiana in Harrison County and was on the Underground Railroad route. Pennington Chapel still stands and is maintained by the Pennington Chapel Cemetery Association.

"The desires of my heart" is a phrase from the book of Psalms (Ps. 37:4). The words tell us that when we find peace and fulfillment with God, when we are extremely pleased with what God has already given us, we are given our innermost desires.

It seemed a fitting title for this novel.

Acknowledgments

*P*erseverance does pay off. Success in reaching a goal depends on one's willingness to never give up even when the reward is delayed. As far back as I can remember, a dream I held was to write a book. I persevered with writing and that goal has now been reached.

I count myself blessed to have family members, friends, and readers who support and encourage me in my writing endeavors. My family helped me more than I can say. To my daughter, Valerie Stice, I say thank you, thank you, thank you. Valerie has been the first reader of my novels and because of her sharp eye has given valuable suggestions on the characters and storyline—what to delete and what to change. I am grateful for my sisters and brothers-in-law, Judy and Will Deuel and Lois and Paul Hartman, for their attention to details in getting the words spelled correctly and in the right order to make a more compelling story. I am also deeply appreciative for my sister-in-law, Barbara Newlin, and her enthusiasm for reading the final draft. To my son and daughter-in-law, Roy (Chip) and Paula Carpenter, I owe gratitude to them for their assistance and patience in providing the technical support I needed.

Furthermore, my heartfelt thanks go to my friends: To Bonnie and Jack Chattin, well-known presenters of prize-winning mules, who answered all my questions on the care and character of the animals, and to Phil Meyer, who reviewed one of the earliest versions and offered advice.

To my readers, I am indebted to them for their confidence in and enjoyment of my writings.

In addition, appreciation goes to Maria Bussabarger for directing my husband and me to the Pennington Chapel in Harrison County, Indiana, and to Teresa Douglass of the Frederick Porter Griffin Center for Local History and Genealogy in Corydon, Indiana. I owe thanks to both of them for their time and attention in helping me.

I am profoundly grateful for my best friend and husband, Roy, who provided encouragement to me. I thank him for his unfailing love and patience and bless God for bestowing upon him the ability to come up with just the right word when I got stuck or needed to test an idea. In more ways than one, he made it possible for me to write this book.

Most importantly, though, is that I give all thanksgiving, glory, honor, and praise to my Savior and Lord Jesus Christ for gifting me with a love for the written word and giving me the mindset to develop the skill of perseverance that was needed to fulfill this dream. Lord, may whatever I write always lift Your name on high.